DIP & DEVOUR

Mary Kate
Kopec

INFINITY
PUBLISHING

ISBN 0-7414-6494-2

Printed in the United States of America

Published June 2011

INFINITY PUBLISHING
1094 New DeHaven Street, Suite 100
West Conshohocken, PA 19428-2713
Toll-free (877) BUY BOOK
Local Phone (610) 941-9999
Fax (610) 941-9959
Info@buybooksontheweb.com
www.buybooksontheweb.com

For my Noney

I love everything about you.
I love your feisty spirit and your loving heart.
I love that you rose up to meet your challenges and that you did the best you could in the face of adversity.
I love that you loved me always, even when I fell.
I loved the early mornings . . . bacon and eggs; and the dusky evenings . . . with the holes you poked in the jar lid so I could collect fireflies. The back rubs when I was a kid. All the hugs, iced tea, laughter, and happy conversation. Your cranberry smash is still the yummiest way to sweeten the holidays.
I love that you were you, no apologies.
I love the sound of your voice and how you said my name.
And I miss you every day, and although you are physically gone from my life, you will never be gone from my heart.

May you always rest in peace and know that you will always be a bright, loving, and wonderful light to me!

This book is a celebration of you and your spunk!!!

Acknowledgements

I would like to share my many happy thanks to all those who helped me bring this story to you.

Brainstorming, problems solving, and endless loving support: Thank you, Paul, my chocolate love muffin for life . . . I couldn't have done it without you!!!

Critique readers: Karen, Meghan, Belinda, Carol, Wendy, Linda, Lucille, Jo Ann and Jim. Thank you for your constant support and honesty, even when it wasn't pretty. You helped to make Kia and Jake's story even more wonderful!

Artistic team: Thank you, Dallas, for your initial cover art ideas and brainstorming; Charlie for your awesome interpretation of the story elements and the cover Dip & Devour has today; and Kathy of Kathryn Schriber Fine Photography for capturing my beautiful headshot.

Cardiovascular surgeon extraordinaire: Thank you, Dr. Sanjaya Gupta, for sharing your excellent expertise and knowledge. I'd say more, but don't want to give anything away!

Culinary expertise: Chef Sandra thank you for the meal planning and the recipe for Chloe's secret syrup.

Practical punctuation: My sincere thank you to Dave and Dave. Your expert knowledge of the English language and its sometimes complex snafus has helped keep Kia and Jake's story clear and fun to read.

Kia

How We Met

I was standing there, bored. Attempting to look entertained. Making small talk and hating fund raisers—and the often "handy" men who found their way to my side.

I'd so much rather be working and luxuriating in the silence of my lab. But knowing better than to bite the hand that feeds me, I glanced around, searching for someone to save me from the suave-turned-slimy check trying to make himself more comfortable as he slithered closer and wrapped his tuxedoed boney arm across my back. Pulling me tight—and cracking *yet another* inane and humorless museum joke.

My overly obsequious employer stood there, dull, dumb, and useless, oblivious to anything other than the dollar bills ca-ching-ing in his brain. If he laughed his horrible twittering laugh one more time at this *generous* idiot's jokes, I might just have to clobber him.

Restraint and poise would be my friends, but they'd skittered out the front door long ago, leaving me to fend for myself. And as my attentive courter stroked my ribcage, I felt my calm flip to sizzle.

I tried to smile and edge away, but the clingy fingers just got clingier, and notes of protest started to rise in my throat. Much more of this, and I'd be fired for sure. Last time I made a scuffle, I was severely reminded to be thankful for my job of which I'd be without if it weren't for the tremendous generosity of our kind and happy benefactors. I did love my job, but if this guy got any closer, he'd be able to tell you who made the bra I *wasn't* wearing, and that wasn't happening.

I politely pried gropey's fingers from my waist and said, "If you gentlemen will excuse me, I need to use the lady's room."

Mr. Touchy-Feely narrowed his eyes and stepped forward. Like he might follow. And my boss gave me *that look*. But I smiled warmly, radiating regret and the promise to return and was reluctantly given silent permission to leave.

Thank God.

I turned and walked toward the restroom, meandering my way through the crowd, when a flicker of male testosterone caught my eye. I scanned to the museum's foyer entrance to see a man—tall, dark, and imposing, impeccably dressed—angle his head in my direction as Marjorie Wilkins, Chair of the museum's Board of Trustees, pointed directly at me and smiled.

Every once in a while you come across one of those perfect specimens. A man. Body carved by the gods into perfection. Face chiseled into exquisite and nearly incomprehensible beauty. Voice deep, rich and smooth, capable of lulling you into a hypnotic state of ecstasy. With thick lustrous hair, seductively inviting your fingers for a tumble. Every warm inch of him a tease and tickle to your senses.

As I watched him walk toward me—my pulse pounding—my every breath an effort—fog beginning to cloud my brain and lips dry, lost for any sound that I could utter that would make sense—I thought, this could be just such a man.

I heaved a heavy sigh of interest and hopeful delight. Thankful my savior had finally arrived. Wondering who he was and where he'd been all my life. Still not sure if when he did speak to me anything recognizable would surface—or if I'd have to return to Touchy-Feely with my tail tucked and my ego crushed. He was after all, stunning, and I was most definitely stunned.

I waited for him to reach me, attempted to collect myself, and realized in a brief moment of panic that he reminded me of a wolf stalking prey. His eyes had locked with mine in certain approach. His confidence absolute, and his intention clear.

He stopped in front of me, and my breath caught just as he said, holding out his hand, "Hi, I'm Jake Davidson. Are you Kia Everet?"

"I think you know I am," I said taking his hand, internally hyperventilating at the delicious warmth of his touch, relieved I could speak. "How can I help you?"

"Actually," he said playfully, still holding my hand, "I'm here to help you."

My brain short-circuited. He *was* a perfect specimen. And he smelled like chocolate and sin.

"Do you smell chocolate?" I asked, and he laughed, a short but cheerful chuckle.

"Beautiful, talented, and highly attuned senses. Just how I like my women."

"Are you flirting with me?"

"If you have to ask," he said laughing again. "The chocolates are for you," he smiled, pulling out a small box from his inside jacket pocket. "I was told you liked yours dark and decadent."

I scoffed at the tiny box. "Ahh, now I know you're trifling with me. A true suitor wouldn't have approached with anything less than a pound."

"You wound me. This is all that would fit in my pocket. I had the rest delivered. It's waiting in your office."

"There's more?" I asked, biting into a rich, ooey caramel. This guy was trouble, no doubt about it. "Mmm, heaven," I said licking my lips and looking up from the box to find Jake amused and *more.*

Smirking suspiciously, I inquired, "And just who would betray my confidence so boldly?"

Giving up the banter, Jake replied, "Why, Marjorie of course."

I looked over to Trustee Wilkins, who nodded and smiled broadly at me from across the room.

"I'm your new Tsarists' Treasures exhibit assistant, on loan from the Detroit Institute of Art, and Marjorie and I are old friends. She told me how much you hated these events and suggested if I wanted to make quick friends, I should bring chocolate. I also just happen to be friends with a guy who owns a chocolate shop. Soooo—"

"So it's a bribe then?" I asked on a playfully disappointed sigh.

"Not if you don't want it to be," he said leaning into me suggestively. "I think you feel it, too."

"What's that?" I asked feigning disinterest.

"You're quick," Jake said. "I also like that in my women."

Real disappointment and regret infused my voice. "Well, Jake," I said; "You look as delicious as this chocolate tastes," and he said, "That sounds like a good start."

"But," I said, and he said, "Oh no, here it comes."

"I don't date or play with people from work."

Dejected, but not deterred, he said "Well, that is a bummer, isn't it?"

The rest of the party flew by with Jake at my side, making me laugh and deflecting would-be grabby hands, yet all the while, we kept the donors entertained and writing those hugely generous checks. Job intact after all, even if my *appetite for perfection* left me unsated, starving, and craving more.

Jake

This One's Gonna Be Trouble

The drive home from the museum was short on distance, long on self-rebuke. I needed the self talking-to. It was six miles of "Jake, Jake, Jake. What *were* you thinking?"

I wasn't really mad at myself—I had it under control, but I shook my head not knowing what in the hell I had been thinking.

"Making nice with the suspect is good, but seriously man. Fifteen minutes alone with her, and she'd have been naked."

I shook my head again. Thank goodness for her No-dating-the-help declaration. It gave me the out I needed.

In my own defense, Kia Everet is H.O.T., *hot.* She's funny, smart . . . *and that body.* I let out a low whistle. I'd read her file, seen photos, knew everything about her, right down to her panty size, but that still hadn't prepared me for the real deal.

I'd walked across that room fully in check, prepared to kiss ass and get my in, but then, *Wham!* Kia in the flesh makes one helluva impact.

I pulled into my drive thinking that I needed to close this case fast. I needed to get 'er done, and get the hell out, before my other brain tried to talk me into something world-class stupid. Like seeing how adamant Kia was about her little rule, and if there was anything I could do to help her change her mind.

Yep, Kia Emily Everet was big trouble. The kind spelled with a capital, bolded, and neon flashing T. R. O. U. B. L. E.

Angling my garnet-red Wrangler into the garage, I shook my head one last time—for good measure—and cut the engine. Tomorrow would be another day, and I'd play it cool, just like always. Grabbing my laptop and duffle, I slid out of my Jeep and headed for the door. As I pushed the key into the lock, I could hear Bullet, my trusty pal and overly excitable Beagle dog, enthusiastically anticipating my return.

I opened the door, and there he was, grinning, bone-in-mouth, tail a-waggin'. "Heya Bullet. How's it goin'?" Shifting my gear into one hand, I gave him a little head scrub. "Give me a second to drop off this stuff, and we'll head out for a walk."

Bullet zipped around, even more excited than before. I'd said the magical word, *walk*. I went in through my mudroom which doubled as a laundry room and entered into my kitchen. Checking my machine for messages and finding none, I set my laptop and bag on the counter, and turned to Bullet.

"Well there, buddy. Do I have a story for you, and I think you're going to like it. It's about a chick." Bullet feigning interest followed me back into the mudroom, and I reached for his lead hanging on the hook on the wall. He dutifully stood still long enough for me to clip it onto his collar. I grabbed a scoop bag, and pulling the door closed, we were off.

I live in a quaint sixties residential area just off Stadium Boulevard in Ann Arbor, Michigan. My tan brick, two-story, with faded black shutters, is situated on a postage stamp lot, conservatively landscaped with boxwoods and aging yew bushes. On game days, I can charge twenty bucks for parking, but only fit three cars on my lawn, due to the huge, zillion year old, but beautiful oak. It was this same oak that Bullet headed for first. His favorite first pit stop. The streets here have just enough roll to make our walks interesting, and at Bullet's eager pace, a little bit of a workout. In my distraction, I'd forgotten to switch into my runners, so I gently pulled back on his lead, and said, "How 'bout more of a stroll tonight?"

The look Bullet threw me told me how he felt about that, but he slowed to trot for him and a moderate walk for me.

"So about Ms. Everet," I said, and Bullet lifted his leg to another tree. "No, seriously, you want to hear about her; she's got *Wham!*" He dropped his leg as if to say, "Alright, let's have it."

"Well," I said. "She's like no other chick I've ever met. She's funny, feisty, smart, and whatta looker. In her heels, she stood at my shoulder—perfect. And she has this long, wavy, honey-brown hair that gently tumbles down her back. It shimmers in the light, and I bet it would feel really good wrapped firmly around my wrist."

Bullet trotted on, tail wagging, nose down in search of his next pee. I could tell he was still on-the-fence.

"Trust me," I chuckled, recalling the irresistible warm scent of her skin. "It took everything I had *not* to pull her into me and nibble on her creamy neck!"

I shook my head, liking the memory. Liking Kia.

"Her eyes are pale green pools, and her lips are plump and kissable. Her body was giving off signals that a fire marshal couldn't stop."

And there it was again. The heat and the want. I shook my head, *again.*

Not gonna happen.

And too bad, because—

"It's been a long time since a woman sent flames up my spine."

Bullet grinned back at me, finally showing his full support, but I said, "Yeah, I know, but it can't happen. She's a suspect, and from the evidence we've gathered, I'm pretty sure she's guilty. So hands off."

Bullet's look was sympathetic, but inquisitive—*not even for a quick spin?*

"No!" I laughed adamantly. "You *are* a dog!" He just wagged his tail and quickened his pace.

Guess that was settled. A few houses later, Bullet sidled off into the yard to do his business, and when he was done, I pulled clean-up. "Well, you ready to head back?" I asked him, and he wagged his tail yes, so we made our way back home. When we got there, I closed up for the night, hitting the button for the garage door and throwing the deadbolt.

I unhooked Bullet's leash, and sated, he walked over to his bowl to take a few laps before settling in for the night on his favorite blanket. It used to be my blanket for winter T.V. watching, but he decided he liked it more, so now it was his.

I checked my watch. Just past midnight. I needed to call Chris, my boss, and report in. Chris Jeffries was a lot like me. Single. Early to mid-thirties. No sustainable life outside the job. Dedicated to catching the bad guys. We were different in that I had a sense of humor, and he was working hard to climb the career ladder. To where I wasn't sure, but I liked it in the field, and he liked fielding red tape, so we made a great pair.

I dialed his number, and he answered on the first ring.

"How'd it go?" Chris asked.

"As planned," I said. "First contact went smoothly. Inside 'chocolate tip' went over well, and we spent the night schmoozing donors. I think she likes me."

"They all like you. Does she trust you?"

Always with Chris, direct, no kidding around. "Well, it's a bit early for trust, but give me another day, and I'll see what I can do." I grinned, but he couldn't see it, not that it would have mattered. I'm telling you, humor is lost on this man. All left brain, no fun at all.

"The informant called with an update."

Our informant was Marjorie Wilkins, the Chair of the museum's Board of Trustees. But that's Chris for you, effortless detachment.

"There's been a change in the timeline," he said. "The Treasures collection is now scheduled to arrive day after tomorrow. Monday, early morning. The opening gala is still scheduled for Friday night, but your time to gather intel and gain Ms. Everet's trust has been significantly reduced. I expect you'll be able to adapt."

Was that sarcasm? Sure it was.

"Of course," I assured him. "Anything else?" I asked, knowing what was coming next.

"Yes," he said strictly serious. "This case is a career maker."

He meant his career, not mine.

"And I need you to play this one clean, Jake."

Only slightly offended, I started to protest, but he kept going.

"Don't even try it, Jake. I know you, and you know it. You're always bending the rules here and there. But none of it. Keep it clean, on the books. In. Catch the bad lady. And get out. Off to jail she goes, and we move on. You get to stay in the field where you like it, with future choice in cases, and I get to keep on moving up."

I tried to protest again. This reminder wasn't necessary, but he said, "I'm serious, Jake. My superiors, and thus your superiors, are watching. This has turned into a high-profile heist, and they want a quick arrest and no complications."

Seriously, this was unnecessary. Something had upped the ante for Chris to be talking to me like this, but before I asked, his tone lightened and he said, "Just promise me. In and out."

"What's—"

"In. And out. That's all I want to hear."

"In and out," I said, irritated and curious at the same time.

"Thank you, Jake. Let me know if you need anything."

"What if I need answers?"

"Good night, Jake."

"Good night, Chris," I said, and he disconnected.

I hung up the phone wondering what in the hell that was all about and thinking that this case just got a whole lot more interesting. And so did Kia Emily Everet, and that was the last thing I needed. That woman was already too interesting for her own good, and mine. I was going to have to keep myself from wanting to *probe deeper*, I thought, smiling, remembering her quick wit and sassy attitude. I was guessing my idea of "in and out" wasn't what Chris had in mind and doubted he would appreciate my take on his command.

Kia

I Want One

"His name is Jake Davidson, and he was born on a Sunday. Smooth talking perfection come to mercilessly tempt me," I said gloomily, and petulantly nudged an offending strawberry across my plate.

My grandmother, Chloe, laughed cheerfully, and said, "Well that is good news isn't it?"

I gave her my best incredulous look, and said, "No Chloe. It's not good news. He's my new *assistant*, and I have to *work* with him. Not think about how good he smells, looks, and likely tastes."

This seemed to delight Chloe to no end, and she gaily laughed again.

I sighed, rolled my eyes, gave into to her amusement, and smiled.

It was Sunday morning, a little after ten, and Chloe sat across from me at my little maple dinette table for two, looking chipper in her pink and peach pastel linen cropped pant set with her short, silvered hair artfully curling this way and that, and her sea green eyes, like mine, sparkling in their usual mischief. Chloe always ate breakfast with me on Sundays. It was our special time together and one of my favorite parts of the week. My family was pretty great, but Chloe was the best, and she was determined to see me happy.

"So what's on your agenda today?" she asked me. "Want to go downtown for a walk. It's a beautiful June day. Seventy-eight and sunny. It will cheer you up. We could do some window shopping and get some lunch."

"I'm good for the walk," I said, "but Phillip called, and my rotational collection is coming in tomorrow, so I have to go to the museum to prepare."

"I'm sure that made your day. Is Phillip treating you any better, yet?"

"You mean, has he stopped treating me like a blond-bimbet?" I rolled my eyes at her. "*No.*"

Chloe's look said it all.

"Yeah, I know," disbelieving sarcasm and more eye rolling making my point for me. "You'd think a PhD in art history addressing the continuity between the Romantic and Victorian Eras would give me some credibility. And if not that, the whole graduating with distinction from the University of Michigan would do it, but *Nooooo*. To Phillip, it would seem that I will always simply be a donor enticing toy."

"That man is an idiot."

"That idiot is my boss."

We both sighed, and the doorbell rang.

"Expecting someone?" Chloe asked getting up to answer the door.

"No."

Chloe peeked out the peek hole and whistled low. "What color hair does Mr. Perfection have?"

"Dark brown, cut short, but thick."

"Crystal clear blue eyes?" she asked, and my stomach sank.

"He's here?" I shrieked, looking down to see I was still in my tank and boxers. "What's he doing here? How does he know where I live?"

The doorbell rang again.

"He's got a bakery bag in his hands. Zingerman's. Do you want me to let him in and ask?" she said opening the door as I dove for my bedroom.

"Hi, I'm Chloe Everet. I'm Kia's grandmother," I heard her say. "How can I help you?"

"Hello Mrs. Everet. Nice to meet you. I'm Jake Davidson. I work with Kia. Is she here?"

Jake's deep, rich voice melted its way back to me, and I swear the air felt warm at my ear, like a caress.

Not good.

"Just a second, Jake. She was just getting ready for work. I'll let her know you're here. Why don't you have a seat in the kitchen."

Chloe's head popped into my room as she opened the door, and her eyes were filled with merriment.

"Jake's here," she said, and came into my room, pushing the door closed again.

"I know," I said, feeling flustered. "Now what?"

"Now you get dressed."

"Did you *see* him?" I said, frantically searching for something pretty to wear.

"I did, and he looks delicious!"

I held out a sleeveless, scooped-neck, light and flowy, white and blue flowered button-up sundress for Chloe to see, and she nodded. So I slipped into it and grabbed for my brush.

"How am I supposed to work with that?" I asked raking the bristles through my thick hair and trying for a gently tossed look.

Chloe shrugged happily and suggested, "Perhaps you should just get it over with and lick him!"

Dabbing on some lip goob, I gaped at her. "What? Like he's a cupcake or something?"

"Yeah," Chloe said. "Just like he's a cupcake."

"That's so not a good idea!"

"Sure it is."

"No offense, Chloe. I don't mean to disparage your age or anything, but have you lost your mind?!"

Chloe was grinning ear-to-ear, happily combative, "Have you lost yours?"

Blowing out a groan, I asked, "How do I look?"

Chloe gave me the thumbs up just as Jake's knock rapped on the door, starling a little yelp from me. *"Sheesh!"* I muttered quietly.

"Kia? Sorry to interrupt, but is everything okay?" Jake asked.

"Yeah," I said skirting past my smiling grandmother and opened the door. "Sorry, wasn't expecting you."

I looked down to see his hands were empty. "I thought you brought Zingerman's."

Jake grinned. "In the kitchen. Thought if I was waking you, I should at least bring breakfast."

Chloe nudged past us both and said, "Well, Jake, it was a pleasure meeting you, but if you'll excuse me, I've got to be going."

She flashed a look back over her shoulder to me, and I flashed her my patented death daggers. "I thought we were going for a walk."

Chloe pointedly eyed the back of Jake's head, and said, "How about later? I don't want to keep you from breakfast, and I know you have to get to work this morning. Call me," she said grabbing her purse and closing the front door behind her.

We both stood there, staring at the door. I was amazed at how quickly Chloe had exited, and I couldn't believe she had abandoned me with absolutely no regret whatsoever.

"Your grandmother's real nice," Jake said smelling like chocolate again, standing so close to me I could feel his breath on my cheek.

I tried to take a step away, but he followed, as if by instinct.

I looked up into his island beautiful blue eyes and asked, "Do you smell chocolate?" And he laughed, smiling down at me. He lifted his finger and lightly tapped the end of my nose, sending a jolt of happy right through me. "Cherry Chocolate Bread. Go with what works," he said and pried himself away from me to walk back to the kitchen.

I don't know which was worse, how great his backside looked walking away, filling out his jeans oh so nicely with his biceps begging to be bitten as they stretched the limit of his black, short-sleeve cotton tee, or the chocolate seduction scene he had going on in my kitchen. And what was with the touching? No touching sinner man. I was going to have to put a stop to this fast, or I was going to cave. Chloe was right. He did look like a cupcake.

Jake

Just Doing My Job

Kia's apartment was small, but comfortable looking. She was neat, didn't appear to like knick-knacks, but loved pastels. Her furniture was overstuffed and inviting, the walls bare. No obvious displays of grandiosity or the lockets that had gone missing from the museum. Nothing here but kitchen, dinette, living space, bedroom, bath, and cozy, warm, chocolate loving Kia, and now, a few discreetly placed bugs. *Yeah, I know.* I hated doing it, but a job's a job.

"So, you still hungry?" I asked staring down at the despondent looking strawberry left abandoned and cold.

"Oh, that," she said, coming up to stand beside me, her tone all airy and dismissive. "He offended me."

"Dared to present himself to you without chocolate?"

Kia shrugged indifferently and cleared the dishes. "A girl has to have her standards."

"You having any?" she asked eyeing the Zingerman's bag.

"And risk losing life or limb? I don't think so."

Kia smiled and took down two plates and set them on the table. "Milk or tea?" she asked.

"Coffee?" I inquired, and she dramatically shuddered at the thought.

"Okay, then," I laughed. "Milk, it is."

I took a seat and opened the bag. The scent of still warm, chocolaty goodness rolled over me, and I had to sigh. This bread was heaven, best served with ice cream, but I figured even for Kia it had to be a bit too early for that. The chocolate chunks were all melty, and the Michigan cherries were an added bonus. My mouth watered, and I reached in to grab a piece.

"Eh-emm," Kia said clearing her throat meaningfully, and I quickly rotated the bag toward her. "Just being helpful," I said, and she said, "Sure you were."

Kia doled out two pieces each, and we dug in, neither of us saying anything at first, too busy reveling in gooey, decadent, chocolate ecstasy to bother with words, but then Kia worked her way past my subterfuge and said, "Thanks for the treat, Jake, but what are you doing here?"

I licked my lips to swallow, and was momentarily distracted when Kia's gaze dropped to watch—trouble, trouble for sure—and said, "I heard the collection is coming in early and thought you might be going in to prep. I'm here to assist."

"You could have just met me at the museum."

"And have you start the day unfed and unsated?" I shook my head. "Definitely not the best course of action. No, this was better." Although the more intelligent part of me, the brain upstairs, disagreed. Seeing the look of unfettered pleasure on Kia's face was probably something my lower brain should not have seen. Now it was feeling challenged, like perhaps, given half a chance, it could do better than the Cherry Chocolate loaf. *Much better.*

Not good.

"But how did you know where I lived?"

"Google and Map Quest can get a guy practically anywhere."

"Too true," she said. "And what if I Googled you? Where would I end up delivering your Starbucks to?"

"I guess you'll have to Google me and find out," I said, fully well knowing she wouldn't find a thing. My information wasn't publicly listed anywhere.

Kia rolled her eyes at me and said, "Too much work. So much for being nice and getting you a cup of coffee."

"You would do that for me?" I asked, my mock doubt making me grin. "After that convulsive demonstration a moment ago, I would think the mere presence of a coffee bean in your proximity could induce apoplectic shock."

"Ha ha, funny man. Laugh if you must, but you just missed out on a once in a lifetime opportunity."

"What? A cup of coffee? I get that everyday."

Kia laughed. "You win," she said finishing off her last bite of bread.

"What do I win?" I asked, hopeful and starting to tread on very thin ice. I needed to get out of her personal space. And fast. The essence of her was everywhere, and it was driving me nuts. She looked good, smelled good, and now she was licking the last bit of chocolate off of her fingers. *Good God, when did it get so hot in here?*

I dragged my eyes north to find her watching me, mischief, laughter, and desire glinting in her beautiful peepers.

I narrowed my brows at her. "You tease," I accused, and she burst out laughing. "Got you, you chocolate charmer."

"Chocolate charmer?" I said, so not insulted. Boy did she ever have my ticket. "I am not!"

"Are too!"

"Well, what if I am? What do I get?"

Still chuckling she got up and said, "You get to do the dishes, while I go brush my teeth."

My jaw dropped. "I bring you some of the most delicious chocolate in the world, and I have to do dishes?!"

"Fair is fair," she trilled gleefully.

I shook my head, but was smiling. "How is that fair?" I asked, going for confused disbelief, but got drop-kicked right back into the kitchen.

"Sponge and soap are under the sink. Be right back." And she disappeared into her bathroom.

"Funny, funny," I smiled and gathered our plates.

By the time I had everything washed and the soap and scrubber put away, Kia had returned and was closing up the bread bag. I was standing with my back to the sink, leaning on the counter, drying my hands with her pale yellow and white checkered kitchen towel, doing my best to calm my craving for just the sight of her, when she looked over and eyed me up and down, *gave me that look*, and saucily sidled over to me. She reached over to put the bag in the breadbox next to me, and breathed, "Get enough?"

My brain went blank, and my blood went hot.

That's it. I'm gonna have to kiss her now. Bad idea, I know, but she started it. I was sounding like I was five, and I didn't care.

Not. Good.

I leaned down, my face an inch away from hers, and we both froze. We were sharing oxygen, and I could feel the enticing warmth of her skin drawing me to her. Then her eyes twitched, and her lips curved into oh so slight of a smile, and I drew back, *had*, and she laughed again.

"I am *so* on to you," was the best I could do.

"What?" she asked all innocence.

"Oh-ho-ho. See if I answer any of your cravings again."

And then she went there. I couldn't believe it.

"What if I'm craving you?" she toyed.

Not buying it again, I said, "*Really?* That's where you're gonna go?" Two can play this game. "Why? Are you?" I asked dropping some seduction into my voice, and she smiled knowingly, "Well, if you have to ask."

She turned toward her door, grabbed her keys and purse, and cheerfully asked, "Coming?"

Kia Emily Everet was playing with fire, and I liked it. We were both fighting the attraction, playing with it anyway, and keeping our eyes on our exit strategies. The good news was that my cover was securely intact. The bad news was, that my cover was securely intact. *Kia, Kia, Kia.* Oh, how I wish you weren't a suspect.

Jake

Say It Isn't So

Kia had refused my offer of a ride, and now I was trailing behind her genuine vintage 1963, cherry-red, Austin Cooper S Mini with white racing stripes, having fun keeping up, and feeling a bit green with envy. What a cool car. It fit her perfectly. Fun and zippy.

Kia had a lead foot and liked punching it, so we got to the museum in no time. She lived a short seven minutes away, but we did it in four.

The Acer Foundation Museum of Art History is a gracefully sculpted, three-story, white stone, brick and glass building nestled back on a gorgeous wooded and manicured plot just off of Plymouth Road. There's a babbling brook that flows through the property and forms the backbone of a reflection walk that in today's sun was looking particularly appealing.

I was thinking how much nicer it would be to take Kia for a stroll rather than heading in to catch a thief. But a thief she was, and to work I go. Maybe after I arrest her and send her to jail for a very long time, she'll let me buy her car from her. Or maybe that would be adding insult to injury, but it didn't hurt to ask, did it? Crass, I know, but it wasn't like she'd be driving it. *You're probably right. Better just to drop it.*

I pulled into a shaded spot near the rear of the lot next to Kia and got out. She was locking up, looking over to the reflection walk, and said wistfully, "What a beautiful day for a walk."

Her sun-kissed honey hair was shimmering in the sunlight, and her eyes sparkled like bright lights glistening off the San Juan waters. She must've touched up her lips somehow, and her skin was glowing. I don't know, but all I could say was that the golden rays made Kia a show-stopper, and I had to pause to catch my breath. I was beginning to think my job would be a helluva lot easier if I didn't have to do it anywhere near her. Every time I got close, my brain waves slowed to a stupor and my blood raced in anticipation. I was acting like a lust-struck idiot, and the next words out of her mouth proved my point.

"Earth to Jake," I heard her say, and focused to see her smiling at me again. Well, at least she found me entertaining.

"*What?*" I said, still staring. "I was just so distracted by that huge glob of chocolate dripping off of your chin. I thought you left the bread at home." I tried for droll, but she didn't let it pass.

"Nice try, handsome, but if you don't stop staring, I'm going to get the right idea, and then what? I'll be out an assistant, and you're not going to let that happen, because we have way too much work to do, and it's the only way you'll be able to stay close to me."

I scoffed. "Yeah, like I want to be close to you."

She laughed a melodious little sound of pure enjoyment and said, "You know you do. Follow me, Starstruck, we've got work to do."

Didn't I just know it?

The display area for the Tsarists' Treasures collection, along with Kia's lab and office, was on the second floor. Marjorie had given me a full, private tour, and I already knew my way around, but I was surprised to find the flurry of activity as we ascended the marble and scroll-worked-iron staircase to the show set. Design staff were busily moving, rearranging, and constructing the showcase displays and backdrops. Kia looked to me, and I made sure my expression read, *business as usual*—didn't want to come off green and draw attention to myself—and she said, "Would you mind to take a moment to look around and familiarize yourself with the layout?"

"Trying to get rid of me already?"

"Pretty much."

"Ouch, my ego," I said, and she said, "Will survive. I just need a moment to check in with Ian, our head designer. He has the updated set plans that we'll need for reconciling the anticipated inventory."

"Suurre," I said. "When you put it like that."

Smiling, Kia pointed out the highlights. "My office and lab are through that door. The restrooms are down that hall. This floor's permanent collection lines the walls and is primarily toward the back, and as you can see from the commotion, the rotational collections take center stage. Look around, and let me know if you have any questions."

"No problem," I said taking it all in.

"Back in a minute," she said, and left me to walk over to a tall, tanned, blonde, well-muscled thirty something who greeted her with a jovial smile and a hand to her back as he led her to his work table.

Woah, buddy, back off, I thought. *She's mine.* But she really wasn't, so I pushed the unanticipated pang that crept up on me out of my mind and wandered about, looking interested in the goings on, but all the while, I kept watch over the interaction between Ian and Kia, telling myself that her professional and personal connections would be important to the case.

Well, they could be.

I'd seen all that there was to see, and Kia came back to me. "Any questions?" she asked.

"No, I'm good."

"Okay then," she said and tapped a portfolio of papers. "I've got what we need right here."

"You've got an All Meat pizza from Cottage Inn in there?" I asked moving my head around to get a better look, and she said, grinning, "You can't possibly be hungry already. You just ate." And I said, "Yeah, dessert, and that's a lot of paperwork you've got there."

"You can call for delivery from my office," she said, and I said, "Now, you're talking," and she led the way.

To get to Kia's office and lab, you need a six digit key code and a bar-coded I.D. badge to swipe. I'd been given the code and a badge, so I got us entry, and she pointed me toward the phone. "Dial nine for an outside line," she said.

I picked up and asked before dialing, "Want anything?"

"Aren't you sharing?"

"Are you buying?"

"No, but you can get me a chicken club, hold the dressing."

"Want anything to drink with that?" I asked, and she said, "No, I've got O.J. in the fridge." I shuddered at the thought. Chicken and orange juice, *blehck*.

I placed the order, hung up, and said, "They've got a rush. It'll be about forty-five minutes."

Kia was spreading papers out on her desk and making organized piles. "Good," she said. "That'll give us some time get set up and started."

Four hours later, lunch devoured, seventy-nine pieces into a hundred twenty-six piece collection, working in near complete silence, pretty much talking only when we had to confer, and my head was humming. I had a double Bachelors—Art History and Accounting—and was a certified CPA. I'd seen my fair share of paperwork and balance sheets, and I knew my way around art, but this was tedious and boring work, and I couldn't imagine Kia actually enjoying this aspect of her job. I'd bounced my head off her desk once already in a head check, and I was about to do it again but was stopped cold in my tracks when she leaned in excitedly and said, "Here it is!" I looked over to see what she was talking about, and my heart sank—*the locket.* So much for her not being guilty.

Kia

I'm in Love

Today it's just a piece of paper, but tomorrow it's reality. The last two years of my work, coordination, and collaboration was staring back at me in realized accomplishment, and to say I was excited was a gross understatement.

"What's so special about this piece?" Jake asked his voice flat, and I looked up to find him staring at me. Something more akin to disappointment rather than his usual heat and flirtation filled his face.

"What's wrong?"

Jake shook his head and rubbed his hand across his eyes. "Sorry. Just getting tired I guess."

"Oh," I apologized. "My fault." I checked my watch. "I'm not good at taking breaks. I get going and next thing you know, it's 3 a.m." It was almost four in the afternoon. What a slave driver, and on a Sunday. "Wanna go for a walk with me? We could take the reflection path along the brook."

"Sure," Jake said brightening. "I just need to make a call and a quick pit stop; can I meet you down there?"

Ten minutes later we were walking along the brook, inches apart, the warm afternoon sun heating our skin, gently baking off the residue of fluorescent lighting, and I couldn't help but to catch wave after wave of Jake's delicious scent. It was the first time since I met him that he didn't smell like chocolate, but now it was worse, because he smelled better. I don't know how you smell better than chocolate, but he did, and I was definitely wanting to lick him.

No, no, no. No licking!

We ambled along, quiet, but strangely content. Jake was mellow, presumably happy to be away from artifact files, and I was enjoying his nearness. I know I shouldn't, but come on. The guy was grade A, and he sent my hormones racing. I knew I couldn't have him, but it didn't mean I couldn't soak a little bit of him up on the sly. No harm, no foul.

I was just getting into a happy place, and I kind of had this heavenly tingling thing going, when my hand accidentally brushed his—*at least I'm pretty sure it was an accident*—and my tingling upgraded to full on flame. He was just too scrumptious for his own good, and mine. I meant to step away, but Jake grabbed my hand, and yanked me close.

He was looking right down at me, his expression pained, restrained, or something like it, and he said with a forced lightness, "If you're going to fondle me," and I panicked, taking a full step back and saying as indifferently as I could, "Accident."

"*Yeah, right!* What about your Not-playing-with-the-help rule?" And he grasped me tighter to his chest.

I might have stopped breathing, but if so, it was only so I wouldn't suck in his amazing scent, hyperventilate, go brain blank, and lick him like he was a cupcake.

We stood there, held fast by the heat, fighting it, at an impasse, and just when I thought I would pass out, Jake smiled, relaxed and released me. He reached up, tucked a strand of my hair behind my ear, and said, "So tell me about the locket. Why do you like it so much?"

Jake-free air. I inhaled deeply, relieved, but not.

The locket. This I could do. Going with his change of subject, I resumed our pace and said, "Well, it kind of goes to the core of who I am."

"Go on."

"It's why I do my job. I get to see, touch, and for a moment, share in the beauty and love of history. I've been waiting for this collection to come here for a long time, and I've spent the last couple of years making arrangements for this showing. This locket is special."

"Why?"

"Well, do you know its story?"

Jake shook his head. "I don't think so."

"What do you know about Russian Imperialist history?"

"Long line of Tsars ended in the Bolshevik Revolution and led to communist rule."

"Do you know about the love story between the last Tsar, Nicholas II, and his wife Alexandra?"

Jake shook his head. "Not so much," he said truly sounding interested.

"Well, the short story is that they were very much in love and fighting the legacy of pain and misery his predecessors' governing rule had made common. They tried desperately to have a happy family and make a positive impact for their country. But they were caught up in circumstance and scandal."

"In scandal, you refer to Rasputin and Alexi's hemophilia?"

"You know the story, then?"

"Vaguely. So how does this make the locket so special?"

"The locket is actually from the Victorian Era, made by a British artisan and given to Sir Alfred, Duke of Edinburgh. Alfred's mom, as you may know, was Queen Victoria of England. And he married, Maria, sister to Tsar Alexander III and father to Nicholas II. So Alfred and Maria were Uncle and Aunt to Nicholas."

Jake's eyes hadn't glazed over yet, so I kept going.

"When Nicholas married Alexandra, Maria wanted to celebrate their love—hers having been an arranged marriage not of affection, but Nicholas and Alexandra were truly in love, so their relationship gave Maria hope and joy. So Maria gave Alexandra the locket as a wedding gift. Four daughters and a hemophilic son later, then fast forward to political upheaval, confinement of the royal family, the women sewing the family jewels in the bodices of their dresses, murder and massacre, and then ninety years later, Anastasia—one of the daughters, thought at first to have survived—her grave is found, and this locket is there with her."

"And that's important because?" Jake asked, interested but not seeing it, yet.

"This locket signifies great love and hope in the face of betrayal, tragedy, and murder. And to top it off, it's beyond beautiful. Twenty-two gorgeous oval garnets and pearls arranged in an enchanting floral pattern. It's Victorian, juxtaposed within the Romantic Era, and it is a gift of romance. It is my study, and it is love, and that's why it is so special to me."

We were on our second go round of the path, on the backside of the museum, shielded from view by a dappling of large evergreen trees. A light breeze had kicked in, and the trickle of the stream over the rock bed inspired relaxation. It's the only explanation I can give for what Jake did next.

There was no rush in his touch, nor hesitation. It was timed just right. His fingers drifted softly up my arm, whispering lightly along my neck to quietly nestle in my hair and caress the base of my head.

With a gentle tug and his warm eyes peering deeply into mine—perhaps searching, he came close, allowing our bodies to linger and languish in the feel of each other, waiting to see if I'd pull away. And then. When I didn't. He kissed me.

It was a soulful outpouring of suppressed attraction and denied interest, and it made me go liquid on the inside. I was flooded with heat, and despite my earlier arguments, I wanted more. I couldn't seem to help myself—didn't want to. I leaned in closer and let his kiss sear through me.

Flame on!

Jake must have felt it, too, because he clenched his hands in my hair and squeezed me tight. His own body tensing against mine.

A lifetime passed as he gradually moved his hands up to cup my face, and with a slow agonizing effort, he broke the kiss.

Standing back a step, he tilted my face up to his and said, "You are driving me nuts. I'll see you back in your lab."

And he dropped his hands and left me standing there in a daze.

Jake
Now What?

I stalked back to Kia's office mentally kicking my ass the whole way. "Great. Just great. One little impassioned speech, and you lose your head. Now what are you going to do?"

This was *so* not good.

Sure the chemistry felt great, amazing in fact, and Kia was definitely beyond spectacular, recently upgraded from show-stopper due to that kiss.

I stopped stomping across the lawn just long enough to pause and relive that kiss.

Oooh my.

Blowing out a hard breath and shaking my head, I acknowledged the facts. *Kia was delicious.* I wanted more. A lot more. And that makes me—in, trouble.

I shook my head.

"*She's a criminal!*" I quietly muttered to myself. "Your suspect, and you're here to catch her in the act and take her down."

Ohhh, I definitely wanted to take her down. Wasn't sure I could stop myself from doing it now. Not sure I wanted to.

That should go over well with the review board. Not to mention Chris and his big "career maker."

Oooh boy. "You need to get a grip, man. And fast."

I slowed my pace, arranged my face into pleasant, and entered the museum. I took the stairs to the second floor where the flurry of activity was still underway and sauntered over to the key-padded door, entered the code, swiped my I.D., and calmly reclaimed my seat at Kia's desk.

She was going to be walking in through that door any second now, and I wasn't sure what to expect, but I was hopeful she'd have forgotten what just happened, and we would finish reconciling the inventory and call it a night.

It could happen. Well, *it could.* Didn't mean it would.

Ten minutes later, three more artifacts down, heat and desire still clinging to me, a touch of guilt for leaving her hanging settling in, and Kia appeared, puffy lipped, glowing, and giving me a look that said the earth hadn't just moved and she wasn't interested.

If only.

I should be relieved, but instead my lower brain stepped up to the challenge and sent a jolt of testosterone laden don't-worry-we'll-show-her coursing through my veins, and I swear, Kia's determined indifference only made me crave her more. Like I said, trouble with a capital T!

She came over and pulled up her chair. She looked over at my pile and asked, "How's it going?"

"Not bad. We have just over forty to go."

Kia nodded and reached for the next file. "I stopped to speak with Ian, and he said the designers are making excellent progress. It's still going to take the week to complete, but when the shipment arrives tomorrow, we'll be able to get the ready displays up."

"Sounds great."

"Tomorrow, I'll need to talk with Karen. She's the curriculum director. And I'm not sure how long it will take. Will you be okay on your own for a bit?"

She was drawing her line and creating distance, which was great in the "avoid the attraction" department, but unacceptable for keeping my professional eye on her, and the locket.

Kia's phone rang, and I was momentarily saved from answering.

She picked up and said, "Kia Everet, Romantics, how may I help you?"

She smiled and replied, "Hi Chloe. How's your day going?" Pausing to listen, she said, "That's great," and looked over at me. "No, he's not here." Kia listened, shaking her head—denial the whole way. "Honest, he's already gone for the day." Pause again. "Well, I'm going to be here kind of late. You know. Until it's done." Another pause. "No, I didn't bring dinner with me. And he's not here."

Apparently Chloe knew her granddaughter all too well, because Kia rolled her eyes and handed me the phone.

I grinned *nice try* and said into the phone, "Hello Mrs. Everet."

"Please. Call me Chloe."

"Chloe," I said, and she said, "Good afternoon, Jake. How's work going?"

"We're making progress."

"That's good to hear. So Jake, I'm calling to see if you two would like to join me for dinner this evening. I've made a lovely Penne Caprese and a chocolate mousse with raspberry sauce."

I looked over to Kia who was working on her impassive, but failing. Her eyes were a big no, as was the tight micro shake of her head.

"Thank you for the invite, but perhaps another night."

"Here's the thing, Jake. Kia's horrible at eating when a new collection comes in. She's easily lost in her work, so this is me making sure she takes care of herself."

"I'd love to, but I need to get home and take care of my dog."

"Couldn't you come after? You could bring Kia with you."

I was looking at Kia when I chuckled and said to Chloe, "You're not going to let this go, are you?" And Kia mouthed, "Sorry," to me.

Chloe laughed and said, "Now you're getting it. Dinner will be ready whenever you are."

"You drive a hard bargain, Chloe."

"Thank you, Jake."

"We'll call when we finish up here. Wanna talk with Kia again?" I asked, ready to hand the phone off, but she said, "No. That should do it. See you soon."

"Alright."

"Bye Jake." And she disconnected.

I hung up the phone, and Kia said, "You don't have to go. She's just making sure I eat."

"And miss out on Penne Caprese and chocolate mousse with raspberry sauce? I don't think so. We're so going."

"Fine. But you know it's a set up, right?"

"Sure," I said, the wind knocked out of my sails a bit, but not about to give in. "We can totally handle it."

That's when Kia truly gave me *that look*, and mumbled something I couldn't quite make out. Rather than push it, I let it drop and grabbed the next file in the pile. Admittedly, I was feeling stupid and satisfied at the same time. Stupid because I didn't catch the set up part, and satisfied because this was my chance to overcome Kia's plan for distance.

It took us another two full hours, plus some, to sift through the remaining files and verify the inventory to set up, but Kia seemed pleased as she collected the pages and organized the portfolio packet.

She looked at her watch and said, "Wow, just after seven. That was fast."

"Sure was," I said totally not thinking so. "How long does it normally take you?"

"Well, normally I'm on my own. And it depends on the size and complexity of the collection. But usually I'm not getting out of here until three, four o'clock in the morning."

"You stay here all night?"

"Not *all* night, but yes, quite late."

"Anyone to keep you company?" If she was here alone, that might be her window of opportunity.

"Not usually. But every once in a while the museum is scheduled to get more than one rotating collection at the same time. Even then, we're all too busy to socialize."

Kia set the portfolio on her desk, called Chloe to give her the heads up, grabbed her purse, and said, "You ready?"

I was starving, and Bullet was probably seeing yellow by now. "Yep," I replied, and we walked to our cars. It was June, and the days were long, so the sun was still up and quite warm. So there was Kia, once again looking delectable, and here I am supposed to be getting a grip.

"So I'll head home, let the dog out, and be over in about forty-five?"

"Sure," Kia said, not sounding all that enthusiastic, looking a little panicked.

"You're going to be there, when I get there, right?"

"Right."

"Seriously. No standing me up, just to get my dessert."

Kia chuckled, "Like you or Chloe would let me get away with that."

"And don't you forget it!"

Kia closed her door, revved up her Mini's engine, and backed out, zippity-split. I watched her drive away as I climbed into my Jeep, and couldn't help but to wonder what in the hell I was doing.

Okay, I know what you're thinking. I shouldn't have said yes, but Kia's plan for distance was a first step to shutting me out, and I couldn't let that happen. Not professionally. And certainly, not personally. And yes, I know, that makes me a first class idiot, but then again, *that kiss*. My, oh my.

Jake

Not a Date, Just Dinner

I hadn't given myself much time to get across town, walk Bullet, and get back. Maybe because I didn't want to give myself time to chicken out. Not that I would. But whatever the reason, Bullet was not happy with me when I announced Potty Stop only.

I grabbed his lead and a scoop bag, got him hooked up, and out we went. Bullet headed for the oak first, lifted his leg, peed forever, and looked over at me, not pleased.

"Sorry Bullet," I said. "I know. It's not ideal, but I'll make it up to you. Couple hours max. Dinner. Conversation. Torture myself with rampant, unabated sexual tension. You know, the usual. It's not like anything is going to happen. Chloe—her grandmother—is going to be there.

He dropped his leg and didn't look convinced.

"Okay. You're right. Maybe she won't. But it's no big deal. It's just dinner."

Bullet wasn't born yesterday, and neither was I. He set his nose to the ground and sniffed in search of his next pee.

I blew out a sigh. "Listen. Let's look at this in a different light. A work light. This is an opportunity for me to do recon and get to know the mindset of my suspect in a more relaxed setting. This could be good."

Bullet had meandered over to the yews, and he lifted his leg again. He wasn't buying it, and why should he? Who was I kidding? One kiss, and I was so charged up, I'd allowed myself to get suckered into a dinner that had disaster written all over it.

I shook my head and looked down to find Bullet staring at me like I was the King of Moronic Moves, but then perhaps that was just me reverse-projecting, and if so, I was truly losing it.

"Well, no hope for it now. It is what it is," I said, and then asked, "You done?" and Bullet wagged his tail and set off for the door.

Eight minutes later, I was freshly scrubbed, brushed, presentable, and on the road. It took about ten minutes to get to Kia's apartment complex. And in the vein of making this a recon experience, I took a good look around. Four older, red brick and wood shingled buildings nestled in among the trees, and another brook. Since both Kia and the museum resided off of Plymouth, it stood to reason it was the same brook. *Wow.* Pathetic, I know. If ever I was grasping at straws. Might as well just shoot me now.

Up I marched, and for as much as I wanted to claim resolutely, in truth, seeing Kia was becoming a craving. And for all my self-reprimand, I felt a calm, a like-it-should-be, when she opened her door and smiled her beautiful, brilliant smile, making my legs go just a bit weak at the knees. She was breathtaking yet again, and this time there was no sun to blame.

"Hiya," she said stepping out and pulling her door to. "Chloe doesn't live far from here. Mind if we walk?"

I stepped aside and said, "Lead the way."

I followed Kia back down the stairs and along the apartment path. Chloe's residence information was part of the file I had on Kia, but I hadn't realized she could just walk through to Chloe's sub. It was a nice convenience for them both, and it took less than five minutes to arrive at Chloe's doorstep.

Chloe was well-off, and despite her house being small, it showed. Her yard was stunning, and should probably be referred to as her gardens. Bright and cheerful flowers filled beds, and a huge, cushioned swing invited idle inactivity under the relaxing shade of a heavy tree canopy. I wasn't surprised to find her home reflected her playful and upbeat personality.

I slowed to pause at the door, but for no good reason. Kia didn't bother to knock or ring the bell. She just sauntered on in. I was close on her heels, and when she turned to close the door, we ended up bumping into each other.

It was one of those moments that you watch in the movies and think how fun and unexpected the actors make it seem—knowing full well how wildly the internal sparks are flying. *Except that we bumbled it*, and it turned into an overreaction of nerves. So I quickly sidestepped out of the way, and said, "Sorry, fumble on the pass."

Kia just smiled, and called out, "Chloe! We're here." Then she turned to me and said, "I don't know why I bother. She's not gonna be here."

We walked in through the foyer to the living room, and Kia guided me to the right. It was even worse than I had imagined. Dinner, sure. The three of us—maybe just the two of us, fighting over who got the extra mousse, but this? This was *Woah*. This was Big Trouble!

Chloe had her ornate cherry table lavishly set for two. Flowers, candlelight, something mellow playing in the background, and the smell of fresh tomatoes and basil floating on the air, hinting at Tuscan flavored romance.

As if my lower brain needed any help. Kia surrounded by soft candlelight and aromatic food. Disaster, disaster, disaster. The image alone had my blood pounding. And she must have been thinking the same thing, because she pulled a cold shower and purposefully strode over to the stereo, pressed the off button, blew out the candles, and moved to flip the lights to bright.

I could just kiss her.

"She's not usually this bad," Kia said and pulled out a chair for me.

I came over and we sat. "It's not that bad," I said, and Kia shook her head. "Just eat."

Chloe had seen to all the details. We each had a leaf lettuce salad with dried Michigan cherries and parmesan cheese, a glass of exquisite red wine, *the uncapped bottle resting next to me*, and a family style bowl of Penne Caprese sat between us to share.

Each and every bite was savory and delicious, so much so, that I turned my attention to my plate and did as Kia ordered; I just ate.

Surprisingly, it was companionable silence, not tense, that filled the space between us, and we took our time enjoying the meal. I reached for the penne serving spoon and asked Kia, "Seconds?"

"No, I'm good. Thanks."

"Mind if I do?"

"Not at all. But I will have another glass of wine, please."

I poured her wine and scooped more penne for myself, and we returned to our silence. It was comfortable, and I felt myself relax.

And that's when it hit me. That Chloe was too smart for her own good, but even though I was on to her wily ways, the true danger was that I knew, and didn't care.

Forking the last bit of penne into my mouth, I grabbed my napkin, wiped, and looked to find Kia gazing at me contentedly.

Before my brain could register any alarm, she offered, "Dessert?"

"Like you have to ask."

Kia got up and went to the fridge. When she returned she had a single plate, but gigantic portion, of mousse draped in raspberry sauce.

"Where's yours?" I asked.

Kia smiled apologetically. "It would seem we are meant to share."

No problem, I thought, in complete denial. *It's just creamy, smooth, decadent, lush, delicious chocolate mousse. It's not like we're talking Kia on a spoon here. Or anything.*

"Just so long as you don't try to eat my half," I said, knowingly.

"Speak for yourself," she said and proceeded to draw a line generously in her favor.

"That's what I'm talking about," I said, protesting, chuckling, and used my spoon to push hers toward half.

She laughed. "Where did you learn math? That's so totally not half!"

"Maybe not *your* idea of half, but mathematically, it's half."

We were laughing and our spoons where shoving back and forth, and the pretty mousse got messy.

"Now look what you did," I said, and she said, "Awww, guess I'm gonna have to eat it all by myself now."

"I don't think so," I said and plunged my spoon in for a huge bite.

"Mmmm," I said, instantly in heaven; and Kia was right behind me. Our playfulness over, we languished in chocolate and raspberry bliss, every dreamy spoonful. I was half tempted to lick the plate, but Kia beat me to it, and I said, "No fair. That's cheating." And she said, "Losers, weepers."

I grabbed for the plate, but motivated by chocolate, Kia was fast and I missed. She was up and heading for the kitchen all the while licking the last of our dessert, and as I jumped up to lay chase—this *was* excellent chocolate we were talking about here—I realized my error.

I wasn't about fun anymore, and it wasn't about chocolate. It was about Kia and how good she looked, and how fun she was, and how I *really* liked being with her.

I slowed my pace, giving her the chance she wanted to finish our dessert, watching her delightful tongue dance across the dish, and giving my blood its chance to go solar.

Knowing what I wanted and not sure what I was going to get, I intently drifted to her side, glutton for certain punishment.

There was a shift in the air and the mood dropped to sensual quiet. Kia held fast to her plate, and her eyes rolled up to find mine.

I reached out, took the plate from her, and placed it in the sink. She had chocolate on the tip of her nose, which made me smile.

Cute.

Not taking my eyes off of her, I lightly wetted a paper towel and with a whisper touch dabbed away the chocolate. I put the towel on the counter, and pushed a wisp of her honeyed hair behind her ear. Kia tried to take a step back, but the counter was there.

"You're pretty," I said.

"You're delusional," she said, wariness working its way into her voice.

I stepped closer, and she held up a hand to stop me. "Feel free to take this personally, but get away from me."

I heard her words, but her eyes were telling me a different story.

The corners of my mouth tipped up, undeterred. Still the fight, but I was ready to give in, and from the looks of things, so was she.

Slowly, eyes still locked, I leaned in. And thankfully, Kia didn't move.

I pressed my lips into hers. Lightly at first. But then we found our place, and there it was again—the heat, the hum, the low timbred vibration in my chest, wiping all thought from my brain. I could only feel. Devour. Consume.

Our lips mated, and our tongues teased.

I needed to get closer.

I threaded my fingers into her hair and held onto her face. Her hands reached up and dug into my chest.

Heat poured through me, over us, and I ran my hands down her back and pulled her tight. For a moment we were a unified force of molten desire. But then—Kia pulled back.

How she did it, I'll never know, but I wanted more, so I angled for her mouth again.

"No more kissing!" she said dodging my attempt.

Dazed and instantly missing her warmth, I said, "You're right. You're right." But I couldn't remember why, so I dove for her delicious, chocolaty, wonderful mouth again.

"Jake!" Kia said sounding flustered.

"What?" I responded, frustrated, wanting to touch her more.

"We're in Chloe's house! What are you going to do? Take me here on the kitchen floor?"

"Perhaps you'd prefer the dining room table," I asked, hopefully.

And then she gave me *the look*.

"Alright, alright," I said and drew in a heavy breath. I took comfort in seeing that Kia wasn't doing much better, and then relented. "I suppose we should do the dishes."

Kia gave a small laugh. "It's the least we could do."

Dishes done, I walked Kia back to her apartment, but domesticity had induced a return to sanity, so there was no more kissing of any kind. I made sure she was safe and locked up, and I drove home. After all it had been dinner, not a date.

Kia

This Could Work

I locked my door, then turned and pressed my back into it. Relief fought against the heat racing through my body, and I stayed there, breathing in the cool air of my apartment, hoping to stabilize my tempted heartbeat. That was a near miss, practically too close to call. Jake with his strong hands, determined eyes, and body that just wouldn't stop. Don't even get me started on his lips. His kisses were gifts from the gods, and my mouth craved more. *I* craved more.

Him and his too sexy self. How was I going to last the week? If he hit me with that come-hither voice again, and those melty eyes. Yep, he was the hook, line, and sinker of seduction, and I was sunk! As it was I'd had to check to see if I was still dressed, standing there in Chloe's kitchen, dazed, and wanting to devour. That man was a disaster in the making. And Chloe!

Yeah, *and Chloe!*

I marched over to my phone and hit the speed dial. She picked up on the first ring and said, with clear accusation in her voice, "You did the dishes."

"I wouldn't have had to if you'd been there," I shot back.

"You should have left them for me. The whole point was—"

"Oh, I think we got the point. Not to worry Chloe. He's a delicious kisser."

"He kissed you?" she asked, trying for shocked, but landing on pleased.

"What'd you expect? He never had a chance after the Italian hookup scene you had going there!"

"Well, I wouldn't have to, if you'd take matters into your own hands."

"Maybe I don't want to," I said sounding like I did but in denial.

"Just because you had one bad experience—"

"That one bad experience sent me reeling for over a year, and I had to find a new job."

"But Kia, honey, life happens. You grow, you move on, *you kiss the new guy* for goodness' sake. Have you looked at this man you are so blithely blowing off."

"It's not so blithely," I said blowing out a breath.

"Well, that's something," Chloe said kindly.

"It's something alright."

"Well, what are you going to do about it," she asked hopefully.

"It's better if I do nothing," I said not believing it.

"How's that?" Chloe asked.

"I don't know. It just is," I said taking a seat on my big, chunky sofa and sinking six inches into the cushions for comfort. "It's all just too good to be true. Too convenient. Too happy."

"How's finding a dream guy too happy?" Chloe wanted to know.

"It's just the timing. The Tsarist collection is here. The locket I love so much. And just when I'm hitting it big at work, along comes Mr. Irresistible. I just don't want to mess it up, or have him messing it up for me. I just have to last the week. He's only on loan from the DIA until Friday night when the show opens. After that, he leaves, and I'll breathe a sigh of relief."

"Will you? Will you breathe a sigh of relief?"

"This is what I know. Jake's kissed me twice. The first time he dragged himself away from me, blaming me for driving him nuts, and left me standing alone glowing, but abandoned. The second time, he practically purred himself across the room, and when he got to me, all thought, all reason was lost. I can't be doing that this week at work. I can't have him coming around inducing stupefied comas. Phillip already suspects I'm a walking dimwit, and the last thing I need to do is prove him right and lose my job."

"Well, what about after this week?" Chloe suggested. "It's obvious you two have chemistry. Maybe after he goes back to the DIA. Once he's not working with you anymore, why not then?"

She had a point. That could work. And why not? Well, if he'd stop fondling my hair and giving me jello bones.

"Maybe," I said. "But—"

"No buts," Chloe said. "Kia, this is the first time in a long time I've seen you flustered over a man. And in a good way. Not many have been able to give you a run for your money, and he's doing it. That tells me that this is worth at least exploring."

"Exploring?" I said, not able to keep my traitorous brain from going rogue and tempting me with visions of my hands roaming the insatiable length of Jake's naked body. We're talking nonstop muscles here! One more thing I had confirmed during our kiss. He was ripped! No way was I going exploring!

"Yes," Chloe said. "See if this is anything more than attraction and smack talk."

"Smack talk?"

"You know you've got sass, and he likes it."

Smack talk made me think of spankings, and it wasn't even my thing, but maybe. If it was Jake. *Oh God.*

"Chloe, you've been great, but I've gotta go."

"You'll do it?"

"I'll think about it."

"Kia—"

"If I say I will, will you stop setting me up and giving me a hard time?"

"Only if you mean it."

"Okay, I mean it," I lied, not sure what I was going to do.

Chloe sighed into the phone. She was hoping, and I wasn't being the picture of cooperation.

"I love you," she said, and I said, "I love you, too!"

"Sleep on it, and I'll give you a call a little later in the week."

Translation, she'd be over in the morning. I smiled.

"Good night, Chloe."

"Sweet dreams, honey," she said, and disconnected.

I checked the clock on my kitchen microwave. Just after ten. It was getting late, and tomorrow was a big day. I needed to get to bed, and somehow sleep. Not sure how that was going to happen, I put the phone away and walked into my kitchen. A cup of Celestial Seasonings Sleepytime tea should do it. Then I'd wash my face, brush my teeth, p.j. up, and crawl neck deep under the covers and drift restfully off to dreamland. *I hoped.*

I was all the way to neck deep under the covers when my phone rang.

"Hello?"

"I can't sleep," Jake said.

"Sounds like a personal problem."

"Where's the sympathy here?"

"Try a cup of Sleepytime tea. You'll be out in a jiffy."

"Blehck. Tea?"

"How'd you get my number?"

"Emergency phone tree from work."

"There isn't an emergency phone tree from work."

"You sure?" he said, sounding happy.

"Yes." I almost laughed, but I didn't want to encourage him.

"Well, actually, it's all part of the info packet Google gives you. Name, address, phone number, bra size."

"I'm trying to sleep here, Jake."

"Yeah, me too. But I can't stop thinking about you kissing me."

"Me kissing you!?"

"So really, I can't sleep, and it's all your fault."

"My fault?!"

"Maybe you should make it up to me and come over here and give me a massage."

"Maybe you should give me a massage. You're the one running around doing all the kissing."

"Be right there," he said, and I sat up in bed, alarmed to say the least. "Jake!" I yelled. "No!"

He chuckled. "You don't have to shout; I'm right here. You sure you don't want me to come over? I give great massages."

I closed my eyes, not wanting to think about it, doing it anyway. "Yes, I'm sure," I said scooching back under the covers, shaking my head. "What do you want, Jake?"

And in an instant he went from playful to all soft and earnest. "I can't help myself," he said, "and I just wanted to hear your voice."

I laid there, breathing, working my play-it-cool.

"Kia?"

"I'm here," I said, and Jake said, "You really are driving me nuts, and I really can't seem to help myself."

He was being sincere, so I didn't think this was a good time to bust his chops. Chloe's plea drifted its way up, and I said, "So what are we going to do about it?"

"What do you want to do about it?" he asked.

"If I tell you, are you going to take me seriously, or you going to give me a hard time?"

"I'm out on a limb here, Kia."

"Fine," I said trying to be hopeful like Chloe. "Your timing is horrible. I have a show to put on, and I need to concentrate. And you're distracting me. And you keep kissing me! And fondling my hair!!" I was escalating unintentionally, so I took a breath and added, "*But*, I like it. I just don't want to like it until Friday."

"Friday?"

"We do our work. We get the show together. We host the gala. And then you go back to the DIA. After that, you can kiss me, fondle my hair, distract me, the works."

"That's what you want?"

"That's what I want," I said, sounding more certain than I felt about the waiting until Friday part. Truth be told, *he could* come over right now and give me that massage. Best to end this phone call before I did or said something stupid. But before I could muster an excuse, Jake's even-timbred voice caressed my ear softly, like he was lying in bed next to me whispering. "Good night Kia Emily Everet. Sweet Dreams. May you float like you're on a cloud."

Now, wasn't that a nice thing to say? I couldn't help but to smile.

"Good night, Jake. Try the tea," I said, happy and hopeful.

He chuckled and said, "Don't need the tea. Got what I came for."

"See you in the morning?"

"Yep, see me in the morning."

Long after I fell asleep and was floating away on my dream cloud, I realized he hadn't agreed to wait until Friday. Thankfully, my state of blissful peace was too complete for the pesky alarm to find its way to the surface. *Sleep, Kia, sleep.* And I did.

Jake

Wishful Thinking

I so wanted it to be true. But every chance she got, Kia gave me another reason to believe she was guilty. What was with Friday? Was she telling me that was the day she was going to pinch the locket? Or could it really be that simple . . . that after the gala we could go spelunking to our hearts' desire? Something was up, and my lower brain didn't want to listen. Truth be told, neither did my upper brain.

My phone rang, and I was tempted not to answer it. I knew who it would be, and I wasn't in the mood. I had Kia racing through my veins, and I wanted to sleep on that, not the dry and dreary rantings of a boss hell bent on making a dent in his career.

I checked the caller I.D., pushed talk, and said, "I don't think she did it."

"Oh God, here we go again," Chris said cutting and resigned.

"Seriously, it doesn't add up."

"Let's review the facts shall we?" Chris said, not sounding patient or tolerant at all, but I interrupted him anyway. "I know, but it's circumstantial, and she doesn't feel good for it."

"I don't care what she 'feels good for.' Every piece that has been stolen has come from collections she's in charge of; each of those lovely—" *note his sarcasm*, "—pieces has been personal favorites of hers; and each piece has gone missing from the museum on nights when Miss Everet has key-passed-in—*alone*—at the museum. She's been taped entering and leaving the premises."

"But we don't have the thefts on tape."

"No, but she did access each of the secure cases belonging to the now missing lockets on the nights of their disappearance!"

Chris was definitely not happy with me right now.

"Do you remember the last time you didn't 'think it was *her*'?" Chris demanded, and I grimaced, resigned and accepting that the conversation was definitely taking a turn for the worst.

"One Miss Victoria LeBrandt as I recall."

Yep. He was going there.

"Correct me if I'm wrong. But you didn't seem to think she was guilty either." He paused, apparently for emphasis. "As I recall, she almost got away!"

If I hadn't been sitting there, reclined on my sofa, Bullet resting across my legs, God I swear I would have needed a blanky, Chris's tone being so freaking disparaging. As it was, I reached for my beer and took a long satisfying pull, working to drown him out, but sadly failing.

"Do I need to remind you of the magnitude of this case?! Or how it's your ass on the line here, should you be stupid enough to screw it up? Or how I will not back you up this time!"

I figured it wouldn't do any good to tell him I searched her place, investigated her haunts—all two of them, the lab and Chloe's—and came up clean. Nothing about Kia matched the profile, except of course, all this highly damning circumstantial evidence. Kia was sassy, but she didn't have the cocky brass and guarded disposition crooks on the job tended to have. Sure, neither did Vicki, but Kia was different. Vicki had been cool, collected, level-headed, playing me for the fool the whole time. Kia was warm and honest, an open book just trying to protect her job, but interested in pursuing some Q.T. with me. Or so I hoped. Regardless, Chris wasn't going to be interested in any of my stellar rationalization, so I sat there waiting for it to be over.

"Jake?"

"Right here."

I heard Chris drag in a heavy sigh. "Jake, just do your job. I don't care how. Schmooze her if you have to—if it will make you happy—but catch her in the act. Catch her at all costs, and let's close this case and move on! Got it?"

"Oh yeah, I got it. But—"

"I don't give a damn about your 'buts.' Let me be clear. She. Is. Guilty. Your job is to catch her in the act, arrest her, and close this case. Move on. I get my promotion. You get to stay in the field with a new boss. Everybody's happy. Capiche?!"

"Yeah, I got it."

"Jake?"

"Loud and clear. Can I go now?"

I was sounding peevish, but I didn't care. Chris was totally pissing me off. Even if he had a reasonable point. I *had* gotten played. And I *had* defended myself, only to find my ass on the chopping block with Vicki almost long gone, headed to a country minus extradition laws. What she would have done in Russia, I didn't know. And here I was doing it again. But really, Kia felt clean. Or was that me just wanting to believe it?

"The locket will be arriving in the morning. I expect a full report. And stay on top of Miss Everet's every waking moment. Feel free to take that as you please. Maybe if she likes you, she'll slip up in front of you, and we'll close this case faster and get the hell out of here, before you do something stupid. Like have the poor judgment to fall in love again!"

"I know how to do my job!" I hadn't meant to raise my voice, but Chris was intentionally pushing my buttons, and it was irritating as hell.

"Good! Then do it!" he said and disconnected, leaving me to sit there, angry, no longer floating on the high of Kia. *Bastard!*

I took another long pull on my Labatt's and drained the bottle. If I didn't have to be at the museum at the crack of dawn, I'd have downed another, but as it was I needed to take my sour mood to bed now and wake up all thrilled to be a schmoozing FBI guy, ready to put Kia behind bars.

I was so not ready to do that. Ready to handcuff her, yes. Tackle her if she resisted. But not for the purposes of taking her in. Only for the purposes of taking her down. Into my bed.

Chris was right. I just didn't want to hear it. So could I do it? Could I play Kia like she was playing me? Even if meant exploring the heated option doing a Samba dance between our pheromone charged bodies. It's like we were stuck in each other's gravitational pull, both fighting to avoid collision, knowing it was impossible, and enjoying it anyway. If I looked at it as it was—a cat and mouse game to the finish—instead of what I wanted it to be—a fresh beginning with a totally *Wham* chick who, by just breathing, rocked my world, then my choice was a no-brainer. Keep up the bait, tempt, and tease, and then, when Kia stole the locket—breaking my heart—arrest her lying, deceiving ass, throw her in the clink, toss away the key, and forget to look back.

If only I believed it. If only I wasn't channeling my burnt trust against Vicki onto Kia, just to please Chris. If only I hadn't already started to fall, and hard.

I reached down with my free hand and gave Bullet a quick ruffle behind his ears. "Come on Bullet. Last time out for the night."

Bullet jumped up and bounded off toward the door. I walked into my kitchen, rinsed out my bottle, and placed it into the empties container. I shook my head, not happy. I was never going to sleep like this.

"Okay, Bullet," I said. "How about we go for a run?" It was the only way I was going to shake this off.

As I laced up my runners and grabbed for Bullet's lead, like the idiot I was, glutton for punishment, I thought, *Kia, you've got me believing in you. Don't make me regret it. Don't make me face the rain-maker and have to walk the walk of shame. Just be real. Please don't make me have to arrest you and Chris be right.* Yeah, I know. I'm a real sucker.

Kia

Tasty Seconds, Please

I woke up to the smell of breakfast yummy floating in from my kitchen. Chloe's Fat French Toast for sure. I was enticed, as Chloe knew I would be. I never could pass up those thick, fluffy slabs of vanilla-custard coated brioche sizzled up to golden perfection. And I'm sure she'd have them slathered in butter and my favorite, cinnamon sugar. Not to mention fresh sliced strawberries. O.J. and a banana would be the predictable accompaniments, and I was salivating just thinking about it. She was going all out, as well she should for such a sucker move, setting me up with Jake like that.

Jake.

That man was just—too much, and he knew it. And now here he was invading my dreams. All that floating on a cloud. Whispering in my ear. And me. Liking it.

Kia, Kia, Kia.

Jake was tempting in my dreams. Molten magic. Lulling me . . . inviting me to linger and bask in the warm glow and tingly sensation of his promises. The delicious and decadent images seduced from the depths of slumber. All I had to do was close my eyes. Instead I bit my lip, smiled, and hoped.

I'm just betting the dream doesn't hold a candle to the real deal.

Shame on me, I know. But with Friday on the week's-end horizon, a girl could spare a little bad, don't-cha think? I breathed a heavy, contented sigh.

"Mmmm, tasty, tasty." And I wasn't just talking about Chloe's French toast.

Chloe knocked on my door, calling out, "Good morning, Kia! Big day! You ready to get this show on the road?"

"Come on in, Chloe."

She popped the door open and peeked in. "Still talking to me?"

"Isn't that what your Fat French Toast is for?"

She smiled. "Did it work?"

"Is the O.J. bottled or fresh squeezed?"

"Nothing but the best for you!"

I pretended to mull it over, and she laughed, "Oh alright, you! Such a tease!"

I chuckled, relenting. "So is everything ready, or do I have time for a shower first?"

"Ready, but if you want I can keep it warm for you."

I sat up, tossed my lavender-flowered summer blanket aside, hustled my feet into my slippers, and asked, "You staying?" and Chloe said "Only for a bit, I know you need to get to the museum."

"Okay, then. I'll hop in the shower and be right out."

Fifteen minutes later, my hair wrapped in a towel, body draped in my plush, hotel-purchased, terry-cloth robe, and feet padding along in my matching bath slippers, I found Chloe waiting for me at the dinette table. She had my plate all set up, and the banana and fresh squeezed O.J. tempted from the sidelines.

"Smells and looks delicious," I said, taking a seat, and Chloe beamed.

I knew it meant the world to her, taking care of me, so it wasn't surprising when she said, "I packed you lunch," and pointed to a medium-sized blue insulated lunch bag.

I swallowed the French toast I was happily chomping on—*heaven in every bite*, and looked over. "What's in there? Food for the entire museum?"

"No, just some lunch for you . . . and . . . maybe Jake."

The look I gave her made her say—all innocent like, *if that were possible*, "What? Can't I look out for you? Make some lunch for you and a friend."

I smiled at her persistence and shook my head. "Yeah, a friend. You're funny Chloe!"

"Well," she said, playfully puffing, "You don't have to share if you don't want to. You can save the second portion for your dinner if you'd like. I'm just saying."

"You're just saying, *what*?"

"I'm just saying it might be a good idea to keep that man near you. Just in case."

"Just in case, *what*?" Incorrigible! That's what she was, and I loved her for it.

"Just in case you two decide to—"

"To *what*? Go 'exploring' in my lab?" I laughed, and so did Chloe.

"No, silly. In case you two decide to continue getting to know one another," she said, going for angelic, but missing her mark by a mile.

"You know Chloe, I hope you never get busted by a cop with that act. 'Cuz you could never pull off, 'Honest, officer. I'm not guilty.' You'd be in lock-up before you could blink."

Her mock indignance was comical, and our laughter rolled on.

"Thank you, Chloe," I said finishing the last of my breakfast. "For the food and the fun. It's been a great start to my day."

"You're welcome, honey," she said. "Why don't you finish getting ready, and I'll clean up here. That way you don't have to worry about it later."

"You're the best," I said, giving her a big hug, and Chloe said, "It's true! Now get a move on before the museum gets going without you!"

"They wouldn't!"

"They might, you slow poke."

I left a vapor trail as I raced through my apartment taking care of my finishing touches. French twist to my hair, for up and out of my face. Teeth flossed and brushed. Pale-yellow linen sleeveless sundress—Jake seemed to like the one from yesterday, maybe he'd like this one too. *I know! Bad, again, but there it is.* Dark leather, side-buckle sandals, and a white summer cardigan to cut the initial chill of the museum. Another hug for Chloe, and her lunch for two strapped across my shoulder, and I was out the door and into my car racing along Plymouth.

Five minutes later, I walked into my office to find Mr. Dream Temptation sitting there at my desk, looking even better than Chloe's Fat French Toast. Impossible, I know. But true. He looked up from the whatever he was looking at and smiled at me.

"Good morning. Did you sleep well?"

His voice was deep, soothing, and sounded sleepy, like maybe he hadn't gotten up yet. *Sexy.* And it sent a happy tingle to the pit of my stomach. I was still high off my dream, and this wasn't helping.

Ignoring it as best I could, I smiled back, and came over to drop Chloe's lunch tote on the floor next to my desk. No way was I going to tell him about my "sweet dreams," so instead I asked, "Sleep much?"

"It's the excitement," he said drolly.

"Me or the collection?"

I shouldn't have asked, but I was having a hard time thinking straight. Might have something to do with the hungry look he drenched me with, and how I was finding it hard to breathe.

When he didn't answer—only continued to eat at me with his eyes—I looked for a quick distraction so I wouldn't do something stupid, like tell him to take me on my desk, and I found a hot mug of something that looked suspiciously like hot chocolate, sitting on a mug warmer, that wasn't mine.

"What's this?"

"Friendship dues, gotta keep the lines of communication open."

"Is it what I think it is?" I asked bending down a little to take a delectable whiff.

"If you're thinking it's your daily chocolate fix, yes."

"Daily?" I scoffed. "This won't last me past morning."

"Give it a chance. It may be disguised as an innocent, steamy mug of milk beverage—but it's potent."

I gave Jake my best I-don't-think-so look, and took a tentative sip.

Cocoa heaven washed over me. The power of dark chocolate, *the really good stuff*, tickled my tongue and sent waves of delicious coursing through me. "Wow! You sure there's any milk in here?!"

"Good, isn't it?"

"This is that guy you know, right?"

"Yep. He makes it from the molten chocolate fountain—*from the gods*—and adds just enough steamed milk so your spoon doesn't stand up straight."

"I have to meet this guy!"

"What? And create competition? No thanks. You get your chocolate fixes through me. Besides, I like my odds just as they are!"

I flashed him my not-a-chance grin and said, "Creating dependency are we?"

"Not at all, just ensuring my place in the servant line."

"So tell me Jake, just what exactly do you think your chances are?"

"Million to one," he shrugged.

"Pretty confident are you?"

"More and more everyday."

Well, that would never do. It might be true, but no way was I going to let him know it!

I took another sinful sip, put the mug back on the warmer, grabbed my files to go see Karen Daniels, my Curriculum Director, and headed for the door. "Don't quit your day job."

"This is my day job!" he said, and I turned to catch him staring at my backside with a very interested and heated eye.

He liked the dress. And he liked me. But he was giving off a funny vibe this morning. Like maybe he wasn't sure if he liked liking me, but then again, he'd brought me chocolate, so I was probably imagining that. *Maybe.*

"I've got a meeting. Will you be okay checking with Phillip to see where we are with the shipment?"

"Got it under control," he said, not looking like he did with his gaze working to devour me, and I said, "Great, see you in a while," and bolted like the sated chocolate chicken I was.

Come on Friday! At this rate, I was never going to make it.

Kia

Business as Usual

Karen's office was tucked away in the Curriculum and Outreach department of the museum, and was located on the third floor. I jetted up the stairwell, anxious to get away from Jake and at the same time missing the fun and sizzle of him.

So not good.

I was getting ideas that were not conducive to my keeping my job here at the Acer, so minus the warmth and banter, I moved upward faster.

Popping out of the stairwell, I veered off to the left to the cache of admin offices, and the C.O.D. I found Karen busily inspecting display materials and ordering her eager minions around. It was organized chaos as usual. We were both always excited to get new collections, and even more excited when everything was out, *correctly*, and educating interested viewers.

"Six seconds," I heard her say to her number two minion, Carrie. "Six seconds is all we've got to get this message across, and I've read it more than twenty times. None of them took less than thirty seconds." She was shaking her head no and grabbed a black permanent marker and started scribbling all over the prop board. "This will never do. We need to separate this into at least three usable chunks," she said to Carrie.

"Hiya Karen, how's it going?" She looked up, and a wee bit of frenzy dashed across her Annette Bening face. "That good, eh?" It was amazing how much she looked liked the actress—except for her funky, fat, black-rimmed glasses—and her family money gave her a sense of distinguished class, but she didn't have any of Annette's grace. She was intelligent, slightly outlandish, and had quite a bit of quirk. It was no wonder why we were friends and comrades-in-arms against Phillip.

"Don't get me started," she said, but smiled. "Same-O, same-o." She looked back at the prop board and said, "I don't know why I bother building these quaint tidbits of educational info, when someone else is just going to ignore my directions and saturate the reader with these giant boards."

She of course meant Phillip. He seemed to revel in making our lives hell, and all just so he could save a few bucks. But unlucky for Phillip, Karen never backed down, and always redid his undoings. You'd think he'd learn, but we've already established that he's an idiot, and Karen had a solid *In* with the Board of Trustees. I'm sure having Ruth Ann Acer as her great-grandmother might have something to do with it, but hey, I guess family money and influence only get you so far! Phillip was truly unbelievably thick.

"Do you have time to talk curricular overview with me?" I asked, and she nodded, handing the heavily defiled prop board to Carrie. "Carrie, please see that these changes get sent to the printer for immediate reprint. Drop my name, and see if you can get me the new boards later today, at the latest, tomorrow in the A.M."

"Sure thing," Carrie said and scurried away.

I took a seat at Karen's gigantic lighted worktable, but before I could open my files, she leaned in and whispered conspiratorially and with more than a hint of suggestion, "So who is this eye candy you've got draped across your arm now? He's yummy!"

"You think?" I asked, playing it cool.

"You know he is!" she said all over my feigned indifference. "Even the men on staff are drooling over him, what with his big muscles and all. Where does someone pick up a bod like that?! He must live at the gym."

We both paused to think about Jake at the gym. I don't know what Karen envisioned, but I saw olive skin, stretched taught across glistening muscles, and loose shorts that might, on a giving day, tease a girl with a sneak peak of future attractions.

It was thirty below in the museum's morning A.C., but that didn't stop us from fanning ourselves.

"God, tell me he's a Neanderthal, make his existence tolerable!"

"Sorry. No can do. He's smart, funny, and he's making it hard for me to breathe. So if you want him, come and get him."

"You don't mean that," she said with a hopeful grin, and I shook my head, smirking, "No. I don't! But he is making my life a bit more challenging, and the irony is that he's been brought in to make my life easier. Help get this collection up and running before Friday. We'll see if I don't pass out first!"

"I heard we got him on loan from the DIA, but I've never heard of him. He must be new out there. I don't know why Phillip would call for back-up. You've never needed the help before."

"Yeah, I don't know, and I didn't ask. Phillip has been giving me a hard time, even more so recently than normal, so when he told me he was getting me help, I figured it would be better if I didn't ask. In the end, it could be worse. Jake could be all that, brains and bod, but be an absolute doof, or something even more wasteful, so—"

"Torture it is," Karen said, and I nodded sullenly, but then smiled, *naughty*, and she said, "You are so bad."

"Don't I know it. I've told myself I have to wait until Friday, and then . . . Well, I might just have to lick him!"

"Lick him?"

"Like a cupcake."

"This is Chloe talking?"

I nodded, and Karen said, "That woman is such a good influence! You have to promise me the details."

I shook my head. "Premium catch. Details will cost you!"

"Guess it's a good thing I'm loaded then," she said, and we both laughed.

"Alright then," I said downshifting to work, definitely needing to change the subject before we really got out of hand. "Let's talk focal points."

"I am going to make your day," Karen said gleefully.

"Phillip resigned and is moving to Siberia?"

"No, but just as good!"

"What can be that good?" I asked, and she got up and said, "Follow me." We walked over to the large display holdings, and Karen moved toward a covered wall board, and said, "Do you remember that beat up photo of Anastasia you gave me?"

"You didn't!"

"I did," Karen smiled and pulled back the sandy colored protective cloth to reveal the restored image of Grand Duchess Anastasia Nikolaevna of Russia, once thought to have survived, but now proven to be dead, murdered, wearing her mother's Garnet Love Locket. Gift from her Great Aunt Maria.

"How's this for a focal point?" Karen wanted to know, cheerfully pleased with herself.

"It's perfection!" I said, awed, and then was startled by a low whistle from behind.

Karen and I turned to find Jake standing behind us, appreciating the wall board. He walked over and introduced himself to Karen and shook her hand. "Hi, I'm Jake Davidson. Nice to meet you."

"Karen Daniels," she replied, sounding smitten, and asked, "Will you be here with us at the Acer for long?"

"Only until Friday," he said, a picture of pleasant politeness, but then the room temp shot up a thousand degrees as he dropped his sinner man, hungry glance on me again and smiled.

I responded with my best withering stare and asked, "Stalking me?" and he said, still smiling, "Not at all, just making sure your chocolate fix was holding." Then he nodded to the resplendent Anastasia and asked, "Where did you get this gem from?"

"I know, but it wasn't much of a gem when we got it. When I requested the pieces for this collection, I also asked if they had any family portraits featuring any of the artifacts being sent, and I hit the jackpot. They sent three paintings and two photographs. This was one of them, but it was in rough shape, burnt edges, and over a third of the photo was missing. But Karen, here, knows a digital wizard, and he restored and enlarged it to this!"

"It's beautiful," Jake said. "And the locket you love so much." He shook his head, and I asked, "What?"

"Nothing. Lucky find."

"I know. That's what Karen and I thought, too. It's never even been on display before, given its condition. So the Acer is able to debut something new. We're going for the personal side during the exhibit, and this is the centerpiece of the show."

"Well," Jake said, "I don't want to burst your bubble, but there's a problem with the shipment. One of the crates is missing."

"Don't tell me."

"Yep, the one containing your locket."

Jake

Just Checking

I watched Kia's face fall, but couldn't gage from her reaction what it meant. Business? Personal? Or both? I was hoping for all business, but reluctantly open to the idea of personal. I don't know exactly what I was waiting for, but if it was Kia exclaiming, "Well damn, that's sure gonna put a kink in my plans to steal it," I didn't get it. She stood there for a moment, blank, processing, and then she came out swinging.

"What do you mean one of the crates is missing? Missing how? Like it didn't make the shipment? Or it's lost, misrouted somehow?"

There was a definite note of panic in her voice.

"Missing as in it was there, and now it's not."

"Well, what does the Hermitage curator say?"

"Nothing so far," I replied, and she looked about to bite, so I quickly added, "Eight hours ahead, remember. Besides, it's Monday; the museum is closed. But I've got a call in to the carrier service, and we should be hearing back from them within the hour."

Karen stepped in and said, "Kia, I've got this here. If you haven't made any changes from our last sit-down, then I'm good. And I promise you, I'll let you know if that at any moment changes."

Kia gave Karen her blank, still processing look, and then said, "It's my centerpiece," and Karen said, "I know." Karen's tone was all over understanding how important this was to Kia, and I would have been a little bit more on top of it, if I hadn't been trying to figure out the business or personal angle, but then Karen said to Kia, "Don't worry. You'll figure this out, and the show will go off without a hitch. There's always one hiccup per exhibit, so here it is, and it's Monday. Four whole days to go. Plenty of time!"

Kia turned to me, looking a lot deflated, but even more determined and said, "I'll need a copy of the manifest to see what other pieces are missing or supposed to be in that crate," and I said,

"Already requested, and we should be receiving a fax copy no later than the return contact from the carrier." And then Kia turned to Karen and said, "Same plan for now. I'll come up with a Plan B, *if this stays south*, and then you and I can dry run it to make sure the presentation is curricularly viable."

"Sounds good," Karen said, and then Kia asked me, "Does Phillip know?"

I nodded, yes, and Kia's nose wrinkled. It was a funny little expression I hadn't yet seen her make, and it shouldn't have been cute, but her look was so resigned and her expression so fitting, I almost kissed her to make it all better. But then she asked, "What did he say?" knowing full well it wasn't going to be good.

I hesitated, not really wanting to relay his offending ignorance, but the look she gave me prompted my speedy reply. "He said it was obvious you were incapable of doing your job, and that even a volunteer temp could manage the receipt of a shipment. He asked me to handle it."

I'd left out his more creative use of the English language, but Karen and Kia exchanged looks, and I knew they knew. The guy was a USDA certified asshole.

Karen made a disgusted sound and said, "No offense to you, Jake, but I don't know what tree trunk crawled up that man's backside. Seriously Kia, what is his problem with you?"

Kia shrugged, and Karen said, "No way is this your fault. And I've never seen you so excited over a collection. It's apparent to anyone paying attention that this is important to you!"

And I thought, *Exactly! Now why is that?*

"No," Kia said, agreeing to the not being her fault part. "But I better make sure it gets fixed and fast. Otherwise, I'm sure this will be just another strike against my continued Acer existence."

"Maybe you should talk to someone," Karen suggested. "Like a Board member."

"Nah. It's okay. I'll take care of it, but thanks. Besides—" Kia said, giving me a meaningful look. "I've got Jake here to help me out."

It was the first time since my arrival that I actually felt like a heel.

I know. Funky. Here I am here to observe, catch her in the act, and arrest her, and I don't feel like a heel until her boss makes me into the bad guy for his benefit. I felt like I should say something supportive, but she beat me to the punch.

"Sorry Jake. It's not you. That man just likes to push my buttons."

I sure knew how that felt. Chris was the same way.

"It's cool. And it's obvious Phillip couldn't tell his arse from his backside where talent and skill are concerned. You're oozing it from every bright and shiny surface, and he's wasteful."

"Awww, what a nice thing to say," Karen said, smiling, and then suggestively offered, "Why don't you two go talk over this 'Plan B,' and let me know if we need to make any changes."

Kia rolled her eyes at Karen's wily ways, and to help lighten the moment some more I protested, "Hey, don't I get a say in this?" and they both pounced on that, letting me know how they felt with a resounding, "NO!"

I put my hands up in surrender. "Okay, okay! Plan B it is." I reached out to drag Kia away, happy to be touching her again, ready to do battle to the death at seeing her downed by Phillip's attack, and knowing I shouldn't be doing either.

We left Karen to her wall boards, signage, and description plates and headed back to Kia's office. Kia was quiet the whole long walk down one flight of stairs and across the display floor, all the way, until we were securely in the privacy of her inner sanctum, and then she let out a frustrated, "That man!" and shook her head.

Kia walked over to her desk and rifled through the papers sitting there.

"What are you looking for?" I asked, trying to be helpful, and walked over to stand beside her. I was so close I could feel her tension crackling around her, elevating her from alive and kicking to alive and just short of screaming.

"Messages about the crate."

She flipped through everything one final time, and then stopped, looked up at me and stared.

"This sucks."

"Don't give up hope."

I couldn't believe I said it, like *Don't worry, the locket will find its way here just in time for you to steal and for me to arrest you.* At least this way, she couldn't lift it, we couldn't prosecute, and I might have half a chance with her.

I know! What was I thinking?!

"It's going to be a long day, Jake. It took Karen and me over sixth months to develop our focus and curriculum. If I have to rebuild it with a new focus, I may not get any sleep this week."

"Let me call the carrier again and see if I can get an update yet, and you can take a moment to collect your thoughts," I offered.

She shook that off and said, "It's okay. You can make the call and check to see if the manifest is in, but I need to check with Ian about the displays." She picked through the mess she'd made on her desk and found the layout plans, and then asked, "So the rest of the shipment arrived okay, though? It's just the one crate not here."

"Yes. All the other crates are here."

"Well, that's something. Maybe we can start matching pieces to Ian's ready displays. I'll be back," she said, and I watched her walk out onto the floor and find Ian. And then I watched Mr. Tan-Fit, Thirty-Something reach around his arm and pull her into his side for a reassuring hug, and I thought, *Hey you! That's my play!*

But it wasn't. And I wanted it to be. *Jake, Jake, Jake. You're falling in deep.*

Kia

Hell and Holding

I was standing there, minding my own business, explaining the snafu to Ian, and discussing possible alternatives, when Phillip came storming up the stairs, purple, waving his arms and a manila folder wildly about, huffing, puffing, spitting mad, and he unfortunately made his way over to me. *Great. This should be fun.*

"Ms. Everet," he boomed, and out of the corner of my eye, I saw Jake emerge from my office and come up quietly behind Phillip. "This exhibit is your brain child *and your responsibility.* Why is that I am the one receiving faxes and phone calls on your behalf?"

"That's my fault Dr. Mann. I was just—" Jake interceded, startling Phillip, causing him to jerk, but in no way did it lessen his ire.

I flashed Jake a thanks-but-I've-got-this look and calmly said, "Thank you Phillip, for bringing me the fax," and I reached out and helpfully grabbed for the folder from his anger flailing arm. "My apologies the phone call was not forwarded appropriately to my office where we have been anxiously waiting to hear from the carrier service."

"You're the Mensa candidate around here," he sneered.

Wow, who knew he thought so highly of me? *Hardly.*

Phillip was escalating, as though I hadn't said a word, and it was just a wee bit mortifying to have him yelling at me in front of Ian and his crew and Jake, but I held my ground, waiting for him to sputter himself out.

"So I'm sure you understand that the gala opening is *this* Friday."

Still Lake Placid on my side, I said, "Yes, Phillip, I am aware."

"So what exactly are you planning to do to get this missing crate here. Lost in transit, by the way!"

My heart sank, but I refused to show it. Lost in transit meant I was at the mercy of the carrier service to retrace the container's steps, the truck's delivery route—*anything*—until it could be found and directed appropriately. There was a good chance it would not make it here by Friday, so I was going to have to find a Plan B.

"You do realize the importance of our gala events, don't you?" he fumed.

Ahhh, here it comes. The money.

"You've already sent out invitations and programs! What will the donors think when—"

This was going nowhere, so I said, "Thank you Phillip for making time in your very busy schedule to bring this information to me. I will get right on it." I was amazed I'd pulled that off without even a hint of sarcasm.

He leaned in to me, lowered his voice—not that everyone couldn't still hear him—but I guess the guy gets an A for his sort-of effort, and said, "Ms. Everet, you've been a tremendous disappointment since the moment you began. I should have paid more attention to the negative reference rather than your resume. So I'm warning you. You either get this right, or you can get yourself a new job."

"Thank you for the clarity, Phillip," I said. "Now, if you'll excuse me, I also have a lot to do."

He pulled back, sucked in a breath, as if preparing to lash out again, but then stopped short when Jake stepped close, put his hand on Phillip's arm, dropped his voice to a whisper, and said with a cold authority I hadn't thought possible from such a fun guy, "You've made your point, Phillip. Now step down."

Everyone on the second floor was watching, and even Karen was standing at the ready on the stairs from the third floor. It was a bad scene. The worst in my Acer time. And I didn't know why Phillip was so bent out of shape, but thankfully he backed off, flashing his angry glance around, and turning to stomp back downstairs.

Immediately Ian nudged closer; Karen quickly closed the distance; and Jake sized me up for breakdown possibility. An absolute silence filled the space Phillip had evacuated, and I'm not sure if any of us were breathing, but then Karen said, "What in the hell. Are you alright?"

Everything about this job was perfect, everything except Phillip. But as bosses go, he could be worse. Right? I mean, as opposed to his crass attitude toward my intelligence and his disgusting sycophantic behavior in front of donors and his demeaning use of my appearance to schmooze, he could be hitting on me, going for sexual harassment instead of discrimination.

I shuddered. The thought was enough to make me vomit.

Yeah, this was way better.

"Kia?" Jake said, and I felt him take my hand. On impact, warmth traveled up the length of my arm, spanned my chest, and filled the pit of my stomach. I closed my eyes, took a deep breath, and shook off the last of Phillip Mann and his contemptuous visit.

I looked at the three faces staring at me, gave Jake's hand a gentle squeeze and let go, and said, "Sorry. Zoned out there, but I'm okay."

They didn't look like they believed me, so I said, "Really. It's cool. Apparently, I just *really* need to find myself a missing crate."

"He can't fire you for this," Karen said adamantly. "I won't let him."

Ian nodded. "It's a shipping error. Is there anything I can do?"

I shook my head. "Thanks, but I've got it. Ian, you're doing a great job here, and after lunch I'd like to start filling the ready displays."

"Sounds great. I'll be here if you need anything," he said. I nodded and smiled thanks, and Ian stepped away to corral his men back into work.

I turned to Karen and opened the folder from Phillip. "I'll be working on a backup just in case," I said and looked down to review the manifest. "It appears that we are missing the Tsarina's settee, her bejeweled writing box, and of course, her Garnet Love Locket." I sighed. "That's all from the same display area. I don't know if that's a good thing or bad thing."

"It probably would have been better if that weren't the case," Karen said. "We would have been able to pretty much stick with the program as it is and just removed the missing items from mention, but now a concentrated chunk from a single presentation point is missing." Karen made a scrunchy face and added, "We'll have to do the same thing, but take extra steps to fill the void to maintain the flow of the show as you intended. Aaand of course, without your centerpiece, we'll have to rethink the entire presentation theme."

She blew out a sigh, and I was right there with her. I shook my head and said, channeling optimism, "Okay then. We need that crate."

"I can start working on some text adjustments, just in case. And you can let me know how we're doing." Karen smiled her best *go get 'em tiger* and started to edge her way back toward the third floor stairwell.

I nodded, gave her a thumbs up, and said, "I'll make some calls, and I'll keep you posted."

"Sounds good," she said, smiling, and disappeared up the stairs, leaving me to stand there with Jake and his warmth. I'd let go of his hand, but he was still there, in my space, breathing my air, soothing me telepathically. He was radiating a calm I didn't feel, and I wondered if he thought I might blow.

"I'm fine," I said, and he said, "I know." He sounded like he cared, not like he was handling me, and that was nice. I blew out the breath I'd been holding, and he asked, "You ready to make some calls?"

I nodded, ready to tackle the world if I had to, and Jake looked like he was right there with me. I'd been right. He was perfection.

Jake

Have a Little Faith

Okay. So watching Phillip Mann, the big, blustering moron that he was, go ballistic on Kia had me going caveman hero. It'd taken restraint, with a capital R, not to blow my cover and kick his worthless, malicious ass on the spot. And Kia, how did she put up with that crap day after day?

This is what I think—a chick about to lift a zillion dollar locket puts up with a lot for an inside chance. So either Kia *really* wants that locket—or it's not her doing the taking. That with her straight-forward-in-your-face thing she had going on, and her obviously solid friendship with Karen, her other personal connections at the Acer, and her not having any signs of being bent or living outside her means, and I don't think she's the thief.

Sure, I know. Saying that out loud will get my teeth kicked in—what with Chris's convictions and all—but I've decided to have some faith, go out on a limb, and get that crate back for Kia, for the Acer. I'm with the freaking FBI, after all, and we've tracked down harder things and people in less time. Sooo, despite what might be my better judgment on a different day, I got on the horn—minus Chris's okay, and made some calls . . . he'll live, I'm sure, *or* not, who cares at this point . . . Kia's job was at stake. If it turns out that she steals the locket, then I'm a dolt, and I'll arrest her faster than she can say Acer, throw away the key, and never look back. Chris gets his promotion, and I get to stay in the field. All's well that ends well. Or so they say.

So a few phone calls later, and I knew getting the locket back was a forgone conclusion. I smiled at my own self-satisfaction and headed back to Kia's office. She was a wreck, but hiding it Oscar well, so this would be a good time to go and give her a hard time about lunch.

Kia was sitting at her desk, ear glued to the phone, doodling her pencil away, and looking despondent but driven. "Well, can you check with them, and see if they have it? It has to be somewhere."

I walked over, and she looked up and mouthed, "Bennington Freight."

No surprise there, so I reached down and picked up the blue, soft-sided cooler Kia had brought in. It had Chloe written all over it, and she made excellent food. I set it on Kia's desk and started to unzip it, but got interrupted by Kia's batting arm. She twisted the receiver away from her mouth and said in a loud whisper, "Hey, that's my lunch!"

"Looks like there's enough here for two," I said peering inside, and Kia grabbed for the bag, but I moved it, and she missed, then said, throwing some attitude into it, "My lunch *and* dinner!" Then she had to return to her phone call.

"Are you sure? You've verified it's not there?" She paused, then said, "Well, where *is* the last place you have a visual record of the crate?"

Kia tried to pry the bag away from me, but she wasn't in the game, being all about her phone call, and I pulled it closer to me and out of her reach. She gave me *that look*, but unless she wanted to dive across her desk, the bag was mine. Ha ha. Inside I found containers labeled sandwiches, fruit salad, condiments, and dessert. I wasn't fighting fair, I know. But tough luck for Kia. Not that it mattered. Neither was Chloe.

I reached in and pulled out a light blue linen envelope with my name on it. *That Chloe.* Poor Kia. She was totally outnumbered. But hey, yay for me! I flipped the envelope over, broke the seal, and opened it to find a note:

> Dear Jake,
> Thank you for making sure Kia eats lunch!
> My special gift to you—double fudge chip brownies, but be nice and share with Kia, I bet she's having a rough day.
> Love,
> Chloe

Chloe was awesome! I wanted her to adopt me, not that I was orphaned or anything, but she didn't know that, and I'd eat like a king forever.

"How long before you can get back with me?" Kia asked the poor schmuck on the other end of the line. "I needed this shipment today, so every day that passes until receipt is critical!" She paused, listening. "Well, thank you. I'm very much looking forward to your call." She stared daggers at the phone, then hung up and sighed. It took her a moment to find her way back to me, but after a much needed deep breath, she looked over and pinned her squinty sights on me.

"Hey! Don't look at me like that. It's not like I took it or anything!"

"No, but you're stealing my food."

Kia was fighting her stress and frustration, and I felt for her, but knew it would be better. Wish I could tell her, but that would be like announcing *FBI guy in the house*. So I did the next best thing.

"Nuh-unh," I said like I was a six year old. "I have a note!" I said waving Chloe's stationary in the air.

"Give me that," she said grasping for it, but I snatched it away.

"It's not polite to read other people's mail!"

"I'm not a polite person!"

"You were."

"That was yesterday, before I got trampled by circumstance. Today, I'm just a mean ol' biddy."

"Unlikely. You don't have it in you."

"How do you know?"

"Too good of a kisser. Rules out all biddiness."

"Jake," she said going all earnest, "I can't let you eat this. No offense."

"None taken. But I'm eating."

"*My dinner?*"

"Nope. Got it covered. We'll order in, just tell me what you want."

"What if I said, 'you'?"

My heart stuttered, and my lower brain gave a hoot and holler, but one look into her eyes, and I knew better. She was just playing me to save her food. I lowered my brows at her. "Not on the menu."

"It is now," she said, adjusting her attitude, throwing a whole lot of sultry into it, and taking a step toward me—and Chloe's lunch bag.

I stood my ground, put my hand over the bag, and countered with, "Nope. Not until Friday. Your rules, not mine."

"I've seen Friday. It's highly overrated."

"Deal's a deal!" I said fully securing our lunch.

"Uhh," she said retreating, and I started breathing again. "You know you're just her food pimp, don't you?"

"Not true. She likes me!"

"She's using you!"

"Says so right here," I said pointing at Chloe's signature line, "*Love, Chloe.*"

Kia shook her head, clearly amused, but thinking better of it. "You going to stand there all day Cabana boy? I'm getting hungry over here."

I smiled. Jake five, Kia zilch. Maybe I should let her win one, just to feel better. I paused, looked upward, and gave that thought all of about a blink before vetoing it. Naaah, where was the fun in that?

I reached into the tote, pulled out the containers and started popping them open. Kia walked over to her improvised kitchen, replete with her office and lab sink, a tiny fridge, and an even tinier microwave. I was luxuriating in the smells of Chloe's culinary delights while Kia washed up and grabbed supplies. When she turned around her hands were full with her O.J., plates, napkins, cups, and plastic silverware.

"Come here often?" I asked, and she shrugged. "Occupational hazard."

"You seem to be the only one at risk," I said, and she said, "Newbie, relatively speaking. Comes with the territory. I have to work harder to prove my worthiness."

Thinking of dear old Phil's gratitude, I rolled my eyes and asked, "How's that working for you?"

Kia found her smiles again and gave me a small knowing one. "Some days are better than others."

"Today must have been stellar," I said reaching for a sandwich to put on the plate she set in front of me, but she intercepted and pointed at the sink, dealing out the goods while I got up to wash. By the time I was done, Kia had our turkey-cheddar on cracked wheat sandwiches and watermelon salad portioned out with her having a suspiciously larger amount of fruit than me. "If you do that," I said looking at her plate, "I'll be forced to eat half of your brownies."

She gave me her look, *daggers*, but cute, and said, "Fine," giving me one small conciliatory spoonful of the melon from her plate.

That's my girl. She was fully recovering and back to her usual tricks.

"So what are these?" I asked taking my knife to what I figured was mayo, and Kia said, "Chloe's brown mustard and homemade herb mayo."

She went to take a bite of her sandwich, and I asked, "You having any?" handing her the dish, and she said, "No. Turkey and cheddar plain is my favorite."

I laughed and set the mayo down. "See! Told you. Chloe loves me. She's even packing for me!"

I was gloating, but Kia wasn't having it. "Don't be ridiculous. Condiments as payment for services rendered is hardly liking you."

"The brownies are payment. The condiments is definitely liking me!" I spread the mayo on my sandwich and took a bite. "Ohmigod, that's a miracle on bread!" I said marveling and in taste heaven.

"Yeah, that's what my dad says, too."

I knew Kia's whole family tree, but given this *in*, I was firmly reminded of why I was here, and this was a good time to "get to know her better." *I was really starting to hate my job.*

"So is Chloe your mom's mom or your dad's mom?"

"My dad's."

"And your grandfather? Chloe's husband?"

"Grandpa Teddy. He passed away about ten years ago. Bad heart, but he was so in love with Chloe. He fought for every day. Lived years longer than the doctors gave him."

Kia took a constructed bite of blueberry and watermelon, looked at me with those beautiful jade pools, genuine and guileless, and offered unsolicited, "Chloe was devastated. Zoe and I became her life. Zoe's my younger sister. She's in grad school. A scientist."

She took another bite of fruit, and added, "I'm closer to Chloe than anyone, and she's my best friend in the whole world. She takes care of me even when I don't."

"Yeah, you two definitely make a pair!"

Kia laughed, happy and at ease, and sparks popped and sizzled in my brain. She so had *Wham*, and I was so sunk. I laughed with her and watched as the play of her lips teased me, and thought how nice it would be to bite them—just a nibble—right before I kissed them numb.

Being the FBI guy that I was, here to bust her, not like her, I should have been more upset about this traitorous turn of events—it's my job we're talking about after all—but I couldn't seem to muster much in the way of getting all worked up. Which was—So. Not. Good.

Kia and her life were digging their way in, and try as I might—even though I wasn't, *not really*—I couldn't fight it. Being by her felt good, felt right. It had only been a few days—I know—but my body hummed when she was near, and I was in constant anticipation of the sight, sound, smell, taste, and feel of her.

Instant chemistry was a bitch when it happened with a suspect, and this was my second go round with it. It was worse when it was backed up with actual *Wham!* Kia was so real and alive and fun and sexy, and I cared. I cared that Chloe took care of her, and was including me. I cared that she loved her job and had friends. And I cared that Phillip needed an attitude adjustment.

This was bad; I know. I was a divided man, part of me fighting to keep my eye on the ball and my job, and the other part kicking and screaming, telling me not to let life pass me by. Kia had potential. She was one in a bazillion, and I was halfway to hooked, ready to sprint the other half.

But then again, maybe that was just my protector complex talking. Phillip had been a dick, and Kia had fallen. It was something I hadn't liked seeing.

"Jake?" Kia asked.

"Yeah?" I said looking to see her plate empty and her O.J. gone. I'd dropped behind, and my thoughts wandered to the brownies, knowing what Kia was thinking.

"So how's your day been going?" I asked.

"Don't even think about it!" she said. "You're sharing those brownies!"

"*What?*" I said. "I'm just making conversation."

We ooooed and aaawwwed our way through Chloe's divine idea of what a brownie should be—dense, moist, chocolate-saturated goodness slathered in a smooth, chocolaty buttercream frosting with these tiny, itty bitty dark chocolate chips that added an initial, satisfying resistance as you bit into them . . . and then melted away like little chocolate dreams. I'd loved the mousse, but these were perfection.

I licked my lips and fingers and searched the lunch tote for more—just in case—and Kia said, smiling, "I know. She's pulling out all the stops and sending in the big guns. I don't know why, but for some reason, she seems to like you."

I grinned triumphantly and Kia shook her head. "Doesn't mean I have to like you, too," she said, and I said, "Yeah, but you know you do."

When we were done, I helped Kia clean up, and then she went off to start setting up displays, leaving me to try my hand at calling the carrier service. Comical, I know. All except the part where I was the FBI guy deceiving her, baiting her, waiting to drop her when she fell.

Heavy sigh. I really hated my job.

Kia

Taking Stock

I was on the fence about how my Monday was shaping up. It had looked a lot better last night, but now that I was in it, I wanted to give it back and try again later.

But it wasn't all bad.

Breakfast and Chloe. Lunch and Jake. Apparently I needed food to successfully navigate from one moment in time to the next. Maybe I just needed to feed Phillip, or rather have Chloe make something I could shove in his mouth to shut him up. What a jerk. I was still shaken, but not stirred, and I did what I did in times like these. Control what I can, and prepare for damage control for those that I can't. Today was now about damage control, and I headed to Shipping and Receiving to see how we were doing with our incoming Tsarist inventory.

Michael Veen was the mastermind behind the comings and goings of all things artifacts at the Acer, and I found him and his two assistants, Vincent Giadarello and Benjamin Nice—yep, that's his name, and he's actually a nice guy—working a steady flow. Each piece had to be checked in, reconciled to manifest, described, photographed, videoed, tagged, and entered into our database—its constant whereabouts monitored and tracked. They had an exhausting job, requiring exquisite attention to detail in the midst of high throughput efficiency, and whenever it was one of my collections coming in, I always went down to help out.

"Hi Mike. How's it going?" I asked coming to stand beside him as he carefully wrenched open one of the larger crates in the holding pattern.

He smiled at me, and said "I think I should be asking the same of you."

"News travels fast," I said, and he said, "Especially when it only has to travel down two floors to the basement."

I shrugged. "Looks like I'm going to need a miracle, but in the meantime, I'm here to help."

Mike looked inside the crate, and called over to his guys, "Writing desk. I believe it's the only one in the shipment," and Ben said, "Yep. Lemme finish with this cameo, and I'll help you film the extraction." Mike turned to me. "You're an angel of mercy, and I'm sure Ben and Vinny will be happy to make some room for you. Phillip's already been down here, and Ben's threatening mutiny if he does it again."

"That bad?"

"You should know," Mike said prying off another crate panel. "Why don't you grab that video cam," he said pointing behind me, "and you can film while Ben and I pull this desk out."

Every aspect of an artifact's arrival, stay, and departure at the Acer was filmed and documented. Every angle covered for insurance purposes and Acer reputation protection. There were cameras covering every inch of Shipping and Receiving, and it was Acer policy to directly film artifact crate removal and packaging. I aimed the camera at the crate, zoomed in for initial image collection, and Ben walked over to help Mike remove the desk. They donned cotton gloves, and very carefully, moved the desk to the recording platform for further documentation. I panned across their path, capturing the entire action, and then handed Mike the camera so he could check the video.

"Looks good," he said, and I came in for a closer look at the desk. "This is Nicholas II's writing desk. The scrollwork is pretty, but manly." The desk was walnut and heavy, well crafted, the sort that makes you want to run your hand across it with pride. "I like it."

"It's fantastic," Ben agreed. "Although how he ever wrote on these angles," he said of the lectern style writing panels, "I'll never know. Better suited to reading. But to each his own."

Ben loved his job, I know, because he never stopped talking about it. He loved that he got to examine each piece up close and personal, and it was like he created a little friendship with every artifact he checked in.

"His desk is nothing compared to Alexandra's Lady's Bureau," Ben said emphatically. "Mahogany and leather. The detail and workmanship are perfection, and it's in mint condition. And neither of their desks hold a candle to the eye popping gem I got to catalogue earlier. Wait 'til you see it Kia. It's gorgeous! A bouquet of flowers made entirely from diamonds and gems set in gold and silver."

Ben was about to add something but was cut short by the dinging of the elevator, and we all looked to the doors.

"If that's Phillip again," Ben said, and Mike countered, "You'll ignore him, and let me handle it."

"But—"

"But nothing. Dr. Mann's in a mood, and I'm not going to let him agitate you into getting canned."

We all stood in frozen animation—none of us apparently looking forward to another Phillip pass—and watched as the elevator burped open to nobody there.

I realized I'd been holding my breath, totally not prepared for more chit-chat with my ill-mannered, disagreeable cretin of a boss, and was relieved to find it empty.

Vacant space stared back at us, and with the anticipated threat over, we returned to the business at hand.

"Like I was saying, Kia—" Ben said, but fell silent again when an ominously suited arm popped through the heavy, stainless doors, right at the last second, halting their late slide progress.

I swallowed and felt the hairs on the back of my neck stand up and overwhelming repulsion kick in. I braced myself for the onslaught, turned to face Phillip directly, and released the breath I found myself holding again, when it was Jake who rolled out of the elevator, phone firmly affixed to his ear, obviously engrossed in his call.

I could just kiss him.

And the expression on my face must have said so, because he looked over to me, roved up and down, and smiled with eyes that said, *Later.*

I shook my head. He was just getting too confident for my own good.

Mike chuckled and asked, "Who's the new guy?"

"Shut up," I said, and he said all fake innocence, "What'd I say?"

Jake flipped his cell closed and extended his hand to Mike. "Hi, I'm Jake Davidson, on loan from the DIA."

"Mike Veen, and this is Ben, and that's Vinny," Mike said by way of a nod.

Ben and Jake shook hands, and Vinny walked over to do the same. Vinny wasn't the social type, so my guess is there was some sizing up going on. Everybody was all smiles, so Jake must've passed, and then he said to me, "I just got off the phone with Bennington."

"And?"

"And they're working on it."

"What's that mean?"

"It means they know where the crate got separated from our shipment, but not where it went from there."

My heart sank for the second time today. This just got better and better. "That doesn't sound reassuring."

Jake smiled supportively, his expression new. Kind. But he was holding something back. It was in his eyes. I just couldn't place it.

His look wasn't his usual heat, but some kind of want. And for Chloe's sake—at least that's the story I was sticking to—I was still working my hopefulness with him. Jake seemed to be on board, so my warm flashes weren't so flashy anymore. They were more of a permanent fluttery tingle that kept frying my circuits every time he got within kissing distance.

I was going to cave; I just knew it. Chloe would be thrilled.

I watched Jake morph from kind to molten, apparently reading me well, and he took a remarkably subtle step back, probably to keep from dragging me to his lips. I'd seen that hungry look before.

I hadn't noticed, but Mike, Ben, and Vinny had faded to black, probably suffocating from the heat waves bouncing off of us, and I looked over to find them *very* focused on anything other than Jake and me.

Jake smiled and said, "Well, I also just spoke with Ian, and he has the display cases and platforms for Nicholas II's items prepped and ready, and security has done their thing, so anytime now." He looked around at the work stations and asked, "What can I do to help?"

Take me, I thought. It's not like I was going to have my job for much longer if that crate didn't turn up. And Phillip was making my existence here less and less appealing by the moment. It was a traitorous thought, and before I could give it the good kicking it needed, Jake leaned in and said just low enough so that only I could hear, "Kia, honey. Friday's a long ways away. You keep that up, and we're never going to make it."

I licked my lips, trying not to think about it, and he shook his head, giving me a low warning. "I'm serious," he said, and I said, "I'm trying," and he said, putting some effort into it, "*Try harder.*"

Right.

"Okay, so let's help with check-in," I offered, but Mike called over—he apparently had ears like a hawk—and said, "That's okay, Kia, we've got it. Why don't you two start moving pieces upstairs?"

Bad, bad, bad.

"You sure, Mike?"

"Yep, we're cool."

Meaning they wouldn't be if we stayed down here.

Mike and the guys were on the ball. With Jake and me on set-up and them on receipt, we got all but two of Nicholas's belongings on display. At least that was something. And Phillip had made himself disappear. I didn't know how or where he went, and I didn't care. I wasn't going looking for him.

We still hadn't heard from Bennington about the crate, so I was making mental plans to work through the night, fixing the design and presentation flow, and prepping curricular changes for Karen to review tomorrow.

Jake angled up next to me, as I surveyed the lay of the land from my office doorway, and said just above a whisper, "I owe you takeout. What are you hungry for?" He paused, looked me straight in the eyes, and added, "And whatever you do . . . don't say or think, *me*. Otherwise, I'm taking you to your car and driving you home, and takeout will no longer be on the menu."

The challenge in his voice put a warm flutter in my belly and sent desire skittering across my skin. I took a deep breath, inhaling his delicious scent, and felt him step into me.

I bit my lip and mentally sighed, *Friday, Friday, Friday.*

My hesitation was just enough for Jake to reach for my hand and say, "Alright, let's go!"

"Bean burrito from Panchero's," I said, and his smile was tight.

He'd called my bluff for an easy reprieve tonight, but tomorrow would be another day, and a lot more heat.

"Be right back," he said and bolted out the door.

Jake

Maybe I Shouldn't Have

Two bean burritos, toppings on the side, a bag of chips and some salsa later, and I was walking back into Kia's office. I'd considered stopping for more chocolate, but then she might come to expect it, and I couldn't have that! Besides I'd already decided not to stay for dinner. I needed to get home to Bullet, and we'd matured into the sharing her chocolate stage, so I wouldn't want to disappoint. Plus, Kia had curriculum plans for the rest of the evening. *No—thank—you.* Not really my thing. Yep, best to get out of Dodge A.S.A.P. Besides, I'd only be in the way. Concentrating, for either one of us, was near impossible when we were in the same room, unless of course you considered desire and distraction concentrating. Which I didn't. Not in the midst of work politics and ogling eyes. Nope, if I'm going to be concentrating on desire and distraction—*the whole-hearted consumption of Kia*—I'll do it when we're alone with no risk of being interrupted.

I quietly drifted over to Kia sitting at her desk. She was flipping through papers and pages, hunkered over a floor plan of her presentation, looking intent and ready to tackle if need be.

Setting our bags down lightly, I asked, "Any last minute calls from Bennington come to save the day?"

Kia stopped shuffling, looked at me—wishful—and shook her head no.

"Sorry to hear that, but I've got your dinner here," I said handing her her bag.

I was still standing, and Kia took note as she opened her Panchero's sack for a peek.

"Deserting me?" she asked.

"Not at all," I said, and she smiled, "Then pull up a chair, looks like you've brought enough for two."

She was so on to me.

"Actually, I have this dog I have to get home to."

"Sure you do," she said and went to her sink to wash up and grab her O.J. "If you can't take the heat . . ."

Sure I could. Shouldn't, but could. It was more like the idea of retrofitting prepared program materials to match a newly diminished artifact flow was giving me hives.

"What happened to Friday?" I asked, and she said, "I don't think we're going to make it."

"Sure we will. We've got self-control."

She came back to her desk, set out a plate and napkin and her O.J., and gave me her unh-hunh look, suggesting I get real. It was the one that made me want to nibble on her lips, and I said, "Besides, you have this gala to prepare for, remember?"

It was time to bolt, before we both got stupid. I grabbed my bag, but she asked, "So what's your dog's name?"

"Bullet."

She pulled her burrito out of the bag and peeled open the foil wrapper. I'd gotten her salsa, guacamole, and sour cream to go, not knowing what she liked, but she didn't add any, just took a big bite, and looked happy.

Swallowing, she said, "Why? Is he faster than a speeding bullet?"

I smiled, "No, he dodged a bullet. He's a rescue."

"Cute."

I took a small step backward toward the door. "So I'm gonna go, let you get some work done."

She rolled her eyes at me, and said—clearly not convinced, "What kind of dog is Bullet?"

"Beagle," I said, and she practically snorted bean through her nose.

"Something funny?" I asked, and she said, "No," but the crinkle lines at the corners of her eyes were telling a different story.

"You don't believe me!"

She grinned and said, "Gonna need proof."

Obviously I wasn't going anywhere just yet—Kia wanted to play—so I let loose of my bag, walked over and washed my hands, and grabbed a cup of water, plate and napkin.

"What kind of proof?" I asked pulling out my seat and arranging my place.

"Visual proof."

I took out the chips and salsa and put them between us, then peeled open my burrito and loaded it up.

"Like a photo?"

She took a chip, shook her head, and suggestively wiggled her brows at me, and I said, *so on to her*, "No way! Not before Friday!" Maybe never. No way was I taking her to my place. I was blinded by her *Wham*, true, but I wasn't prepared to lose my job, *not yet anyway*, probably never.

"Your loss," she said, so totally full of herself, and I dug into my burrito buying time, humored by her sass, and not wanting to slip up and say something truly idiotic like, *Let's go*, especially since that's exactly what I wanted to do.

Kia was motoring through her dinner at warp speed. I'm guessing having a day like hers built up an appetite, but if I wanted any of those chips, I was going to have get going.

"You know all about me," she said, "but I don't know anything about you."

"What do I know?" I asked, knowing where this was going—not wanting to lie—prepared to do exactly that if I had to.

"You know where I live, what I eat, where I work, what I do, you've met my friends, need I go on?"

She reached down, picked up fallen beans, and plopped them into her mouth, clearly enjoying herself.

I grabbed for some chips and countered, "You know where I work, what I do, what I eat, who my friends are."

"Don't tell me Bullet's your only friend!"

"Nope, now I have you, too."

She grinned, "I don't know. I'm not really looking for any new friends right now, and I'm not sure you're friend material."

"Of course I am," I said, so not offended. "I'm fun. I share my chocolate, and I'm good in a pinch."

"Well, you are at that. But what about family? You've met Chloe, and at the rate she's going, the rest aren't far behind."

"Orphan," I said, and she gave me a sideways-narrowed glance and said, "No you're not."

"If it will get Chloe to adopt me, sure I am."

"Ohmigod, you're using me for her food!"

"Am not!"

"Sure you are! Not that I blame you, she's an excellent cook. But still."

"Honestly, it's not like that."

"Then what is it like?"

I swallowed my big bite, hit her full on, all serious like, with my baby blues and jacked up the charm. "It's your car. I want to drive your car!"

She burst out laughing, and my brain did its fireworks thing again.

"You're too tall for my Mini."

"Am not."

"Have you ever driven one?"

"No."

"Trust me. You're too tall."

"You're just saying that so you don't have to share!"

She finished off the last of her burrito, crumpled the foil, and tossed it in the recycle.

"Too true. I'm no good at sharing, but if you want to cram yourself in for a go, you're welcome to it, but only if I get something I want."

Uh-oh, this was trouble for sure. "Is this the Friday thing again?"

Her eyes glinted my doom and she cracked a sly smile, both of which set my blood on fire and sent my lower brain into overdrive. I was equally dreading and craving her next words, hoping for more, when she leaned in, reached across the table, dropped her hand to mine—drawing little finger-tip circles and sending jolts of heat racing up my arm to short circuit my brain—and said with a whole lot of seduction on her side, "Be my date for the gala."

Slam on the brakes. What?

"Hunh?" I had been expecting something completely different, and my brain choked, my reaction time froze.

She smiled her gotcha smile, and I retracted my hand from her tempting, teasing, taunting touches. "Hey! No fair."

"What?" she asked, a picture of innocence, like babies, puppies, and kittens.

"*What*, my backside!"

"Well, will you?"

"Will I take you to the gala?"

"Yeah. Fair's fair. You're using me for my car, and I'm using you as a deterrent."

"Doesn't seem like a fair trade to me," I said. Two could play at this game.

"You're right," she said, seeming to mull it over. "You should bring the chocolate, too."

Sass and *Wham!* If it weren't for the delectable image that flooded my mind, I would have gone for the hard time. But this way, I had a bargaining chip to make sure I got what I wanted. Kia naked with chocolate. The best dessert ever.

"Alright," I said. "You've got yourself a date."

"Good. Now finish your burrito and get a move on. Bullet's probably seeing yellow by now!"

"Now you believe me!" I said, finishing off the last big bite and drinking down my water.

We gathered up the trash and tossed it, and I pulled out my keys and said, "You gonna be okay here?" looking at the work in front of her.

She nodded, totally confident. "Nuther day, nuther dollar."

"O-kay. If you say so. See you in the morning."

"See you," she said, but our eyes held steady. We lingered, then smiled. She looked back to her desk, and I headed for my car.

From there, my night went as usual. Bullet and I tackled the neighborhood, *twice*, as he was feeling frisky and needed to work off some of his excess energy. Or maybe that was me, but he hadn't complained. Chris called to annoy me and get an update, and I gave him the low-down. *Locket's M.I.A., the Acer and Kia are working hard to ensure on-time shipment for Friday's gala.* He wanted to know if I had anything more on Kia, and I told him what he wanted to hear. *Nothing new, but he was right. Guilty for sure. And I was on top of it, ready to do my thing.* We both knew I was being patronizing, but he'd let it pass, knowing I'd already gotten the message.

Midnight, Bullet's tummy massaged, two beers, and an old black and white spilling mystery and high hopes later, and I heard Chloe's voice coming through on the recorder, the bugs I'd placed in Kia's apartment doing their job.

"Kia, honey, are you there?" Pause. "I've tried the museum, and you're not picking up either place. I'm getting worried; secretly hoping you're with Jake, forgetting me with good reason. Please give me a call when you get this."

Okay, conundrum. I'm not supposed to know about this call. But if Chloe was worried, something was wrong. Kia wasn't going to be one for leaving her best friend in the world hanging. I knew she hadn't come home. I'd have heard it on the recorder, so my guess was that she was somewhere in the museum—which given that the locket wasn't in house, was not troublesome on its own—or she was somewhere along the route to her apartment. Knowing she was a fast driver, I'd give her five minutes, then I was going looking.

Five minutes passed, and no sounds of Kia in her place came across the recorder, so I slid my runners on, laced them up, and called out to Bullet, "Be back in a bit."

I hit Stadium in a flash and waggled my way to Plymouth to find Kia's Mini still parked in the museum lot. I angled my Jeep next to her car, and beeped it locked on my way inside. Sprinting up to the second floor, I crossed the showcase to Kia's door and key-coded my way in.

Kia was bent over her desk, head propped on her left arm, pen still standing in her right, out like a light. Long, wavy wisps of her hair had fallen from her do and gently spilled around her face, some tucked behind her ear, and one of them playfully puffed and fell in time to her silent breathing. She was so irresistibly pretty, and for a moment I froze, stuck in an impossible eternity, standing there falling further—feeling happy—taking in the peaceful sight of her. It was a stolen moment, and I wanted to reach out and caress those soft hairs back and run my fingers through her long locks. But if I did that, I'd have some *splainin'* to do. And Kia might just take me up on the offer. We were both wavering and really didn't need any more temptation. So instead—I moved to wake her.

I didn't want to startle her. I just couldn't see any way around it. She wasn't expecting anybody, least of all, me.

I stepped up next to her and very gently shook her shoulder. "Kia. You should go home now."

I watched her blink and take a heavy breath. She sat up slowly, looking beat but not ready to call it a night.

"What time is it?"

"Just after midnight."

Kia checked her microwave for the time and said, "How can that be?" She reached for a sheet of notes and checked off three more items on the bullet list, and groaned.

"Maybe you should pick this back up in the morning," I suggested, and she asked, "Why, when you've come back to help?" She paused and looked up at me. "Speaking of which. What are you doing here?"

"I was just in the neighborhood and saw your car parked. Knew you were a die hard, but tomorrow's another day."

She looked like she might try to think about that for a moment, and I didn't want her coming to any detrimental conclusions, so I asked, "Have you been asleep for a while? Should you call Chloe?"

"Chloe!"

Kia grabbed the phone and dialed Chloe's number and waited, then said, "Hi Chloe. I'm so sorry." She paused, listened, then added, "I'm still at work. I fell asleep." Another pause. "Yeah, I will." Pause again. "I'm packing now. See you in the morning." Kia listened for a moment more and then added, "Yeah, I love you, too. Sweet dreams." Then she hung up and looked back to me.

"Thanks. It's been a long day."

"I know. Lemme help you here. What do you need to pack up?" I asked, and she said, "Purse and Chloe's lunch tote."

She grabbed her purse, and I snagged the tote.

Kia took one last look at her desk and shook her head, looking exhausted, yet expectant with lots still to do.

"You ready?"

"Not really," she said but nodded anyway, and we headed for the door. Kia flipped the lights, and we let the auto-lock take over as we exited for our cars.

"I'm going to follow you home, just to make sure you get there okay."

"That's not necessary," she said opening her door and tossing her purse to the passenger side, and I said, "Sure it is," and followed with Chloe's tote. I gave her my best not-taking-no-for-an-answer look and said, "Now get in and drive."

Her lids were still heavy with sleep, and her eye roll didn't quite work, which made me smile, but it didn't keep me from nudging her into her seat and closing her door.

"Don't forget to buckle," I said as I pulled my door open and slid behind the wheel of my Jeep.

Kia turned her engine over, and I did the same. We backed up and wound our way to Plymouth. Tired or not, she still made the drive in under five, and when we pulled into her lot, I got out and walked over to her car and opened her door for her. "Let's go sleepy head."

I walked around to the passenger side, popped open the door and hoisted Chloe's tote and Kia's bag over my shoulder, then tightly shut the door again. Walking back to Kia, I reached for her hand, and she beeped her doors locked. Gently tugging and guiding, I got her to her door. The hallway light overhead gave her sight to her lock, and she slid the key home and twisted the knob open. She turned to me all petered out, smiled, and said, "Thanks."

Kia didn't mean to, but she looked sexy and relaxed, tired too, but soft and kissable with drowsy eyes and mussy hair, and before I could say, "No problem," it happened again. I got hit square in the solar plexus with a sucker punch of want, and unable to stop myself I drifted closer, a moth drawn to flame. Kia looked like Sunday morning, or at least how I thought my Sunday mornings should look, and an electric vibe sizzled up my chest and went straight to my brain, telling me here was my chance.

Catapulted back into my impossible eternity moment of happiness, lost on any sense of sanity, I took another step forward, and Kia's eyes, becoming ever more alert, swung up to meet mine. I'd closed the distance, eye on the prize, and time stalled. The calm before the storm. We'd flitted and floated all day around the attraction. Teasing and baiting each other. And now here we were, a thin sliver of air between us, breathing each other in, waiting for what could happen next. Neither making a move. Neither daring to . . . when Kia glinted invitation and challenge, smiling again and dropping her gaze to my mouth.

I was hungry for her, and I did what I'd wanted to do all day long. I reached for her, releasing her hand on the door, pulling it shut, and kissed her. Reveling once again in the delicious taste of Kia's lips on mine. I angled closer still, and she fell into me, kissing back, giving it some gusto. I nibbled, delved, devoured, took all that she offered and more.

My brain started going blank, and my body begged for more. There was a bed behind that door, and we should be in it. I dropped the bags to the floor and threaded my fingers into her hair, pulling her skin close. And she followed. Biting back. Mouth pleading for more.

Our limbs became tangled as we fought for air. And release. And each other's clothes.

We were sliding toward out of control, and Friday was days away. Shocking that I could even process that, but I no longer cared, and I bumped her backward into the door.

Kia clawed at my shirt. My hands raked through her hair and down her body, seeking a way in, but found the doorknob instead, *and* a flicker of unwanted reason—*damn!*

My eyes squeezed tight in disbelief at what I was about to do. I rotated the knob and gently, but firmly, pushed her inside. Our lips were still locked, and I worked hard to pull myself back. I dragged in a heavy breath, fought for my right mind, and questioned my sanity for not following her in.

"Lock this door," I said with difficulty, not believing the words had actually found their way out.

"But don't you want to come inside?" Kia looked hot and stunned, and I made myself stand firm.

"You know I do."

"Then why don't you?"

"Friday."

She dismissed that idea, smiled her come-hither smile at me, and said, "Now," reaching for me. But I took a step back and pulled the door closed.

"Do not open this door."

"But—"

"Kia, I want to hear you lock it."

"But I want you to come inside with me."

"Lock the door, Kia." I closed my eyes, trying to pull myself in check. "Please."

There was hesitation, but then I heard the tumblers reluctantly fall into place. I took another step back, and shook my head when I tripped over her purse and Chloe's tote. *Just my damned luck.*

I picked up the bags and called out, "Kia, open the door."

Her triumphant "Yay" almost broke my will, but as soon as I saw her excited face, I pushed the bags inside and yanked the door closed again.

"Hey!" she said.

Jake, Jake, Jake, what in the hell are you doing?

"Good night, Kia. Get some sleep," I said, and dragged my sorry ass home.

Kia

Don't Make Me Beg

Jake was a cupcake, no doubt about it, and he was driving me crazy. It was my own fault really. It was my stupid Friday rule. But it was like I'd waved a red flag, and he was charging, except that his attack plan was tactical, calculated, intense, *flawless*. Every look, every laugh, every bite of chocolate, each of those soulful kisses, hit deep, sending little zappy lightening bolts racing around in my body, electrifying my every nerve, making me crave him until I couldn't think straight. So what had started out in theory as a good plan, in practice was turning out to be my own personal bait, lure, bite, incite, and retreat torture plan. He was taking me down, and I wanted to go, but he kept leaving me there, flames building to a roaring fire, stunned and fighting the aftermath of unslaked, provoked desire. Mr. Sinner Man held promise, and it was time to pay up. He and his touchy-feely, hot and spicy kisses. He'd made me want him—admittedly, it hadn't taken much, but that's how it is when your packin' the kind of heat he has—and now I wanted him to finish what he started. So if he tried it again, I wasn't responsible for my actions. If he ended up tied to my desk, okay, maybe not my desk—I had a job to preserve—but if he ended up tied to something, forced to go the distance, it was his own fault. He'd brought this on himself, and it was time he held up his end of the bargain.

It was Tuesday morning, and I'd slept for crap. Between my missing crate and my hormones on overdrive, I'd done the best I could, eventually giving up the fight, and was now trying to wake up in the shower, tussling with crankiness. I needed a better day and was working on my Chloe inspired hopefulness when I dropped my shampoo bottle—almost missing my baby toe—but not quite.

"Owwww!" I yelped doing a hoppity-ouch dance trying to nurse my poor digit.

So far it was not looking too good.

I reached down to grab the kamikaze anvil and heard a tap on my bathroom door. Chloe called in, "Kia. You're up early. Didn't sleep well?" She sounded amused, so I grunted at her, and she chuckled. "So things are moving right along then."

I refused to dignify that with a response, and I could feel her smiling from the other side of my shower curtain.

"Don't make me come out there," I threatened, and Chloe said, still having fun, "Well, how else will you get to eat your waffle?"

"*Waffle?*" I asked my interest piqued.

"Belgian waffle, just the way you like it. Fresh strawberries and turkey sausage. O.J. of course, but if you plan on staying in there."

Her *oh well, if you must you must* tone issued an effective challenge, and I rolled my eyes in defeat.

"Did you bring your secret syrup?"

"Of course." Like there was ever a question.

"I'll be out in ten," I said, and Chloe retreated whistling a merry tune.

Terry-wrapped hair, robe and slippers, steam rolling out with me, and I was greeted by Chloe with a, "Bad day yesterday, huh?"

She looked tired, too. Her pale yellow cotton pant set had gone without ironing, her hair was flat on the left side, needing to be brushed and fluffed, and the lines around her eyes were deeper than usual. It didn't take much of a guess to know she had worried about me and stayed up, waiting for my call.

"The worst," I said. "The shipping crate with the locket was lost in transit, and Phillip blames me."

Chloe shook her head, fully able to imagine the whole disastrous impact of that and said, offering me a supportive smile, "I'm sorry. Well, come on over here and eat. This will help you survive today."

"Sorry for keeping you up," I said feeling really bad that I had.

"It's okay. I'll get a nap today, but you won't. I'm making sure you've got the fuel you'll need to survive."

I pulled up my chair to Chloe's spoil-me-rotten breakfast and inhaled the scrumptious vapors floating up to me, cheering me immensely. "So," I said feeling myself relax a little. "Where's your secret syrup?"

Chloe smiled and handed me the gravy boat. "I just knew this would do the trick."

It was closing in on eight, and I'd been working for almost an hour. Chloe had helped me get my move on fast. I was filled up on mmm-yummy breakfast, and while I ate, she had picked out my clothes for me and ironed them. I'm telling you that woman has a one track mind. Like I was her personal Barbie or something. I looked down at myself and smiled. If this didn't send Jake for a spin, I'd eat dirt and let him eat my entire dessert. And that was saying something, because Chloe had made one of my favorites last night while waiting for me to call. Chocolate chunk cookies with microscopically-fine chopped walnuts. Simple, but the best! And I loved them with a tall, frosty mug of milk. I'd already put two mugs in the common kitchen freezer in anticipation of lunch.

I was back to staring at my floor plan, feeling like I'd worked out a feasible redirect for the presentation, and now I just needed to draft up some ideas for the graphic displays to run by Karen. Chloe had sent another tote filled with lunch for two or lunch and dinner for me. No big surprise which she hoped for. She was probably calling Jake right now to let him know, and not even I had Jake's number, *and* I'm the one he's been kissing.

So my day was set. Call Bennington for an update. Get the crate back. Meet with Karen to get this show on the road. And dazzle Jake into a stunned stupor—payback time.

I picked up my phone, punched in Bennington's number, and listened to it ring and ring, all the while absently doodling, waiting for an answer. If they had caller I.D., they were probably on the run not wanting to deal with the crazy, irate lady from the museum. Sure enough, I got sent to voicemail, so I put a little chipper in my tone and left a supportive, but firm message. "Hello. This is Kia Everet from the Acer Foundation Museum of Art History. I'm just calling for an update about the crate missing from our shipment yesterday." I added in the crate info and my phone number. "I would greatly appreciate a follow-up return phone call this morning, and I look forward to hearing from you soon. Thank you, and have a nice morning."

"How diplomatic of you."

I looked up from my doodle paper to find Jake standing in my doorway looking drop dead gorgeous, *again*. And just that quick, the fluttery butterflies attacked my stomach and sent my heartbeat into overdrive. My lips and body remembered his kiss, and traitors that they were—they wanted more.

No fair. It was my turn to stun, and he'd stolen my thunder. I suppressed the urge to stand up and do a little runway march around him. Deciding, instead, to bide my time. So I flashed him my bedroom eyes and sassy smile, and had the satisfaction of watching him stumble his step. *Yay, small victory for Kia!*

He was wearing a black silk, two-button suit with pants pressed into razor sharp creases, classic white shirt, black-n-white artsy, geometric design tie, with black, square-toed, lace-up oxfords, oozing a sense of power and sex, and it made me want to bite him, *playfully of course*, and then strip him naked.

Having regained his step, he crossed to my desk and asked, "What'd I do?"

Like he didn't know.

His hands were empty, and I adjusted my glance to squinty and asked, "What? No chocolate?"

Jake smiled, big, and moved to the lunch tote Chloe had packed and confidently patted the top. "I'm sure Chloe's taken care of everything," he said, and I said, "I can't believe you'd leave it to chance."

His grin still in place, he shifted his eyes to me, and caught a full view of my dress.

"More like certainty," he said, showing sudden interest and coming closer. "You're shimmering. Is that on purpose?" he asked suspiciously.

"It's just a dress," I said lightly and looked back to my desk, knowing full well it wasn't, and pinched my lips to keep from smiling. *I've got you now*, I thought cheerfully. And I'm sure it had nothing to do with the fact that my skirt was slit miles high to my thigh, giving him a tantalizing glance of my entire leg.

"Stand up."

"What?"

"You heard me."

My look was *I-don't-think-so*, but he took the final steps to reach me and pulled me up to full height in front of him.

"I see," he said, stepping back, and I watched as his Adam's apple bobbed on his swallow.

I'd be lying if I said I didn't feel satisfaction, but as it was, I rolled my eyes at him, threw every ounce of innocence I could into it, and said, "You see what?"

"So it's to be shock and awe today, then?"

I just smiled at him, sweetly, and said, "Chloe picked it out. You like it?"

His eyes were practically sweating, his smile tight, and he said, "Let's get this over with."

"What are you talking about?"

"Five o'clock is nine hours away. If I'm going to have to work with you like this all day, then you're going to have to get this show and tell over with now. So walk."

I may have overshot my mark by a bit more than a smidgeon, and it was my turn to swallow. Jake's look was rigid control, but his eyes were eating me alive, and it made me burn, low and deep. I momentarily forgot where I was and practically lunged for him. But Jake easily sidestepped me and balanced my missed attempt with one hand, sending even more fire through me.

"Kia," he said, lowering his mouth to my ear, tempting me with the hint of a kiss. The feel of his warm breath was intoxicating, and my body hummed with wanting him. But he held his ground, and with a voice heat saturated to thick and quiet, he said, "I get it. Playtime is over. And I assure you, I'm happy about it. But for now, we work. So walk."

Jake

Oxygen Please

I'd slipped on my Ray-Ban Aviators and was in my Jeep, dawdling up Plymouth and heading toward downtown Ann Arbor, hoping to hit every light along the way, and back. I needed time to cool off, so I'd appointed myself as the go to guy for getting the missing crate back, and even though I'd already made the necessary calls—Kia didn't know that—I was out of the office and on my way to the local branch of Bennington Freight.

Kia and that dress.

Ho-ly crap. My eyes had practically popped out of my head.

Sure. I'd kissed us senseless last night, but that was different. There was no call for violence. But in one fell swoop, Kia had more than evened the score. And to blame it on Chloe. I shook my head, smiling. But then again, maybe. Chloe was more than capable, and definitely willing.

I was on Broadway, near Main, and thankfully, the light changed to red. I pressed the brake, and closed my eyes and watched again as Kia—calm, enjoying herself, walked past me, sashaying her delectable self, acting innocent, and intentionally charging my guns—called quits to her Friday rule. She was a flaming siren at sunset in that dress, and I did what any rational man in my position would do. I bolted. So now here I was inch worming my way across town—in no hurry to get anywhere fast—and taking a much needed breather, so I could relive the vision of Kia in her sun-goddess dress at a safe distance, in a safe place.

In and of itself, her dress was simple—a two-piece number that shot straight to her calves. A red-coral silk with some kind of gold sheen in it. Sleeveless. With an eye bursting scoopy, cleavage enticing neck. And it kind of flounced at her waist, calling out, "*Here kitty, kitty*" to my eager fingers. Which had been bad enough. But *that skirt.* We're talking temptation in a bull fight, and I'd made the unfortunate mistake of touching it. It had been cool in my palm, but I was still burning from it. And all I could think of was using those thigh high slits as starter marks for ripping it right off of Kia's perfect ass.

I know. How caveman was that?

Kia and her legs. *Mmm, mmm, mmm.* Just the thought forced a swallow. Nonstop creamy delights. Firm and begging to be climbed. Every step she'd taken had taunted me with a touch-me-if-you-dare.

Oh, I dared. Just give me the chance.

Someone behind me honked, and I looked up to see a green light. Hitting the gas, I shook my head. I was losing it.

It's just a freaking dress, Jake.

But I knew it wasn't the dress. It was Kia's unabashed offer sending crackling shock waves straight to my lower brain, and had him fighting for air.

Bottom line—I'd left Kia standing, kissed and hot, again. And this was payback. Plain and simple. But no way had I seen that dress coming.

Oh my!

I managed to drag a fifteen minute drive out to almost thirty, but I still hadn't cooled off. It was definitely time to focus on something else.

I took a right onto West Liberty and followed it past Wagner to the more industrial section and found Bennington Freight's yellow and gray cinderblock building and loading docks located at the end of a long, concrete drive on a large, weedy-grass lot. There weren't many trees, just a few spruces clustered at the corners, and the space looked hot and didn't exactly set out a welcome mat.

I pulled in and drove the distance to the parking lot, and cut my engine. I grabbed my window visor, just in case I was going to be here for a while, and tucked it up on the dash. Locking up, I crossed the blacktop, yanked open the door, and was blasted by a wave of arctic air and found my Aviators useful in fighting off the fluorescent glare from above.

The customer receiving office was mid-size, heavily used, overdone in the Bennington's yellow and gray motif, and had three service counters in a U-shape formation. No one was to the left; straight ahead, another client was being helped; and off to my right, the counter was clear, and a Bennington worker sat incognito behind his computer. The sluffer. Just my luck. I walked over to find *Craig,* paunchy, salt and peppered, forty-something, cramming a breakfast biscuit sandwich into his face. He looked up from behind his screen, not all that happy or helpful, and around a mouthful, giving me a show I didn't need, he asked "Can I help you?"

I peeled off my Aviators and went for pleasant, trying to cut the guy some slack. He was washed-up and unhappy about it, so nice first, then work it if I have to. Smiling, I said, "I hope so. My name is Jake Davidson, and I'm with the Acer Foundation Museum of Art History."

Craig's face took on the look of the damned, and he said, "It's like I told the lady on the phone, I checked, and it's still missing." He didn't make a move to get up or try to be helpful, and he added with growing irritation, "I don't know what you all expect me to do about it. My hands are tied until corporate locates it."

Moving to the "work it" strategy.

Smile still in place, encouraging cooperation; tone, even and calm, but hinting at you're-going-to-help-me-whether-you-like-it-or-not; and I said, "I understand. But since I'm here, I was hoping you'd be willing to check the file again. See if there's been any update since my associate spoke with you on the phone."

You'd think I'd poked him in the eye with my keys or something with the "Fine," he gave me, but he started pounding on his keyboard, and that was progress.

Out of my peripheral, I caught the other service agent finish with his customer, and he walked over to investigate the hullaballoo.

"Hi, I'm Rob Matheson, Branch Manager. How's it going here?"

Ahh, now I get it. Rob, much younger, thin, blonde, handsome, pleasant, and in charge, on his way moving up the corporate ladder, leaving Craig here, to fester in his going-no-where dismal attitude.

I extended my hand, and Rob shook it. "Hello Mr. Matheson. I'm Jake Davidson, and I'm just here to follow-up on the hopeful whereabouts of a missing crate."

Rob looked to Craig, noticed his half eaten sandwich, and offered on a suppressed sigh, "I can handle this," by way of an invitation to let Craig finish his breakfast.

Craig's mood didn't improve, but he picked up his sandwich and took another large bite.

Rob motioned me to his counter and said, "Do you have the crate I.D. number?"

I pulled a copy of the manifest from my inside pocket and read the number off.

Rob typed away at his computer and said, "The crate cleared Customs in New York and was lost in transit."

This we knew.

He typed something else in, then added, "Our Pittsburg branch has reported receipt of the carton. And a note has been added. It appears that your crate was misdirected to the Carnegie Museum of Art during intake at Customs. The Pittsburg branch reports the crate has already been shipped, and we are due to receive it this afternoon."

Hip hip hooray. "Do you have an E.T.A.?"

Rob looked up from his computer and said, "It's due here at two."

"Excellent news. Thank you. I'm going to run out and take care of a few errands, but I'll be back. I'd like to follow the delivery truck over to the Acer."

"Sure thing," Rob said, and I asked, writing my cell number on a slip of scratch paper, "Would you mind calling me if it arrives early?"

"No problem."

Aviators and errands. I was back in my Jeep, flipping through the radio stations, getting happy, rocking out to *Radar Love*. Great song! I was looking for anything to eat up time until the crate came in. No way was I going back to the Acer empty handed. So I grabbed a Dimo's glazed donut and coffee; called Chris—giving him the latest—and got another speech; made a pit stop at the pharmacy and purchased some *incidentals*—just in case; picked up a jar of chocolate body paint—thinking Kia might like the fun—and a dozen chocolate covered strawberries—given that she had a penchant for disregarding the plain ones; and then went home to walk Bullet.

That's me. Mr. Wishful Thinking.

Kia

My Hero

It was just after two, and I'd worked through lunch. Tuesday was quickly becoming a faint memory, and I had two days to wrap things up, so despite the grumbling in my tummy and Chloe's ready made lunch, I kept working. Ian and his guys were making good time with the displays and were way ahead of schedule, so Karen and I kept moving. I was sitting in her office listening to her cajole her digital wizard into meeting our deadlines with the new displays, looking over our miniature, rough mock-ups, and noting that she sounded happy, so my fingers were crossed.

Karen hung up, thumbs up, and said, "Theo says they can do it. But we're going to have to bribe his design team with something out of this world for the overtime."

"Yay! Decapitating fate, a zillion; Kia, one. Now if only we just don't have to do it—that will be great!"

"Have you heard from Jake, yet?"

"Not a word."

"Well, he's probably still in shock," Karen said goggling at my dress. "I want to bite you, and I'm not even into chicks."

"Ha ha," I said. "It's not my fault. Chloe made me do it."

"Lame," Karen said, gleefully refusing my excuse. "But good for Chloe, and hopefully good for you. Remember. I get details. I'm willing to pay!"

"If he's any good, there won't be any details, because—"

"Ehem." Karen cleared her throat and raised her eyebrows meaningfully, looking past me, and smiled. "Hi Jake," she said, her voice ridiculously nice, and I turned to find him standing there in the doorway looking like the cat that caught the mouse.

He flashed his glance at me, purposefully scanned my leg from toe to hip, and my body went incandescent, again.

How inconvenient.

A warm radiating hum settled into my chest, and I felt my mouth go dry. This whole Friday thing had turned into foreplay, and my body was beyond my control. Heat, *the good kind*, had reached my fingertips and ears, and was blocking any functional brainwaves from making it to the surface. Horrifyingly, I just stared.

Jake smiled, *Gotcha*, and my lovely heat evaporated in an instant. I shot him squinty daggers, and he smiled bigger.

"Would you ladies like to join me in the basement?"

Lust fog forgotten, I jumped up and asked, "You got it?"

"Why don't we all go and see. Mike's waiting for us."

I blew by him, racing for the elevator, and heard him say to Karen, "I think she might be happy."

"Ya think?" Karen said, and I said, "Come on, come on. Let's go."

We all piled into the elevator. I punched B on the button panel, and the doors slid closed. It took a hundred years for the doors to swing wide again, but there was Mike, crowbar in hand, waiting with a smile.

"Kia," he said, patting a very large wooden crate sitting next to him. "It's here."

I was practically jumping up and down, unable to contain my excitement.

Ben came over to help Mike with the contents, and Vinny was on the ready with the video cam. Jake and Karen stood next to me, and other than watching with enthusiastic fascination, I was momentarily useless.

Mike carefully pried a short side panel away, and Ben reached for it, placing it off to the side on the floor. Mike set the crow bar on top of the crate, and both Ben and Mike donned cotton gloves and reached in to pull out Alexandra's settee. Protective foam boards fell away from the cloth covered chair, and Ben pulled back the covering to reveal the lovely design. The frame was intricately carved dark walnut, and the fabric was a rosy pink and floral silk. Pretty.

"One thing's for sure," Ben said, moving his cotton-gloved hand along the wood. "The Tsarina had good taste."

We waited while Ben and Mike moved the settee to the recording platform and Vinny recorded receipt and condition. Ben grabbed for the R.F.I.D. handheld scanner and bleeped it into the inventory.

This was taking forever, and I craned my neck to see what else might be in the box. It wasn't the guys' fault. They had to follow protocol. It's just that I was anxious. Thank goodness Mike was on it.

"Alright, Kia, hang on," he said and looked into the crate. "There's another box inside at the other end."

He grabbed for the crowbar again, walked around to the other short end, and pried it off. He used his knee to support the panel, set the crowbar down again, and lowered the wood side to the floor. There was a storage box sitting on a raised support inside the crate, and Mike lifted it out and moved it to the now clear recording platform. Vinny and Ben had moved the settee into the *For Display* hold.

Vinny was on the ready with the camera, and Mike lifted the lid on the box. Inside was the Tsarina's writing box. It was made of gold and covered in bright rubies and sapphires and sprinkled with smaller diamonds and other stones. It, too, was pretty. But still not the locket. So we waited again for the guys to go through receipt protocol, and in the process, remove the writing box from the storage container to reveal another much smaller case. The locket.

I held my breath, and Karen nudged closer. She was excited, too. As well we should be, especially after all of Phillip's theatrics. My centerpiece was here, and we could move forward. No more need for Plan B. I couldn't remember anticipating an artifact this much, *ever*, and as Ben extracted the beautiful jewel from its encasement, Karen, Jake, and I all moved forward in a sort of suspended animation, momentarily mesmerized.

And there it was. Alexandra's Garnet Love Locket. My career to date in a piece of jewelry. The pearls gave the locket a delicate, sophisticated look, but the garnets were a bit fiery and against the silver gave it a brilliance not appreciated by photos. It lie nestled in Ben's palm, quietly winking at me, showing a bit of attitude and letting me know that everything was going to be A-okay. I couldn't help myself. I gushed relief.

Karen gave my arm a little squeeze and said, "There you go Kia. Job intact."

I nodded, and she added, "I'm going to call Theo and let him know we're good."

Jake had stood silent this entire time, and I looked up to find him studying me. There was a small pinch to his brow, and if I had to place it, I'd say quizzical concern, but that didn't make sense, and I was so high on giddiness that I just smiled and said, "God, I'm hungry."

Jake's brow shifted to exasperation, but he smiled and shook his head at me. "Don't tell me you haven't eaten."

"I was busy."

He reached for my hand and pulled me toward the elevator. "Come on. Let's go. You being a martyr for the cause won't keep me in Chloe's good graces. And I'm not missing out on whatever delicacy she's packed for you."

"Food pimp," I laughed, and pulled my hand back. I looked over to Mike and the guys, already back to work, and called, "Thanks, Mike. Let me know when I can move these to display."

"Sure thing, Kia." He looked relieved, like me. This should shut Phillip up, and keep Ben from jumping ship. Happiness for everyone.

Chloe's homemade chicken potpie was comfort food for the gods, and fighting off starvation, I busied myself with polishing mine off, all the while watching Jake watch me from across my desk. He wasn't talking, just following me with his eyes. It was almost a lazy, comfortable kind of gaze, but there was that quizzical look again, buried beneath the relaxed, as if he couldn't shake off something, and somewhere between my potpie and side of watermelon and blueberries, I asked, "What?"

His face went surprisingly blank, and he said, heavy on the accusation, "So what's with the dress?"

I rolled my eyes at him, and he said, "You do that a lot," and I said, "Take it personally. It's you. And not my dress—not again."

His pupils dilated and heat roiled in his oceanic eyes. "You'll be singing a different tune later."

I rolled my eyes again, and he smiled, all knowing, and shrugged. "So where's Chloe's chocolate treat, and my note?"

"I don't know what you're talking about."

"Kia, two potpies means a note. For me."

I scrunched my face, *Pshaaw*, and shook my head. "Didn't happen."

Jake smiled a very sinful smile, ripped my dress off with his eyes, and quietly said, "I'd be happy to do a strip search."

My mouth went dry, and flames licked up my spine, but I swerved with a playful, "What are we talking about?"

He got up from his chair and made to move toward me.

"Oh. You mean this note," I said, quickly extracting Chloe's signature blue stationary from my desk drawer.

Overly smug, Jake took the note from my hand, read it and said, "So it's chocolate chip cookies today. I hope you brought the milk."

The last two hours of my work day flew by in a blur. Jake and I kept time with Ian, Karen, Mike and the guys, security, and our set designers. We moved cleared pieces to their cases, marked them off on the layout plan, and inched our way toward completion. I green-lighted the final mailers for the gala to be sent, and I confirmed my updo and makeup appointment for Friday. At this rate, we were going to make it, and I was thankful Jake was here to help. I know. That meant Phillip actually did something nice. I wasn't ready to stomach that, so I dismissed his random act of kindness, knowing that there was no way Phillip would have done it, had he known how much I'd like Jake. And as if on cue, Phillip emerged from his cave, sending workers everywhere scurrying as he B-lined it for me.

I sucked in a sigh. *So much for rounding out on a high note.*

"Kia," he said with his characteristic oily tone oozing from his pores. *At least it wasn't his angry, malicious tone.*

I resisted the urge to cringe, and waited for the predictable shift toward money.

Jake was standing in my doorway at the ready, and Phillip flashed a glance at him, making sure he was a safe distance away, and I hid my smile.

No need. Phillip wiped it off my face for me.

"Good thing Jake was here. Lucky for you, he's been able to save your show. I expect you'll be able to manage under his direction until Friday."

Bastard. Phillip not Jake.

Phillip oozed on. "So now that Jake has done his part, you just need to make sure his efforts don't go to waste."

His eyes dropped to my chest and then lower. "I see we understand each other," he said taking in my dress and making me feel dirty in it.

I stood my ground, gave him my best blank face, and waited for it to be over. It was the closest thing to feeling violated I'd ever had, and Phillip had moved from monumental irritant to hellishly loathsome in my book. Maybe I would take Karen up on her advice. Talking to a Board member had to be better than this.

His objectifying inspection ended abruptly, and he shifted a glare at me. "I won't be here tomorrow."

Wednesday's appeal just shot through the roof.

"I can't keep my eye on you all the time." *Thank God.* "Try not to screw up again. You're running out of time, and Jake and I can't be running around putting out all your fires." *Go to hell.* "I trust you'll be able to manage for one day without me." *I can manage without you everyday of the week, Asshole.*

He smiled his slithery, cutting smile at me, and left.

I breathed in a heavy sigh of relief, and Jake came up behind me, grabbed my hand, smiled, and said cheerfully, "Come with me."

Jake pulled me down the staircase to the first floor and out the doors into the bright sunshine and stopped only when we were at my car. I hurried to keep up, and he said, "Soak up some sun, babe. Burn it off."

Somewhere in Phillip's sneering address, Jake had grabbed my lunch tote and purse, and looking into my bag, he said, "Do you mind?"

I shook my head *no*, and he reached in to find my keys. He beeped my car door open, threw the bags to the passenger seat, pushed me in, and said, "Last one to your apartment is a rotten egg."

What a doof! But it made me smile. And then he left me to climb into his Jeep. We revved our engines, and I threw my car into reverse. No way was I going to be a rotten egg!

Jake

Mine, Mine, Mine

I had Kia all the way to the stop light at the entrance to her apartment complex, but then it turned red, and on green she punched it, zipping around me, oh, just a wee bit illegally. Apparently she really didn't want to be a rotten egg. I just wanted to wipe the angry devastation that had settled onto her face away. Phillip was not a nice man. But he was smart, and being a dick wasn't illegal. Otherwise, I'd arrest him flat.

As it was now, my goal was to get her out of that dress, and make sure it was a happy memory, not the filthy one Dr. Mann had implied. There was nothing sleazy or dirty about Kia. She was beautiful, funny, and all circumstantial evidence aside, a good person. I really liked her. More than I should given my position. But it is what it is, and I wanted more.

I watched as Kia slid her car into her spot, pop out with bags in hand, and race for her door. No way was I going to make this easy for her, so I grabbed my sack of chocolate goodies, followed hot on her heels, and caught up to her just as she slid the key into her door.

I helped her turn the knob and pushed her through, glued to her side, and called, "Tie!"

She tried for indignant, holding back her laughter, and said, "So *not* a tie! I was miles ahead of you."

"Right here, babe," I said walking to her fridge. I opened the door and put the sack inside.

"What's in the cute paper brown bag?" Kia asked, curious, craning her head to see.

"What bag?"

She eyed the fridge meaningfully, and my look said, *You're seeing things.*

Willing to play along, she marched over to me—just like I'd hoped she would—and reached for the fridge door.

Buuut I had to block her path. Had to.

Zing. Pow. And Bam. *God, how I love that spark!*

Kia stopped breathing-distance away from me, poked me lightly in the chest—sending heat racing around my body and letting my lower brain know we were at DEFCON 1—and said, "Are you holding out on me? Is that chocolate from your chocolate guy?"

"You're touching me," I said, and she said, "Well, if you gave me the chocolate you're hoarding, I wouldn't be touching you, I'd be touching it instead."

"Are you calling me a tease?"

"If the shoe fits."

My jaw dropped in mock insult. "I was trying to help you get to Friday."

Kia smiled, vixen all the way, curled her fingers into my shirt, and tiptoed up to kiss me. I pulled her tight, and kissed her back. *Hard.* I'd had my fill of waiting, and after a long day of dress-inspired desire, I was hungry for Kia.

"Are you sure this is what you want?" I asked biting her lips, and she bit back, "Not if you keep talking me to death."

Done, done, and done.

I scooped her up and hauled her into her bedroom.

My brain was oxygen depleted, *all my blood had gone south*, and I was left to feel my way through this field op. I broke our kiss long enough to find the bed. Far left corner. Target sighted, I let Kia pull me back into our lip frenzy and knew my knees would tell me when to dive. A few steps further, I bumped into her mattress and merrily toppled us onto the downy pillow top. We were rough and tumble as she grabbed for my jacket and jostled it off of me. My tie followed, and her nimble fingers made quick work of my shirt buttons.

I, on the other hand, had found Kia's long, creamy thigh, and my fingers wanted to know what was to the immediate north. Sliding my palm up, edging under the silkiness of her skirt, I found a tiny little string spanning from an even tinier front to back, and dragged myself away from our kiss to look Kia in her temptress little eyes and demand, "Did Chloe pick out your panties, too."

She pursed her lips, *sly beguiler*, and happy heat glinted in her sea green pools. I shook my head, dropped my lips to hers, and said on a nibble, "Just for that."

A flick of my wrist later, and Kia's string bikini panties were no more. She narrowed her glance at me and bit back, but spread her legs, just in case I wanted to explore some more, not the least bit concerned, and my fingers were happy to oblige. Kia purred a little moan, and deepened our kiss with her tongue teasing mine the way my fingers teased her.

She was hot. I was hot. And I felt her reach for my belt.

This was getting good.

I kept playing with her delectable wetness, and she unzipped my pants. We were moments to launch, our bodies a go, ready for more, but then the doorbell rang.

"Ignore it," I said, and Kia said, "Plan to."

But we heard it ring again, more insistently this time, and then I heard Kia's front door push open.

My brain registered alarm and fought hard against the sex cobwebs blocking reason.

We heard Chloe call out, "Kia," and looked at each other with concern. Something wasn't right with the tone of Chloe's voice, and Kia and I both flew out of bed. Kia raced to smooth her skirt down over her now pantiless bottom, and I grabbed for my pants, zipped them back up, and wrestled my way back into my shirt, fastening a couple of buttons.

I quickly followed Kia into her living room, *we were a scruffy picture of sexus interruptus*, but one look at Chloe and none of that mattered. Her hand was on her heart, and she looked pained. She angled her head up at us, apologetic recognition hitting her, mouthed, "Sorry," and collapsed to the floor. Kia ran for Chloe, and I ran for Kia's phone. I dialed 9-1-1 and heard Kia cry out, "Chloe!"

Dispatch picked up, and I looked over to find Chloe lying on the floor. Kia was kneeling beside her, feeling for a pulse and checking her breathing.

"Please state your emergency."

"My name is Jake Davidson, I have a potential heart attack victim in need of immediate medical assistance."

I asked Kia, "Is she still breathing?"

Kia nodded. "She's trying, and her heart's racing."

Kia's voice was wobbly and panicked, and I suspected her heart was doing flip flops right along with Chloe's. It was not a good scene, and even though by training I was calm and in control, I was concerned for them both.

The dispatch operator toned in and confirmed Kia's address. "EMS has been deployed and is on the way."

Twenty minutes later, Kia's small living room was bursting at its seams with us, a paramedic and two E.M.T.s, their equipment, and Chloe trundled up on a stretcher. Kia was intensely focused on Chloe—the rest of the world lost to them—and she was holding Chloe's hand, talking to her, reassuring her, and ready to move with the responders to the ambulance. I grabbed Kia's purse and keys—she wasn't thinking about them—and followed everyone out the door, pulling it to and locking it.

At the ambulance, I watched as the E.M.T.s loaded Chloe, and Kia clambered up with her. Kia flashed a quick glance my way, and I told her, "Right behind you." Her eyes were strained with worry and fear, but her face was fighting it. She nodded and returned her attention to Chloe, and I followed the driver to the cab.

"Which hospital?" I asked, knowing it would likely be the University of Michigan's. It was the closest.

"U of M," he replied and climbed into the driver's seat. I pushed his door shut, and raced around to my Jeep. The ambulance would be flashing lights and sirens the whole way through, but I'd have to obey regular traffic laws, and it was going to take me longer to get there. I didn't want to leave Kia alone when they wheeled Chloe into the procedure room, so I was going to have to do some fancy footwork.

It was almost a straight shot to the hospital, just up Plymouth to Maiden Lane which turned into East Medical Center Drive, and I was there. Chloe's ambulance had left me behind at Kia's apartment's stoplight, but I'd made good time, and I wound my way into the parking ramp, and B-lined it for the emergency room.

Kia was sitting in the waiting room, staring at a clipboard, holding a pen, and Zoe was there with her. Zoe was easy to recognize. Over and above the fact that I had her picture as part of Kia's file, Zoe was a darker, slightly younger version of Kia. Her hair hung long, black, and bone-straight to her mid-back. She had Kia and Chloe's sea green eyes, full lips, and creamy skin. She got a little extra decoration with freckles sprinkled across her nose, and she was a knock-out just like Kia.

I took a mental pause. This was going to turn into a family affair, which made it inherently more complicated for me. Liking Kia and balancing that against her potential future bust was bad enough; meeting her entire family and feeling their vibe, well . . . that was tricky. I was getting sucked into the land of no return and unchartered waters. I'd fallen hard for Vicki, but never met a single family member in our time together. Now with Kia—four days in, reason going by the wayside—I'd already met Chloe and adored her. I couldn't imagine what it was going to be like if I fell for the rest of the family, too.

Kia hadn't spotted me yet, so I stepped off to the side, watching her and Zoe discuss the medical forms in front of them, weighing my options.

Hang onto the faith or cut and run?

Less than a half hour ago, Kia and I had been T minus nothing to being naked and deep into each other. Good! Great! Wonderful! *But so Not Good.*

It should be easy. I just walk over, give Kia her bag, and tell her I'll see her at work tomorrow. My head made it sound like a cake walk, but my heart held me still. I was falling and didn't know what I was going to do about it. The smart thing was to follow my head, but my heart wasn't going to let me. Indecision wrangled my brain, and uncertainty mangled my gut, but then Kia looked up and spotted me standing there. Our eyes met, and her will dissolved. She burst into tears, and my will went with hers.

I crossed the distance, and in a single breath, Kia was in my arms. I cradled her head into my shoulder, and she held on for dear life. Zoe stood up, and I angled us around, smiling supportively, extending my hand to her.

"Hi. I'm Jake Davidson. You must be Zoe."

She took my hand briefly, gave me a small smile, and said, "Nice to meet you, Jake. Thanks for being here."

"No problem." And I realized it wasn't. I was right where I should be.

Kia lifted her head, and Zoe offered her a Kleenex.

"I've already called our mom and dad, and they're on their way," Zoe said.

"Have you had any word on Chloe, yet?" I asked.

Kia shook her head and blotted at the new tears welling.

"We got here, and a doctor met us at the door. The E.M.T.s briefed him, and I got directed here. Zoe was still working in her lab, and I called her on an inside line. A nurse just brought us these forms." She pointed at the clipboard now in Zoe's hands. "And we need dad to fill them out."

Kia looked fragile, and I guided her into the chair she had been sitting in. Zoe sat, too, and I handed Kia her bag. "I grabbed this for you."

"Thanks. That was quick thinking."

"Why don't I go see if I can get an update on Chloe?"

I'd no sooner said the words—in the same instant, Kia's parents showed up and the doctor came out. Family introductions delayed, the doctor said, "Hello. I'm Doctor Gupta. Are you Chloe Everet's family?"

Kia's dad answered for all of us. "Yes, I'm James Everet. Chloe's my mother. How is she?"

Kia reached for my hand, and I took the seat next to her.

"Your mother presented with severe chest pressure and associated symptoms. These along with an E.K.G., suggesting heart injury, lead us to suspect that she may be having a heart attack. We are currently treating her for this possibility, and we are running tests to help us confirm this diagnosis. She has stabilized, but we'll need to keep her here for a few days for further testing, observation, and continued treatment. When we have the results from her tests, we'll know more about what her next steps will be."

Doctor Gupta's pager beeped, and he looked down at the readout. "I have to go," he said, and James asked, "Will we be able to see her tonight?"

"She's being moved to a room, and a nurse will be out to direct you shortly."

"Thank you for the update," James said, and Doctor Gupta smiled, nodded, and left.

There was a heavy pause while we all absorbed the news and breathed a collective sigh of relief at Chloe being stable. Then James, looking every inch the powerful corporate lawyer that he was, turned to me, all six-feet-two forbidding inches and two-hundred-twenty imposing pounds of him, sandy blonde hair, business man cut, and those Everet trademark green eyes, looking polite but unhappily uniformed and said, "Hi. I'm James and this is my wife Celeste." He looked at Kia's hand in mine and asked, "Who, may I ask, are you?"

As meeting the parents go, this could have been better, but here we were, and Kia protested, "*Dad!*"

"Well, Sugarplum, you've been keeping a secret, and you know I don't like secrets."

Sugarplum? This was so not the time to laugh, but . . . *Sugarplum?* I bit my cheeks, and Kia gave me her dagger glance, then squeezed my hand tighter, and said, "Mom, dad, this is Jake Davidson. I'm working with him at the Acer, and you haven't met him until now, because we're on deadline for my gala opening this Friday."

I extended the hand Kia wasn't still holding onto, and both James and Celeste shook it respectfully.

"That's fine, honey," Celeste said, tall, thin, and beautiful with her deep blue eyes and dark, curly, shoulder length hair. She looked at me and asked us both, "Pardon our confusion, but this is an awkward time to be meeting a new *friend*."

Celeste's emphasis had been on the word "friend," but it was the stress of the awkward time that was making this more uncomfortable than it should be. I offered—trying hard not to think about what Kia and I had been doing at the moment Chloe stumbled into Kia's apartment—"My apologies Mr. and Mrs. Everet. Kia and I had been thinking of going to dinner when Chloe came in. It was obvious she needed immediate medical assistance, and after I called for the ambulance, things got a bit confusing. I'm just here being helpful. But now that you're here, I can see Kia later."

I didn't want to leave Kia, but I didn't want a stress induced parental showdown in the middle of Chloe's health emergency either, so I made to let go of Kia, but she stepped closer and said, "You can't leave Jake. Chloe will want to see you." She rolled her eyes at me, then added, for everyone's benefit, "Jake's her food pimp, and he hasn't fed me dinner yet. If he leaves, Chloe will not be pleased!"

Kia

Not Now

It was a ludicrous thing to say, but my parents were overreacting. Sure, I didn't bring guys home often. Okay, never. Not since undergrad. Except for the last time—which was the only time. And sure, that guy'd been worse than a dud. He'd tried to ruin my career and reputation all over a tiny misunderstanding. If you call him being my bosses boss and deciding that me being nice, showing some interest, and going on a few dates with him was an open invitation for sex—on his terms and his terms only—a tiny misunderstanding.

Dad had sent in a clean-up crew to legally lessen the intended damage, and now he was way over the top overprotective, and his lawyerly predisposition toward the third degree only added to my lack of willingness to bring guys home. I dated, but nothing had added up to surmounting the interrogation potential my father was primed for. I figured I'd be walking down the aisle and halfway to the altar before I told my parents about another guy. And of course, be exceptionally careful who I played with. And no way did Jake actually qualify on either of these counts.

I didn't want him being raked over the curiosity coals, and certainly I didn't know him long enough to be thinking aisles and altars, but that hadn't kept me from tempting him and letting his hand search out my unmentionables. And now here I was, facing down my folks, minus my underwear, terrified for Chloe, and not wanting Jake to leave my side. So I went with the absurd, and it showed, then backfired.

"Kia, honey, if you haven't eaten, we'll be sure to see to it," my mom said. "Just as soon as we all see Chloe. Certainly Jake has better things to do with his time."

I felt Jake's hand tense around mine, fully well knowing that he liked Chloe, and that "better things" smacked of insult and dis-invitation.

I smiled, difficult given my stress-induced fatigue, and deflected my mom's poorly worded mama bear tactic and said, "Thanks, but I want Jake to stay. And Chloe really will want to see him."

Thankfully, I was saved any further defense. The nurse the doctor had promised finally arrived.

Hip hip hooray! Now just let me see Chloe!

"Hello. I'm Nurse Ryerson. Today has been moving along a bit more smoothly than normal, so Mrs. Everet is already being moved into a room. By the time we get there, she should be ready for visitors. However, the doctor has provided a few restrictions."

We all nodded, and Nurse Ryerson went on. "The doctor has insisted that no more than two visitors are in the room at a time, and each visit needs to be limited to just a few minutes. Mrs. Everet has had a taxing day, and she very much needs her rest."

She looked at us to make sure we understood, and then said, "There is a small waiting area near her room." Nurse Ryerson looked at the clipboard in Zoe's hand and added, "You can finish filling out the intake forms there."

Zoe quickly handed them off to my dad, and the nurse said, "If you'll follow me, I'll take you to Mrs. Everet's room now. It's located on the seventh floor of the Cardiovascular Center. At the moment, the room she is in has no other occupant, so it's nice. You'll have a little extra privacy."

My mom, dad, and Zoe waited in the waiting room, while Jake and I went in to see Chloe first. My dad didn't look happy, but I reminded him that Jake had made the 9-1-1 call, and he gave in.

Chloe was resting, propped-up a little, wired for sound, oxygenated, and medicated to within an inch of her life with her I.V. pumping help straight into her system. Jake and I walked over to her bedside, and she smiled big.

"Close call there. I'm glad you two were home." Her smile said cheerful, but her eyes were wry apology.

I leaned in for a gentle hug and batted at the stinging in my eyes. "Me, too."

Chloe hugged me back, and said, "Don't you worry. I'm going to be fine. Doctor says so. I just need a few days, and then I'll be back on my feet in no time."

I tried to smile, but it was watery and flopped. "Chloe, I was so scared."

"Me, too, honey."

"What happened?" I asked, standing up but keeping hold of Chloe's hand. Jake pushed a chair up behind me to sit, smiled at Chloe, and said, "Hi, Chloe," to which she smiled back, then he joined me in another and we settled.

"I dunno. I was taking my afternoon walk, just like always. Thought I'd stop by to see if you were home and needed any dinner. I took the stairs up, and by the time I got to your door, I couldn't catch my breath, and my chest felt like an elephant was sitting on it. It all happened pretty fast."

I lightly rubbed my thumb along her knuckles, adamantly ignoring the "what ifs" of not being home, and said on a thin string of bravado, "Not to worry. Your food pimp was hard at work."

I was referring to the chocolate he'd brought and the dinner he promised, but Chloe grinned, shifted her look from me to Jake, *knowingly*, way too happy for someone trying to have a heart attack, and said, "Yeah, sorry about that."

She was all *my-plan-is-working*, and I laughed. I couldn't help it. "You're incorrigible!"

"Too true," she said playfully, and I felt the heaviness squashing my heart lift. Chloe was back to her usual tricks, and I wanted to do back-flips of joy.

She turned her amiable eye toward Jake, and said with apology in her voice, "Don't suppose you met my son in all of this?"

Jake smiled a quiet snort and said, "Don't suppose."

"That bad?" Chloe said scrunching her face with *that-had-to-hurt*, and Jake said, sounding completely okay with it, "He went for imposing, and I didn't think it was good time to contradict him."

"A looker *and smart*. Kia, you're gonna wanna keep your eye on this one."

I looked at Jake, whose eyes beamed "told you." I'm sure in reference to his belief that she liked him, and I shook my head at both of them.

"Speaking of dad. He's waiting. You know how he hates waiting."

"Your father needs to take a chill pill. He's wound so tight, you could play a symphony on him."

"True, but still. Maybe not the best day to tell him that," I said, shifting my eyes toward Jake, and Chloe said, totally on top of it,

"Maybe not," and Jake said, "Hellooo. I'm right here," and we laughed.

"So you'll call me tonight?" Chloe asked.

"Absolutely," I said squeezing her hand. "And I'll be back in the morning."

"I love you, Kia," Chloe said and pulled me in for a hug.

It was a quiet moment acknowledging what had just happened, and my heart remembered the fear and concern, and I was so glad she was going to be okay. I hugged her, gently and tightly all rolled into a ball of loving encouragement, and said, "I love you, too." Chloe squeezed me back, and I knew she'd been frightened, and it choked my heart even more.

"I'll call you when I get home."

Reluctantly, I let go my hug on her, and stood to go.

Chloe looked at Jake meaningfully. "Food's on you for the next few days."

"No worries. I've got it covered."

She smiled at him, and her tone was all gleeful approval. "I'm sure you do." And I said, mimicking Jake's earlier indignation, "Hellooo, I'm right here."

Jake and I made our escape to mom and dad's disapproving eye. Not so much of Jake, but of not having control, feeling protective, and missing a whole lot of information. If they knew Jake, they'd love him, I'm sure. Probably. *Maybe.* But mostly it was just loving, parental concern. And as much as it was uncomfortably inconveniencing at the moment, it was nice. I have a great family, sometimes too pushy, sometimes too interfering, always loving and supportive. Jake—if ever—would fit right in.

Kia

Let's Try This Again

Having seen Chloe—seeing the color back in her cheeks, hearing the perky back in her voice, and catching the merry mischievous glint back in her eyes—I felt better. Don't get me wrong. She was in the hospital, and that made me choke on a hearty *ugh.* Likely heart attack. Tubes, bright lights, and whirring, beeping monitors. So I was still concerned, and was anxiously awaiting her all-clear, back-to-healthy, comfortable, and back in her home. But this was way better than what I had feared just a few hours ago—that I would lose her, my best friend and most supportive family member. Even thinking about it left me cold with rising grief. I had felt sick, sad, immobilizing fear, but now—here she was laughing and back to her loving, conniving matchmaking. *Yay!*

But the rest of our not-fun evening had taken its toll. My head was giving in to gravity and my legs were ten ton weights dragging me forward, by rote, following Jake to his Jeep.

"So where to?" Jake asked me opening his passenger side door.

I crawled in, tired, starving, craving comfort food and sleep. "Home."

"Home it is," he said, and closed my door.

He walked around and climbed in his side, quietly supportive, and cranked the engine over, paid the parking fee, and pulled into traffic.

I was sandman droopy, but Jake had been perfect and survived the initial parental blast, so I worked my chipper and took a look around.

His Jeep was very Jake—dark, sexy, capable, and fun with muscles. But it lacked the peppy zing my Mini has. She gets me where I'm going with zip-zing-zadoo. Jake's Jeep had a mellow undercurrent, that at the moment was really working for me—but that didn't keep me from dealing out some guff.

"Well, no wonder you want my Mini."

Appropriately sounding accosted he said, "Hey—don't pick on Chuck."

"You named your Jeep, Chuck?" My disbelief floated across the cabin and fell flat in his lap.

"Yeah." He was playing along, and tossed back a defensive, "What'd you name your Mini?"

"Molly, which of course fits her perfectly," I said filled with air, and then flipped to grieving friend for his Jeep. "Why did you name your poor Jeep Chuck? Don't tell me it's because you like a good steak?"

Jake checked me with his *I'm-going-to-get-you* smile, then said "I do, but then I would have went with something like T-Bone. I named him Chuck so I could hop in and say, 'What's up Chuck?' And that makes me laugh, which comes in handy on days like today."

Days like today. He wasn't kidding. It'd been a roller coaster of ups and downs.

"You're feeling feisty," he said, not sounding unhappy about it.

"I need food and sleep." I turned to him with a genuine smile. "But you've been supremely magnificent—way beyond the call of duty—and I don't know what I would have done without you!"

"Ahhh, perfect. Just how I like my women. Indebted and grateful!"

"Women?"

Jake tilted his head toward me and dropped his interested glance from my head to my toe, setting little fires all along the way.

"In general," he said. "Currently working on *woman.*"

"And how's that going for you?"

"I'll know better after I feed her some more chocolate."

"Food pimp and chocolate charmer. Got anything else up your sleeve?"

"Why don't you take a look and find out for yourself?"

Tempting tempter. I could have done better, but my brain was running on fumes, so I held back saying it out loud. Avoiding embarrassment by exhaustion when engaged in a sexually intensified battle of the wits seemed my wisest move at the moment. No need turning him off after he just endured my parents.

Jake veered into the parking lot of my apartment complex and rolled to a sexy, confident, lazy stop. Cutting the engine and throwing his emergency break, he shifted toward me, and asked, "Do you want me to come up?"

"Are you hungry?"

"Is this a trick question?" he said, looking at me with eyes that were already volcanic and very interested in devouring me.

"I was thinking grilled cheese and Chloe's veggie soup."

"Sure you were."

Well I had been, until he slid his finger down the side of my face and gave me his smoldering look. Now I was thinking I wasn't so tired. Maybe I could muster up the strength to rip off his clothes before I passed out. But then he said, "I love grilled cheese. You're on K.P."

"K.P.?"

"Kitchen Patrol."

"I don't think so. You've still got your underpants on."

"But I like you naked."

"I'm sure you do, but I'm gonna catch cold."

"I don't think that's how you catch colds," he said with that fiery glint burning through.

"And you're an expert?"

"On certain things."

I was curious, but had a good idea what things he was talking about. He was caressing my face again, melting me, directing my thoughts south, and my stomach growled.

"I should feed you." He said looking down at my tummy and grinning.

"Yes, food pimp, you should. And that's why *you're* on K.P."

He narrowed his eyes at me, calculating, and pushed me toward my door. I opened it and climbed out, and he followed on his side. "I'll cook; you clean," he said, and I countered, "You cook, you clean."

He beeped his doors locked and we headed for my apartment, "That's hardly fair. Where's the fifty-fifty in that?"

"Who said anything about fifty-fifty? You willingly volunteered for Chloe's service, and that means feed and follow-through."

We got to my door, and I slipped the key in to unlock it, and we found our way to my kitchen, me dropping my purse on my couch along the way.

I stepped to my sink and washed my hands with Jake right behind me. "Tell me more about this 'follow-through'," he said with a suggestive wiggle of his brow, and I chuckled, reaching for the skillet and a spatula.

"Here. You'll need these."

I opened my fridge, aimed for the butter and cheese, but grabbed the cute little brown bag of presumed-chocolates Jake had brought instead, and he said, taking the bag away from me, "Unh-unh-unh. You don't want to spoil your dinner."

"Sure I do," I said rallying and reaching for the bag again, but Jake deftly sidestepped me.

"What if I crash before dessert?"

"You won't want to do that," he said, unmoved by my protest and hinting at the good stuff.

I was really wanting the good stuff, especially with Jake, but on the inside my body was already in a full-body yawn, and I knew we were talking long shots for tonight.

Hmmm.

"So you're saying there's nothing that could persuade you to share now."

"Not if I'm on solo K.P."

Nuff said.

"Okay. Bread's in the cabinet. Butter and cheese are in the fridge. Chloe's soup is in the freezer, labeled up, and serving dishes are behind you. I'll be back in a bit."

I heard Jake's lazy laughter chase me down my short hallway all the way to my bedroom. I slid my door open and turned to shut it, actually surprised not to find Jake already there. But then I heard the quiet sizzle of butter in the skillet and my stomach grumbled again. I was craving food, sleep, and Jake, and not necessarily in that order.

I had to get out of my skirt and into something more comfortable, but I didn't want to go with real clothes—it was late—and I didn't want to do sweats. That would be so unsexy. I rifled through my drawers looking for something suitable. Not finding much, I turned up my light flannel p.j.'s. They were pink with funky little chomped-on hearts that said things like *bite-me*. Chloe had gotten them for me for Valentine's one year. I thought the *bite-me* was sufficiently inviting enough to overcome the flannel, and they were p.j.'s. Reasonable invitation with that, right? I piled the jammies and some panties into a heap across my arm with some footies for my feet and hurried into my bathroom.

I tied my hair back and scrubbed my face into a dewy glow. More incentive for Jake. Not that he needed it. But when you're that hot and tasty looking, I didn't want to disappoint. I switched into my flannels and let my hair loose, finger tossing it into what I hoped was a sexy, mussed temptation. I looked in the mirror and smiled. Yep. That should do it.

I heard Jake call out from the kitchen, "Dinner's ready."

And I thought, *So is dessert.*

Jake

Hunger Pangs

Kia came out looking cute and sexy as hell, and I was definitely interested in biting her, just like her jammies suggested. If she hadn't had the day she had, I think I could've convinced her that food was highly overrated. As it was, she was working hard to play along—fighting fatal fatigue. And despite her will power, I didn't think she had it in her, at least not enough to really enjoy. No way was I wasting our first time on something less than rocket-ships-to-the-moon spectacular. No second rate roll in the hay for us. So food first, then see.

Kia padded her way to the table and took in the sight of my semi-stupendous cooking efforts. Soup heated in bowls, *not burnt.* Grilled cheese sandwiches, buttered and lightly browned, cheese oozing out the sides, *not burnt.* It was a reasonably successful outcome, and she said, "Smells great!"

"Just doing my job."

I offered her her usual O.J., and poured a full glass when she nodded.

"It looks like you found everything okay," she said taking her seat, and I said, "Hard not to with all the labels everywhere."

Kia, smiled and shook her head at me, picked up her grilled cheese sandwich and inhaled it, retorting in between bites, "If you put labels in my kitchen, I'll beat you silly."

"Me?" I said wide-eyed and smiled back, returning the O.J. to the fridge and joining Kia at the table. "If you get anymore organized in your kitchen, I'm going to have to report you to O.C.D. anonymous."

"My kitchen is two cabinets and a drawer. No room for disarray, and if you report me, it's not anonymous."

And this is where I get lost in the fine lines between black and white. I knew I had this job to do, and I knew Kia was my suspect, but I really didn't believe she was guilty, and this ease and fun and sensual heat, her *Wham*, is where I wanted to be. I loved being with her. She kept me on my toes and she made me laugh, and every moment made me look forward to the next. This, right here my friend, is the good stuff.

I dipped my grilled cheese into my soup and took a big, satisfying bite. "Mmmm." Talk about hitting the spot. It's hard to screw up grilled cheese, but Chloe's veggie soup was a ringer for the Soup Hall of Fame. It was the perfect blend of tomato base, basil, rosemary, and country vegetables. It felt like home, and as always, my mouth was in heaven when Chloe was behind the meal.

"Ohmigod, that's good!"

"I know," Kia said. "Her soup is the best. She makes it up in bulk, and then replenishes my freezer whenever it gets low. It's like I have a soup fairy from above."

Kia said it with joy on her face, but her eyes recalled the day's events and concern wilted their brightness.

"She's going to be okay."

Kia nodded, her sad moment over, and chuckled wryly. "Seems likely. She's too determined to see me happy to throw in the towel mid-fight."

Kia spooned up the last of her soup, having made record time, and I said, finishing mine off, too, "So you're telling me I have a chance?"

"I think you know you do, but it really all hinges on your next move."

"We're back to the bag," I said, and she nodded her *you-know-it* look.

"One-track mind," I said, shaking my head, and she smiled.

I gathered our dishes together and cleared the table to her wiggling her shapely brows at me suggestively. But I wasn't buying it. No way was she playing that game, so I stayed on course.

"Well, I'd love to serve you dessert, but I'm busy with K.P."

"No problem," she countered. "I can get it myself."

Kia got up and tried to make her way to the fridge, but I intercepted, one hand on the door, the other depositing dishes in the sink. "Nope. You don't get to eat, if I don't get to watch. You'll have to wait."

"Unh," she pouted. "I'm beginning to think you're a tease for sure."

"Bad-mouthing me is not getting you to that chocolate any faster. You want dessert, help me clean up."

"Bully."

"Ahh, you're just saying that 'cuz you think I'm cute."

"You are *not* cute!"

"Am too!" I put the stopper in the sink, turned the water to semi-hot and added some soap. "You helping or not?"

Kia grabbed her pale yellow, plaid kitchen towel, and said, "Fine! You wash; I'll dry."

I smiled and picked up the sponge. To be honest, there wasn't enough room for the two of us in her two-cabinet, one-drawer kitchen, so we were standing in each other's oxygen again, and I'd be lying if I said it wasn't exactly what I wanted. Kia close to me was where I wanted her always. And already, the sparks were sparking, and the pheromones were pheromoning. The sliver of space between us vibrated with cresting, unslaked heat, and in a blink the dishes were done; the kitchen was clean; and we were caught in our sexual vortex again.

Kia looked up at me, suspicious, and I bent to kiss away her *not-born-yesterday* look, but she narrowed her brows at me, stepped back, and said, "Nice try, Chocolate Charmer. Now fess up and charm me with some chocolate!"

I smiled and finger nipped the tip of her nose. "Aye, aye."

Reaching into her fridge and pulling out the coveted bag of goodies, I found Kia was all expectant jubilation, but before I handed over the delectables, I said, "One condition."

"What's that?"

"There's something in this bag I'd like to keep secret for a while."

"How long's a while?"

"Not today, maybe tomorrow."

"Sounds reasonable, but it depends on what else you've got."

"Now who's the bully?"

"From where I'm standing, still you; since, you're still hogging the chocolate."

Kia's amused exasperation was cute and merited reward, so I selected the largest chocolate covered strawberry and held it out for her to bite.

Her eyes went wide, and she stepped in close to me to taste her treat. I'm terrible I know, but I couldn't help myself—before she could sink her teeth into the strawberry, I inched it closer to me so that she had to *lean* into my chest. She gave me her suspicious eyes again, and I said, all innocent, "Don't you want any?"

Me or the chocolate, either way I was a winner, winner!

She smartly stood her ground and reached for my hand. Keeping her eyes locked with mine, she pulled the succulent strawberry to her mouth, and then took a big, messy, sexy, hot bite. Chocolate melted onto her lips and strawberry juice dribbled at her chin. She finger wiped at the sweetness before it dripped, and my body lit up like a Christmas tree.

Chocolate bag firmly secured in my left hand, strawberry still in my right, I wrapped my bag arm around her, yanking her into me, and kissed the sweetness away, licking and nibbling at her juicy, chocolaty lips.

Kia tasted like desire. And as I watched her lids drop curtain, her nimble fingers curled into my shirt, scraping at my roughened nipples—like she might be holding on for dear life—and my eyes followed, drifting shut—leaving me to focus on the wetness of her mouth against mine and the warmth of her body as it nestled perfectly into me.

Oh my!

Heat shot south, and I steadied my hold on her, deepening our kiss.

The desired effect was achieved, and Kia moaned into my mouth. We both knew we had to stop eating chocolate or start hitting the sheets.

Kia arched into me, making contact in all the right places, and our kiss went *four alarm fire*. I was still holding her close and was thinking we had too many clothes on, when I felt her hands spread slowly across my chest. This was good, and I wanted more. I took our kiss to the next level, teasing her lips with little laps from my tongue, and she got in on the action, returning my punts. Then, while I was distracted by her *got-game* kissing assault, I felt her hand slowly closing in on my little bag of chocolate seduction and knew she was playing me for my tempting confections.

I abruptly broke the kiss and pushed back, a picture of mock indignation. "You sneaky scamp!"

My breathing was a little ragged, and I wanted her back in my arms, but she gave me her look and smirked. *Oh-ho-ho*, I thought and firmed my stance.

She laughed. "Great kiss, but I almost had you!"

I kept my jaw from dropping and narrowed my eyes at her. "Not by a long shot, missy!"

"Admit it. If I would have went full on tongue, you'd be out that bag of strawberries, clueless as to what hit you."

"A little confident are we?"

"You seemed to like it."

Like it? I loved it. Couldn't seem to get enough.

Stumped for a verbal response, my troglodytic instincts took over, and I scooped her up, *much to her squealish surprise*, hauled her over my shoulder and playfully flopped her onto her big, cushy sofa, where she immediately sunk in a good six inches. If her pillowy cushions had given way any more, I would have had to go diving to find her in the deep folds of flowers and fluff. As it was, she floated up to the surface, giggles galore, waiting for her promised fruity delights.

I heavy sighed my playful resignation, shaking my head in disbelief at being duped, *again*, and did my best not to crack a smile. Like I said, Kia was fun, and she made me feel happy.

"Will that be one or two strawberries for your highness?"

Kia looked up at me, a kid in a candy shop, finger-signaled two, and then audaciously demanded, "And bring me a napkin, too, please!"

I'm sure she added the "please" only to soften the defeating blow to her helpless servant. I put the chocolates on a plate, grabbed some napkins, put the bag and its remaining contents back in the fridge, and joined Kia on the couch, sitting at the end with her feet. I passed the plate off to her with the napkin, smiled at her mmm-delicious expression, and reaching for her foot, removed her sock and gently rubbed at her arch.

I don't know if her eyes rolling up and into the back of her head was in delight over the strawberries or the foot massage, but my guess was that it was the scrumptious combination.

When she returned back to earth, Kia said, "You're really good at this."

"Foot rubs?"

"The seduction scene."

"You think this is me trying to seduce you?"

She smiled and nodded a definitive, "Mmm-hmm."

"Not in the least. I'm not actually all that interested in you. I just thought given your difficult day, you could use a break."

I'm surprised she didn't sputter strawberry at me with the impact of her scoffing snort, or worse, choke, but she finally managed with, "If this is you not being interested in me—" And then she left it hanging for me to fill in the obvious blanks.

"Sooooo," I said, stroking her foot and gently kneading her toes, "You going in to work tomorrow?"

Kia's microwave read nine thirty-seven. It was getting late for fun and games, and I suspected Kia had a long day planned for tomorrow.

She licked at her fingers, demolishing off the last of her strawberries, and said, just as I expected she would, "Have to. Too much to do. But I'm going to see Chloe first thing."

I finished coaxing the tension from her foot and returned it to its sock, then gently picking up her other foot, started again.

"Well, I can go in and get things rolling with Ian and Karen. Is there anything special you wanted to do next, or just keep on keepin' on with plan?"

"Keep on keepin' on. Now that the locket's here, everyone can breathe easy again. Now it's just a race against the clock."

The locket. Every time Kia mentioned it, I watched her face, her expression, her body language, *everything*, looking for any hint the locket was on her list of things to do, but got nothing. Just a normal work vibe. My judgment might be getting clouded by my libido, but she honestly didn't have any of the signs. This just wasn't adding up. But hey, that was good news. Right?! Just so long as the locket didn't come up missing, we were in the black, and all was cool.

"You'll have to tell Chloe I said, 'Hello.' I can stop by later in the day, unless you think it's gonna freak out your folks."

"Oh, if they're there, it's going to freak them out. But if you don't stop in, there'll be hell to pay. Chloe will not be pleased. And I'm sure that's not something you want marring your excellent record with her!"

I switched from foot rub to tickle at her sass, and Kia laughed, trying to pull her foot away, but I held on tight.

"Hey, no fair. That's misappropriation of your servant-ly station."

I gave her my best scolding look and said, "Then behave," and made to tickle her again, but she quickly said, "Okay, okay. I'll behave, *if* that's what you *really* want."

Kia's switch-and-bait indifference routine was entertaining to say the least, and I shook my head. What a little rabble rousing instigator.

"You're gonna be a handful aren't you?"

"It's why you like me."

"If you say so."

"See. Told you you were interested me."

I shook my head, smiling. *Incorrigible woman.*

"You going to be okay for breakfast in the morning? I don't want Chloe thinking I'm derelict in my duties."

Kia yawned a giganormous yawn. She was tired and trying hard to fight it. Her look was disappointed resignation, and it made me smile. She liked me and wanted me to stay, but knew she'd never make it.

Warmth filled empty spaces I didn't even know I had. I liked being wanted by Kia, and knowing we were over our hesitations. We were getting there. Just not tonight.

"Sorry," she said, not meaning the yawn.

"Nothing to be sorry about. You've had a rough day. Besides . . . there's always tomorrow," I grinned.

I finished massaging Kia's foot, resocked it, and gave it back.

"Thanks," she smiled, taking in her cotton clad piggies. "That was wonderful."

"Anytime."

I stood up, leaving Kia on the couch, relaxed and reclined, and walked over to the fridge, retrieving my bag.

No way did I trust her with my next surprise treat.

She heard the rustle and looked over.

"I was hoping you'd forget that," she said wistfully.

I smiled. "I bet you were, but not a chance!"

Coming back to stand by her, I asked, "You want me to get your pillow and blanket?"

"No, I'm good, but thanks," she said swiveling around to put her feet on the floor. No easy feat, given the fluff friction holding her down.

"So you didn't answer earlier. You cool for breakfast?"

"Yeah. Chloe has an emergency stash of waffles in my freezer. Besides, I'm pretty sure she'll somehow have managed to have my breakfast brought to me at the hospital."

We both smiled. It was probably true.

"Okay then," I said and bent down to kiss her square and full on the lips. It wasn't a passionate kiss, but it held longing and interest and intention, and it was nice.

"Tomorrow," I said, and she said, "Give Bullet some scritches for me."

"Will do."

Her eyes were already beginning to drift. "Sleep well, Kia. Dream of me."

I left Kia looking drowsy, warm, and want-able, and headed for my car. When I hit the pavement, I pulled out my cell and dialed Chris. He picked up on the first ring.

"So you met the family did you?"

I opened my door and climbed in. "Wow. Mr. Everet was fast with that security check."

I cranked my engine over, put Chuck in gear, and backed out.

"How'd it go?" Chris asked.

I shifted to drive and aimed for Plymouth. "Fine. Chloe had what appears to be a heart attack. I was on the scene and dialed 9-1-1. We all ended up at the hospital."

"I guess it was an unavoidable complication."

Complication for sure, but Chris's implied accusation of fault on my part rode up my backside and chaffed. He just never quit.

This was going to deteriorate fast, so I made quick to disconnect.

"Just checking-in. We're still moving forward as planned. I'll be with locket at the museum in the morning, while Kia is at the hospital. I'll verify the extra security measures have been taken."

Chris apparently got the hint, because he grunted, "Fine," at me and hung up.

He really needed that promotion, and I really needed him off my back.

I drove the rest of the way home in silence, thinking of Kia, seeing her fun, sexy, smart, and hot, and not being able to imagine her as a thief. Which got me to thinking—*If not her, who then?* Some one was taking those lockets, and so far, that someone was getting away with it.

Kia

Finders, Keepers

Chloe was sitting propped up in her bed flipping through an entertainment magazine with the same bored attention one might give to doodling while waiting on hold for a cable company rep. Hospital beds were so not her thing.

"How's it going?" I asked, walking into her still private room.

"Kia, honey!" Chloe said, brightening to day-at-the-beach and laid the magazine aside. "I'm so glad to see you. I'm going bonkers just sitting here."

"I figured as much, so I brought these for you." I handed her a bag of her favorite books, and set a giant vase of flowers on the bedside stand. "Thought you might like some cheering."

"Are those from my gardens?"

"Yeah," I said pulling up a chair. "I thought they might help you feel more at home while you're being incarcerated."

Chloe gave a dry chuckle. "Good thinking. The doctor came by today already, and I have to stay here until Saturday. What am I going to do in here until Saturday?"

I gave her a compassionate grimace, "Oh, Chloe. I know you hate being cooped up, but apparently you need some rest."

"Rest, schmest!"

We laughed.

"It's all this matchmaking that's got you so worked up, so maybe now we'll both get a break," I teased, and Chloe looked even happier.

"Speaking of Jake," she said, and I said, "Were we?"

"How's it going?"

Chloe was not one to let loose of something once she got her teeth into it.

I let out a playful sigh and said, "Well, if you must know."

"I must," she said, and I chuckled.

"We seem to have come to an agreement that something between us is happening."

"Mmm-hmmm, go on."

Shaking my head at her gleeful encouragement, I said, "You're very bad, Chloe." To which she replied, "I know, and I hope it's being helpful. You were saying."

"I was saying, *and we like it.* But I told him I wanted to wait until Friday. Then wanted to take it back and tried attacking him, but now we keep experiencing near misses."

Chloe's eyes were all mirthful anticipation and she wore a little happy smile, like everything was going just as she planned. She did everything but laugh an evil laugh and tap her fingertips together.

"And he keeps feeding me chocolate. Really excellent chocolate. It's cheating, but it's working!"

"It's foreplay."

"Chloe!"

"Well, it is."

She was so matter-of-fact. It was hilarious. My own grandmother trying to get me together with a man. My mother would be aghast at Chloe's meddling and directness—which is why they don't hang in the same circles, except when supporting my father. And it's another reason why I love Chloe so much. My mom is a perfect wife to a big-time lawyer with a potential future in politics, and sometimes her expectations of perfection can be a little intense. Chloe kept levity alive and kicking in our family, and she made sure that I had lots of fun growing up.

"So what's next?" she asked.

"Don't know. The next couple of days are going to be sooo busy. You know me."

"Yes, I do. Which means you'll be working like a fiend until Friday."

I scrunched my face, total *bleh*, and agreed. "Pretty much. There's so much to do, and Phillip has just been being awful. Worse than usual, and I don't know why."

"No social skills," Chloe quipped, and I smiled.

"Well, there's that, but it feels like he's moved from condescension and inappropriate lasciviousness to hate. He's been being really loathsome when he addresses me, and he essentially threatened to fire me."

"On what grounds?"

Chloe was totally indignant on my behalf, and I could tell she was getting upset. I didn't want her getting worked up, so I aimed us back to happy.

"Same-O, same-o," I said putting a whadda-you-gonna-do look on my face, and shifted optimistically to, "The good news is he won't even be in to work today, and Jake's been pulling knight-in-shining-armor every time Phillip gets cranky. So we'll get to Friday, and maybe then Phillip will chill out."

"Hopefully," she said, and then smiled, taking the Jake bait I'd laid out. "So Jake's good for more than just feeding you."

"As I'm sure you hoped he would be."

"Well, he's so handsome, and he fills out his suit so nicely. It'd be a shame if he didn't have anything else to back-up those good looks."

"True. All buff with no stuff—those boys are just for fun, not keepers."

"Jake's a keeper."

"Too soon to tell, but he's got excellent cupcake lick-able-ness going for him."

"Yes, he does," Chloe said emphatically, giving me her just-go-for-it look, making me chuckle again.

"You're so funny, Chloe. You know—he told me to tell you he's feeding me, and he'll stop in to see you later."

"And you're not already convinced he's a keeper?" Chloe shook her head at me sadly, like I needed to get my head out of the sand and smell the roses. "Who comes to see an old lady in the hospital and diplomatically discharges your father's surly protective streak?"

She might be onto something there, but—

Okay maybe there weren't any buts. But it's been less than a week, so other than the working my cheerful maybe-ness, let's not go counting our chickens before they hatch.

"Just for you," I said. "I'm keeping my fingers crossed, and I'm ready to lick at a moment's notice."

Chloe laughed, "Deal. So what are you wearing to the gala?"

"I bought something new, Chloe. It's the most beautiful gown you've ever seen. I wanted to surprise you, but now you won't get to see it."

My lip puffed into a sad pout all on its own, and Chloe said, "Oh honey, I'm sure you'll be beautiful, and you can show me after. For now, you can tell me all about it."

"I'll make sure to take pictures," I said, promising, "but for now—" I held up my hands to indicate that the dress was off my shoulders. "It kind of wraps around with these cap-like sleeves that drape right below my shoulders, and it's made of the most beautiful pale blush chiffon, so soft looking and light, that's kind of layered and draped. It's a dream in a dress. Very romantic and sexy at the same time." I pointed at the upper swell of my left breast. "A fabricy flower looking adornment is here, and it has this thigh high slit in the front with a hint of delicate lace that peeks out. I'm thinking, now that there's Jake—he's a goner!"

Chloe laughed and said, "It sounds lovely, and I think Jake is definitely in trouble. What about your hair and make-up?"

"Bethany," I said by way of explanation, knowing Chloe would immediately be able to imagine.

"You'll be a knock-out for sure. Is she doing your hair up or down?"

"I'm not sure. She told me to bring a picture from my fitting, and she'll figure it out when I get there."

"You'll definitely have to take pictures. I'm sorry I'm going to miss it."

I got up and gave Chloe a big hug. "Me, too! And that's why you have to do whatever the doctors tell you, so you can get better fast!"

"I'm going to be fine."

I stepped back and took my seat again, giving Chloe a stubborn look. "I know you are, because you're going to follow your doctor's orders."

"I want to go home now," Chloe said wistfully. "But you're right. I'm hoping they'll have a definitive diagnosis for me later today."

"Will you call me at work? It's going to be a hectic day, filled with meetings and busy work, but I want you to call me as soon as you hear anything."

"Sure honey, I'll call you."

"Promise me. No matter what the news is, you'll call."

"Promise."

"I hate to go, but I have to get to work. Jake went in to get the ball rolling, but I want to make sure we're not hitting any more snags. Friday's racing here fast, and we don't have time for anymore complications."

"It's okay. You've brought me my favorite reads," she said patting her bag. "And I'm sure your father is going to be coming by soon. And Zoe will probably sneak in at lunch time, most likely wanting my pudding!"

"Yeah, you've got to watch out for her. She always stealing people's dessert!"

I got up again, and gave Chloe another hug. "I'm not sure what time we'll wrap up tonight, but I'll stop in on my way home. Or if it gets too late, I'll at least call you. But I'll work really hard to get here."

"I know you will. You make sure Jake feeds you, and when I get out of here, we'll have ourselves a little celebratory jailbreak party!"

"Sounds like a plan!"

I gave Chloe another hug, and she said, "Have a nice, productive day at work," and I said, "Try not to harass your doctors too much, but give dad a hard time as always!"

Chloe smiled and said, "You bet."

It was hard leaving. She looked a little lost in the hospital, and definitely didn't want to be there or have anything wrong with her. It was a bit heart wrenching.

"I love you," I said on another big squeeze, and she said, "I love you, too. Now get to work, before Jake has to send out a rescue crew."

"Bye."

"Bye, honey."

We exchanged smiles and waves, and I forced myself out the door, through the hospital and to my car, all the way to the Acer and up to the second floor.

When I got there, the rest of my Wednesday and Thursday turned into a blur of frantic activity, with Jake by my side, working just as hard as me, feeding me, rushing out for dinners and to see Chloe, getting me in my car and sending me home—and telling me he'd break my legs if I tried to come back in during the middle of the night—which was absolutely silly, because how would he know?

I met with the caterers and the first floor decorators, successfully avoided Phillip like the plague, finalized my dress pick-up, re-confirmed my Bethany appointment, and collectively, we at the Acer got the Tsarists' Treasures exhibit up and going, and then celebrated with an apple piroshky, a Russian pastry Karen made for us.

Both nights, I visited Chloe on my way home from work, then dragged my exhausted bones home, and crawled into bed. And when Chloe had called me to tell me the doctors were able to confirm that she had had a heart attack, I cried like a baby, and Jake came in to hold my hand and pass me the Kleenex.

As Thursday night came to a close, I had the happy news that with rehabilitative therapy, Chloe was going to be back to almost good as new. She'd have to make a few lifestyle changes, and she would have some new medication in her daily routine, but otherwise, I was getting my fun and playful Chloe back. Jake and I celebrated with some hot chocolate and another one of his mind-bending, body-melting, clothes-ripping kisses, and some hot promises for Friday night that left my body humming with electric excitement that chased me all the way into my dreams.

Cue Friday morning. I woke to a bright, blue-skied, sunny day, practically beside myself with high-hopes, delirious with anticipation, giddy with Jake butterflies, and as silly as it may sound, I declared it *My Day!* I had my dream dress and Bethany, the locket and my dream show, and Jake who rocked with dream guy potential as my date. And tomorrow Chloe was coming home. It just doesn't get much more perfect than this. I sunk my teeth into my bottom lip and smiled—goofy, happy, and hopeful! Ready to get this show on the road.

Jake

Stunned Speechless

I'm not normally a nervous guy. It's one of my greatest field assets. I don't get shaken, not easily, and if I do, I can pull off impassive like nobody's business, and that's saved my ass more than once. But today, I was feeling it. And I hated it.

I'd put myself in a position where I had something to lose if this went south, and I was betting against the odds. Life wasn't one to treat me favorably, *not in the personal department*, and my risk to benefit ratio for the next few days was threatening to hang me out to dry.

A sinking feeling had taken up residence in the pit of my stomach as the realization that there was a part of me that *needed* Kia to be innocent. For whatever you can learn about a person in a week, I'd seen her in her element, at home, with family, and for all that she was selling herself as. And if it was all true, I was a goner. I'd fallen, and her reality of me was a shadow of a wisp of the truth. She knew the real me, all except my family, friends, history, interests, job and my reason for being here. I'd sold her a bill of goods that was rotten to the core, and if she was innocent, I was going to have some serious explaining to do.

But to cross that bridge—later. Hopefully *much* later.

My current cover was only good through the gala. After that, I'm supposed to be heading back to the DIA, but the Tsarists' collection was scheduled to be here for a month. I needed a reason to stay in house and keep an eye on the locket, and make Chris's career by catching Kia in the act and arresting her. Chris had told me he'd handled it, and guaranteed me I'd *love* his solution, but refused to tell me, claiming some crap about genuine response. It was the smug sound of his voice that had my hackles up.

I wasn't sure how tonight was going to add up, but I knew Kia was excited, and for her, I wanted to make the evening perfect.

It was a black tie event, and I rented a black, Lincoln Town Car to match my penguin suit. I thought it might be a nice touch and a surprise to begin Kia's night. And having given it much thought, I decided I would be taking Kia back to my place after the opening. I was going with faith and probable stupidity, but the way I saw it was that if she was guilty, she'd be going to jail for a long time, and it wouldn't matter. If she wasn't, then it wouldn't matter. There wasn't anything at my house to indicate my FBI guy status, except the recording equipment for all the bugs, and since Kia was going to be with me, I put it away, so my cover would be intact. Instead, I had strawberries in the fridge, champagne chilling on ice, clean sheets, a whole lot of hope, a ton of desire, and my secret chocolate surprise waiting to temp her.

Kia requested I bring a camera and pick her up at Chloe's at six. I checked my black-leather banded Bulova dress watch—right on time—and pulled into Chloe's drive. I hadn't seen Kia yet today. Only talked to her on the phone. And now here I was, with all my anticipation, electric hum, and reservation clashing together in a bizarre mix of contented bliss and dread.

Stepping up to Chloe's front door, I rang the bell and waited. I could hear the click clack of Kia's heels on the tile, and then with a *whoosh*, Chloe's front door pulled wide. And it happened again. *Wham!* And I almost lost my footing.

Good Lord, Kia packed a punch. She was resplendent, and for an instant, my brain froze, and I forgot how to breathe. I meant to say something, I really did. But I just stood there staring, like an idiot, momentarily struck speechless.

Kia tilted her head sideways, and smiled. "Hiya."

I still just stood there, fighting the full body contraction throwing me off balance. Fuddled, muddled, and a little blurred—I felt dizzy drinking in the sight of her, and all the while I was fumbling to voice something coherent.

If I hadn't already fallen, seeing her like this would have sealed the deal.

Kia's look turned gotcha-pleased, and she chuckled, saying, "Can I get you anything? Paper bag, perhaps."

Droll. Always witty this one.

"I'm not hyperventilating." I was blown away, and now that I'd found my voice, I was surprised my tone was level.

"You sure? Maybe you just need to sit down for a minute."

"You know. Normally—" I said, hearing my voice thicken and my breathing go quiet.

"Normally?" she asked, biting her lip and dropping her lids to follow my hand as it slowly reached for her.

"Normally," I calmly said again, trickling my fingers down the length of her soft, warm arm, "I'd be game for the banter, but—"

I wasn't sure if it was the dress, the hair, her eyes . . . I don't know. But she was breathtaking. Truly enchanting.

"Buuut?" she asked still biting her lip in a hopeful smile.

"But," I said getting my footing back and stepping into her space. "You're beautiful."

I smiled and bit a soft kiss into the crook of her neck and had the satisfaction of seeing a shiver ripple through her. I raised my lips to her ear, sprinkling little kisses all along the way, taking my time, and breathing in the soft scent of her, whispering, "You look like a goddess, princess, and angel all rolled up into one delectable bite, and I'm thinking tonight just got a whole helluva lot longer."

Kia beamed, her smile radiant like the sun. "You like it?"

"I don't think like is the right word. What did you do to your hair?"

Kia's sun-kissed, honeyed-brown hair was half up, half loose loopy large enticing curls, framing her face, and it shimmered somehow, giving her an impossibly soft, ethereal look.

"Bethany."

"Bethany?"

"She does my hair and make-up. She's awesome, and she works magical miracles. Did you want to come in for a minute?"

That was not a good idea. Kia was porcelain perfection, and I could just look at her like this all night long. But at the same time, we were a week into waiting and wanting, and I needed to rake my fingers through her hair, bury myself deep, and take us to the other side of never-never land.

"No. If I come in there, you won't make it to the gala." My tone had dropped to flat, but that was just me suppressing my he-man-gone-wild response to wanting to permanently claim her for my own.

Kia had the wherewithal to blush, not in embarrassment, but in knowing what was to come, and that just made my blood pound harder. I looked her over, needing to get us out of there, and took stock—Kia, dress, shoes. "Do you have a purse or something?"

She nodded, *her turn to be speechless*, and I said, "Grab it, and let's go."

Kia reached over to Chloe's foyer table and picked up a matching, delicate, slender-thin, hand-sized clutch, and then walked out, turning to pull Chloe's door shut, and locked it.

I escorted her to the Lincoln, realizing that with her heels, she now stood at my eye level, and I got a tantalizing future flash of Kia's leg making use of that thigh high slit and wrapping itself around my waist.

Oh my!

"Where's Chuck?"

I shook off the image, looking forward to later, and said, "I gave him the night off. Thought the Town Car would fit the occasion nicely."

Kia stopped, leaned into me, and gave me a happy kiss. "There's more where that came from, but I have to watch my make-up."

"Like I said . . . it's going to be a long night."

She smiled and reached out to squeeze my hand.

I helped her into the Lincoln, gently tucking the bottom of her dress in with her, and she carefully fastened her seatbelt. I walked around to my side of the car, sucking in some much needed steadying breaths, and thought wryly, *Well, at least I don't feel dread anymore.*

I angled into my seat, pulled my door closed, and fastened my belt. Kia reached over, touching my hand again, and said, "Jake?"

"Yeah?"

"Thanks, you're making my night."

We were halfway through the gala, and Kia was making the rounds. She'd given her opening speech to the enraptured applause of all. I don't think there was a single soul there—with the exception of Dr. Phillip Mann, who simply had no excuse other than his own ignorance and ill-begotten attitude—that hadn't been taken in by Kia's mythical beauty and her passionate story telling. She'd hit big with that dress and hair and her obvious intelligence and fascination with the history of the Tsars. Her decision to showcase the humanity of Tsar Nicholas the Second through his love for his wife and his family had earned her high praise. And in my brief conversation with Trustee Marjorie Wilkins, I learned that the museum had already received four times what they had hoped for in donations and pledges, and the evening was still young.

Guests were alternately hovering in clusters, networking their wealth, or migrating through the exhibit, chatting up how much they were enjoying the displays. Either way, the champagne was flowing freely, the food was disappearing quickly, and Kia was earning her keep.

I'd taken up a quiet post near Kia's office door. It gave me a great vantage point for keeping an eye on the locket, and it got me out of the fray. Kia was my social hero. How she could carry on that much meaningful small talk without having her head explode was beyond me, but she was a natural, and it was a shame Phillip refused to see that.

My drink of the night was a steady stream of iced club soda. I intended to keep my wits about me, and I was saving myself for sipping champagne off of Kia's belly, just a little bit later. I was letting myself savor that thought, when I noticed Kia edging her way toward me. She looked happy, with her eyes bright and sparkly against her skin. Earlier I'd gotten a close-up look at Kia, and found that Bethany had woven pinkish crystals into Kia's hair, and that was what was making it shimmer. And her eyes, shoulders, and chest were showstoppers with their own sprinkling of iridescence. Secrets revealed, but she still looked like a goddess in a fairy tale to me.

"Hi," Kia said, landing at my side.

"Hi," I smiled back at her, wanting to be in her glow. "How's it going?"

"It's perfect! I'm having a wonderful evening. And if you can believe it, I've not gotten groped once."

"They're afraid Zeus will strike them dead if they touch you."

"Wrong exhibit silly," she said. "Greek mythology is on the first floor."

Kia eyed my club soda, and asked, "Mind if I have a sip. I'm getting parched from all the conversation."

"Sure," I said handing her my glass, and catching Dr. Mann's approach out of the corner of my right eye.

"Incoming," I said. "Brace yourself. Here comes Phillip."

Kia stiffened and steeled herself, but kept her smile firmly fixed on her face.

"There you are!" Phillip exultantly whooped, crossing the last few yards to us. "I've been looking all over for you."

Kia's shoulders relaxed in relief and she turned to meet his approach, but it wasn't to her he was speaking.

Dr. Mann came bounding up, hand extended, and practically bellowed, "Jake, my man! You've done a bang-up job getting this exhibit together. Everyone's talking, and you should be damn proud of your hard work."

I didn't offer my hand, so he dropped his, but remained undeterred.

"Thank you, Phillip, but it's Kia's hard work that has gotten us here. You should be congratulating her."

Phillip let my comment pass with barely an acknowledgement, and he didn't even deign to notice Kia standing right there.

"Jake," he said, "I have good news. That is, if I can compel you to take me up on my offer."

I gave him my quizzical look, and caught Kia staring a bit dumbfounded at the two of us, right there with me in not knowing what in the hell was going on.

"I've taken the liberty to speak with the DIA on your behalf, and they support the offer I'm making you."

"And what offer would that be?"

"Well, Curator of the Romantics Department, of course."

I watched as Kia's jaw dropped in stunned disbelief. I mean it was Kia's job that he'd just offered me, plain as day, right in front of Kia, as though she didn't even exist.

"Phillip," I said sternly, unable to keep the unfriendly tone out of my voice, "That's Kia's job."

He still refused to acknowledge her presence, and instead, he leaned in close to me and said, "I'll understand if you choose to keep her on your staff. She is quite the looker, but looks aren't everything, and this job is obviously way above her intellect. I can see you need some time to think about this, so I'll leave you to it."

And before either one of us could object, Phillip left Kia and me standing there watching his backside fade into the crowd.

Fuck! If this is what Chris meant by taking care of it, he was a dead man. I know I needed a firm position here at the Acer to have reason to continue my watch, but Kia's job! What in the hell had he been thinking?

And Phillip.

What a freaking ballsy delivery. Right in front of Kia, and during her perfect night. I wanted to kill him.

"Did I just get fired?"

Kia's face had gone blank with incomprehension, and I didn't know what to say. Phillip had blindsided her, and I wasn't doing much better.

I didn't think Kia would appreciate me pointing out that she could still have her job if I hired her as my assistant. And the irony was that she was perfect for the job, and I was FBI undercover.

What the hell?

"I think it's time you had that talk with one of the trustees. Maybe Marjorie Wilkins. She seems to like you."

"Can he do that? Just fire me without even telling me."

"No, Kia. This is all wrong."

Kia's gaze came back into focus, and she snapped her eyes to me. She was fighting back tears, and I didn't think she had much longer.

"Jake, I'd like to leave now."

I grabbed her hand and made our way to the back exit. No sense dragging her through the crowd, adding further insult to injury. So much for her perfect evening.

I felt her start to sag, and I pulled her to my side.

"Oh no you don't! You will not give him that satisfaction. You hang tight. We're almost outta here."

Kia tried hard to squelch her sob, but up it came anyway, and on a hiccup of a wail in progress, Kia cried, "Ohmigod, Jake. What just happened?"

Kia

Chocolate! Now!

Jake whisked me to the Lincoln before I could say *That sucks*, and as the dam started to break, he handed me a handkerchief and gripped my shoulders more tightly. I blotted at the offending waterworks, and tried to shake it off, but it just hurt so badly.

I was lost somewhere in the middle of stunned disbelief and grief saturated anger. It was one thing to tolerate Phillip's condescending attitude practically on a daily basis, but for him to fire me on *My Day* without evening stooping low enough to look me in the eye to do it, or even at me at all. Granted he didn't know it was *My Day*, but I'd just pulled off one of the most successful gala openings and exhibits in the history of the Acer, and instead of finally giving me an ounce of credit or praise, he gave my job to Jake. How could that be? What did it take to please that man? And what was I going to do for a job now? I'd had two jobs since graduating grad school, and both times ended badly. Who was going to hire me now? *Oh God.*

It was becoming apparent to me that bosses and bosses of bosses, where I was concerned, were not a good idea. No matter how hard I worked, how educated or talented I was, or what I accomplished, it just didn't seem to matter. Not even when I didn't go on a couple of dates with the jerk. And now Phillip wanted Jake to be my boss.

My brain was starting to take a downward spiral, and I felt like a scream might be trying to escape. I clenched my hands into fists and willed myself to get a grip, but my frustration at the injustice was doing its best to claw its way to the surface. And anguish at really loving my job, and it not being mine anymore, because a narrow-minded, sycophantic, womanizing pig was my employer, banged painfully around in my chest.

I felt raw, stripped bare, angry. Dizzy. I couldn't breathe.

I looked around and realized we were on Stadium, no where near my apartment, and I didn't know where we were going, but we needed to stop the car.

"Air! I need air!"

"We're almost there," Jake said rolling my window down.

Jake had turned into a residential area, but it was unfamiliar to me.

"Stop the car, Jake. Please just stop the car."

Jake pulled over to the curb, and I popped the lock on my door and got out. Jake was right behind me, and now that we were standing on the sidewalk, I didn't know what I wanted or where to go. I just couldn't seem to breathe and my chest burned.

Jake stood there for a moment, looking uncertain. We were in unchartered territory. We did fun and jest; this was real life, and it had just beat me up. He looked like he wanted to say something, but what do you say to the person whose job you just got offered? He stepped into me and pulled me tight, embracing me in all his warmth, and then the tears really did start.

"This isn't fair. I'm an excellent curator," I cried.

"I know," he said cradling me in his hug.

"Phillip's a complete ass!"

"What was your first clue?"

It wasn't much, but it got a tiny smile out of me, and Jake's expression was all *hang-in-there*. "I live just a few houses up the street. Let me lock up the Lincoln, and we can walk the rest of the way."

I nodded *okay*, and Jake went over to the driver's side and climbed in. A second later, my window slid up, and he stepped back out to beep the car locked.

He came back by me and took my hand, and we started walking.

"I'm not taking your job," he said, looking over at me. "I seriously think you should talk to the Board. He's sexually discriminating against you, and he can't do that."

"He's probably got a file a mile thick filled with all my incompetencies."

"But you're not incompetent. Far from it in fact. Phillip's just choosing not to see."

"Phillip never wanted me there. My dad pulled some strings after my last job went south, and I thought if I just worked really hard, proved my worth, it would be okay. My guess is Phillip's been gunning for this moment every since."

"Even if strings were pulled. You're qualified and great at your job. Everyone can see that except Phillip."

"And now he has you."

"No, he doesn't. I have a job."

"You say that like you mean it."

"Because I do."

"But the Acer is so much closer than Detroit."

"Commute is only one factor. And I don't mind. I'm not taking your job."

He couldn't possibly know how much that meant to me, and even though I was down, it helped.

"Thanks," I said, and Jake steered me up a driveway and over to a front walk.

"We're here," he said with bright eyes working their sincere cheer.

We heard rhapsodic barking from the other side of the door, and Jake looked down, taking in my dress. "Bullet's not normally a jumper, but I don't want to risk your dress, so give me a moment. He's excited I'm home."

"And here I thought Bullet was just a good excuse."

Jake grinned and lightly clipped my nose with his fingertip. "Silly."

He unlocked and opened his door. I heard small, clawed paws tearing around, and Jake stepped inside and said, "Heya Bullet. What's up?" I heard a sharp bark, and Jake laughed, and said, "Well, hang on. Let me get your lead." And then there was some scrambling about, then silence, and then I heard the garage door behind me open, and Jake walked out with Bullet-the-happy-Beagle rushing toward a giant oak tree in the front lawn.

Jake followed behind and looked over to me. "We'll be in in a moment. Why don't you go on in and make yourself at home?"

"Okay."

Jake with his dog. Who knew? It was one of those *awwww* moments, which totally contradicted the sexy Jake, but worked perfectly with his fun, Jeep-driving side.

I opened his front door, stepped in and entered the Jake cave. Closing the door behind me, I walked into the living room and smiled. It looked like the comfortable, mellow Jake, not his suit-at-work, knight in shining armor Jake. A large, walnuty wall unit lined one wall and had a gigantic flat-screen TV set in the center. Books, CDs, and DVDs lined the shelves. He had a manly-sized, cushy, matching living room suit, made of soft-looking brown leather. And a big, square walnuty coffee table sat in the center. A deep burgundy plush rug contained the space and covered up old, worn wood floors. Framed print art hung on the clay-tinted walls, but no pictures of family were anywhere to be seen.

I was used to Jake in my space—my apartment, my work, Chloe's. This was new, and felt tingly, private. A secret shared.

From where I stood, I could see part of the dining room, and stairs leading upstairs were at my right. Everything was tidy and had a homey feel. Despite Jake's on-top-of-it, crisp, well-organized work corners, here was exhibit A—he was easy going, chilled to perfection, and now, even more alluring. Not that he needed it. I was already in over my head.

I slipped my heels off, and walked over to the sofa. I'd been on my feet all night, and sitting sounded perfect. The leather was a little cool to the touch, but it was baby-bottom soft and the cushions had just the perfect amount of give. I sunk in, feeling the promised calm seep into me, and thought, *Now we're talking.* I smoothed out my dress, and let the relaxation set in.

A door opened somewhere in the house, presumably the garage entrance, and Jake said, "It's like we talked about Bullet. No jumping, or it's the basement for you." *Bark!* "Okay, then."

The garage door began its decent, and the house door closed. There was a bit of a jostling about, then the pitter-patter, tip-tap of Bullet's paws as he came racing into the living room. He looked like he wanted to jump up and see who I was, but Jake's voice called out, over water running in a sink, and said with friendly warning, "Bullet."

Bark!

But then all the commotion died down, as Bullet, eyed me happily, wagging his tail, then turned a few circles before settling down on the carpet at my feet.

"Good job, Bullet," Jake said walking in and taking a seat beside me. Bullet raised his eyebrows and swacked his tail around a bit.

Bullet was happiness in a dog, and he was the most adorable Beagle I'd ever seen with his little brown-patched face and legs, big black ink spot on his back, and expressive eyes. He used his eyebrows a lot, and it was kind of funny.

"Can I pet him?"

"Sure, after we get you out of that dress."

"Is that a come on?"

"It's me protecting your dress, but it could be a come on, too."

"You're funny."

"Really? I was being serious."

I smirked ha-ha, and Jake smiled, loosened his tie, and popped the top two buttons on his shirt. "Can I get you anything?"

"Hemlock."

"I was thinking champagne."

"You got anything harder?" I asked, thinking vodka sounded better, and he said, "Is this a trick question?"

"You're still being funny."

"No, I'm not," he said, but grinned.

"What about chocolate? Usually you've got chocolate ready and waiting."

"Hmmm. Except that the chocolate I have tonight, might not be what you want right now."

"If it's chocolate, I want it."

Jake gave me an *alright-but-I-warned-you* look, stood up, held out his hand, and said, "Come with me."

It was the understated, playful, yet suggestive tone in his voice that reminded where I was, and I looked around again. Jake's place. Champagne, Friday night, chocolate.

Oooooooooh. Right.

Before my night had gone wrong, we'd made plans, and now Jake was looking down at me, holding out his hand—no pressure—but definitely still interested.

He was so beautiful, standing there, tall, dark . . . crystal-clear blue eyes, perfect lips, comfort and confidence in one sexy package. How could I refuse?

"Where are we going?" I asked, placing my hand in his. Liking the warmth traveling up my arm, into my chest and down into my belly.

Jake walked me into his kitchen and said, "Did I tell you how beautiful you are?"

"I don't think so," I said, watching the corner of his mouth rise.

He quietly pressed me into his counter-top, and said on a low hum, "Now who's being funny?"

It occurred to me that he had home court advantage, *not that I cared* . . . I was thinking Jake was all about win-win, and I was up for some winning.

He leaned in closer and breathed in the scent of me, starting at my hair and slow-poking it to my neck.

"Is it getting hot in here?"

He smiled, a heated, sexy, *you-know-it-babe* smile, teasing out a little titter on my bated breath.

Jake was still holding my hand, and he used it to pin me to him as he slid his other hand up my arm, going to his fingertips, and traced along my shoulder, down to the hollow of my throat, and back up to my collarbone.

I bit my lip, loving the heavenly glow trailing his feather-light touch.

He drew a lazy X on my tingling skin and said, "I've wanted to kiss you here all night." Then he bent to do just that.

My eyes drifted shut, and I titled my head just so. I wanted Jake to place all those little kisses in just the right spot. His lips danced across my skin, and my chest tightened with delicious heat, then heaved in delight as his kisses turned to a firm and sensual bite.

I let loose his hand and grasped his shirt, curling my fingers into it, wanting access, and craving the feel of his skin, and he dove for my mouth.

"How do I get you out of this dress?" he breathed against my lips.

"Buttons at the back."

Jake flipped me over and leaned us into the counter, dropping a few more nibbles and kisses on my shoulder. He leaned back to take a look, and said, "Oh God. Isn't there a faster way?"

Twenty delicate, fabric-covered, tiny, round buttons stood in his way, and I chuckled at his *you've-got-to-be-kidding-me* tone.

"How much do you like this dress?" he asked.

"Don't even think about it," I said. "I love this dress. It's pretty."

"Okay, then," he said, and nibbled my shoulder again. "This could take a while."

I felt him hike up the skirt of my dress and place his hand on my thigh. He breathed into my ear, "Maybe I'll get lucky again, and you'll be wearing some of those barely there panties."

I sucked in my breath as his hand slid up to find the little lace-let dainties I had donned, just for him, and then he kissed my ear and said, "Yep." And just like before, a flick of his wrist later, and I felt them drift to the floor.

Jake

Now We're Talking

I was just buying time while I worked at the buttons on Kia's dress, but my frisky fingers had ideas of their own. It wasn't long before they had sauntered their way up Kia's impeccably soft and smooth thigh, and back down again heading on a one-way trip to Camp Everet.

Through her curls, to her wet and waiting folds, they found Kia was game. I inserted one finger, then two and played with rhythmic variations, searching for the one that would send Kia soaring, and I knew I'd hit it when she arched her delectable bottom into my groin, and began a bob and arch dance, following in time with my stroke. She seemed to prefer the in-out-sliiide, in-out-sliiide motion, and as I picked up the pace, she rolled her head back to rest on my shoulders and moaned.

"Mmm-hmmm. Yep. *Oh . . . yeah.*"

Kia's voice was thick and building, and I knew she was getting close. She kept her head on my shoulder, but as her body stiffened with the impact, she clutched the counter in a death grip, moaned like she meant it, and rode the cresting waves over and over. Her sexy moan intensified, and her voice got throaty with pleasure. Her "Yes. Yes. Yes. Unhhh. Ooooh. Mmmmm," were tough to take in my position. My lower brain was listening and had heard the *all-systems-go* signal, and now he wanted to come out and play, too.

While Kia floated back to Earth, my button's hand continued its task. And when Kia turned to face me—her cheeks flushed and glowing—her dress fell to her waist, and I said, cheerfully, "Well, that was productive."

Kia chuckled on the breath she was working hard to catch, and her hand held her dress up to keep it from falling to the floor. She, however, didn't jump to cover up, so I reached out my fingers to caress her fluttering chest, feeling her pert, round breast, and gently thumbing her raspberry pink nipples until they puckered up into stiff, bright peaks.

This put the happy on my face, and hers.

"I think you're gonna want to wash your hands."

Kia gave me a *what-for* look, and I held up my jar of chocolate body paint. I'd noticed she liked clean hands before she ate, and this was definitely for eating.

"You said you wanted chocolate."

She shook her head, smiling, moved in for a closer look, and said, "What's in the bottle Jake? A new treat from your chocolate guy?"

She moved to the sink, and I nudged up behind her. She finished washing, and I handed her my kitchen towel.

"Unh-huh. Chocolate you can play with. As long as you play with it on me!"

Kia's eyes went mischievous, and she licked her lips, apparently quite interested. "So you're saying I get my chocolate, and you, in the same bite? Like a Jake sundae? Or a chocolate covered Jake?"

It was the reaction I'd hoped for, but apparently hadn't expected, because my brains shorted together, and threw me into action. I handed Kia the jar, scooped her up in one swift swoop, and while she giggled, my blood pounded around, encouraging me to move faster.

I passed through the living room, where Bullet lifted a brow in question, but was too comfortable to get up and see what all the fuss was about. When I hit the stairs, I adjusted my grip on Kia, and she said, "Don't you dare drop me!"

I gave her my he-man muscle flex and a no-sweat grin, and said, "Never."

"Good. I'd hate to waste any of this premium body chocolate, just because you weren't up to the task at hand."

The lip on this one—I'm telling you.

"Oh, I don't know, I think I handled the task at hand quite well."

Kia leaned in and nipped at my ear, "Well, Chocolate Charmer, I hope you've got a few more rounds in you still, 'cuz there's a lot of chocolate here, and I'm hungry."

She drew out the word hungry, like she could never be sated, and the challenge set flames to my already burning body.

I got us up those stairs and down the hall in a flash. My door was closed to keep Bullet from sleeping on my bed, and I wiggled a hand free enough to twist the knob and shove it open. The door banged off my wall, but we were already in and crossing the room. My bed was dead center on the far side, under the skylight, next to a picture window, and I made it in two long strides.

"That's what I like to see, gumption."

I had planned to follow her down, but Kia's sass called for payback, so I tossed her onto the bed, and said, "I think I can show you something a bit better than gumption!"

She swallowed her next words and handed me the jar, but eyed me gleefully.

Kia was witty, wisecracking, flirtatious, and fun. Everything about her sucked me in, and left me begging for more. How we'd made it until Friday, I'll never know. And now that I had her here, touching her, coaxing her, loving her, I was almost deafened by the rush coursing through my veins. It was going to be a long, satisfying night. And thinking of all the things I planned to do to Kia had me retorting with a *be-careful-what-you-wish-for* smile.

I shook my head at the chocolate and said, "No. That's for you right now."

Her eyes widened and she bit her lip, totally cheeky, not the least bit concerned, and I said, "You might want to hold that thought."

Kia chuckled, sexy, waiting-for-you.

I pulled at my tie and tossed it on the floor. Next, one by one, I snapped the buttons on my shirt, and little black beady balls fell, rattled, and rolled across the aged wood. I could have unbuttoned them, but I was going for effect.

Kia tilted her head off to the side, and batted her long lashes at my effort. "I like the show, but do I get to play?"

She was cruising for a bruising, and her hot little bottom was begging to be spanked.

Kia didn't wait for my answer; she stood and let her dress fall to the floor.

More sass. More *Wham!*

She'd dropped her voice to sultry sex kitten, and if I thought she packed a punch before, it was nothing to having her standing buff, brazen, and playful, with wanton eyes eating me up like I was dessert.

Kia reached out her hand and slid it inside my shirt, touching my chest and setting off fire alarms in the process.

"I was just wondering," she said, glancing up to meet my eyes, then back at my chest. "Are you a cupcake?"

"How's that?" I said, impressed at my self-control.

"Well, I was just wondering. If you're a cupcake, and I lick you, do I get to keep you?"

Two could play this game.

"Why don't you lick me and find out?"

"Good idea," she said, pulling my shirt wide, nothing tentative about her approach, and laid the tip of her tongue to my chest and licked little, red-hot hearts around my nipple.

"Okay, playtime's over," I said, and she said, "Finally."

The score . . . Kia six, Jake four, and I was utterly spent; whereas, Kia had that glint in her eyes again, the one that had earlier made me very happy, but now had my guys running for cover.

They needed a Time-Out.

But Kia didn't seem interested in taking a break. She was all bright-eyed and bushy-tailed, with Wonder Woman stamina. I definitely wanted her more than ever, I just wanted a nap first, and maybe a huge steak dinner. We were almost five hours into our *getting-to-know-you* marathon, and if Kia's cheerful gleam was any indication, she was ready to go another five.

It was late, probably around two or three in the morning. My watch was somewhere on the floor, and my clock had gotten knocked off my bedstand somewhere in all the melee. We'd cracked the window for air, and a comfortably cool breeze drifted in, soothing and relaxing. Stars twinkled from above, and a sliver moon decorated the dark sky. All in all, it had turned into a beautiful evening, and I was blissed-out just shy of a coma, but Kia was up for some more fireworks.

Her fingers added to my tranquil repose, being so soft and traveling the length of my body in a lazy, exploratory, hopeful trek.

She leaned into me and kissed my chest, leaving a little trail of baby bites as she meandered her way south, passing my belly button, and all the while, humming a merry tune.

A tiny spark of *want-to* tried to fire its way up my spine, but my jello body laughed at the thought. I draped my arm across her back, and made to redirect her upward for some kissing and sleeping, but she turned toward my hand and started kissing it—apparently happy to kiss any part of me, as long as we kept going.

"I'm done Kia. I was a good man, but then you broke me."

Kia moved to sitting and held up the unopened jar of chocolate body paint and put on a sexy pout. "But you said I could have some chocolate."

"Run down to the kitchen and grab yourself a spoon. You can have as much as you want."

"That's not the same," she said with a face so long it was comical, cute, and so very tempting.

"I'm telling you, you've sent my guys to the locker room. They're down for the count."

Kia smiled, like she knew better, and popped the top on the jar. Chocolate vapors permeated the space and attempted to revive the undead.

"Not gonna happen," I said.

But Kia remained undeterred. A woman on a mission. And my little spinal sparks tried harder.

"Well, no one says you have to move or anything. I can just put a little chocolate here," she said and dipped her finger into the thick, creamy cocoa and dotted each of my nipples.

It was starting to get hotter again, but still the sparks weren't enough to get a full-body turnover.

Kia tilted her head, taking in her initial efforts, and decided to continue her stipple art down my chest and onto my lower brain, which she had affectionately named, Hercules.

"Hiya Hercules," she said to my overly unimpressive looking penis. Not that it was his fault. Kia with all her *Wham* was a lot to handle, and for his first try, he'd done well.

"I think you're good for one more time," she said encouragingly.

Speak for yourself the-little-spark-that-could said.

But then Kia bent her head to my nipples and licked. And sucked. Devouring me in the most heavenly way. Reigniting brain waves I didn't know I had. By the time she was half way down my chest, Hercules was showing signs of life.

"See," she said. "I knew you could do it."

Signs of life and doing it were so not the same thing.

But then, turns out, Kia is not only an excellent curator and talented chocolate painter, she's also an excellent sculptor, patient and persistent, molding, massaging and kneading until the desired effect is achieved.

Hercules was once again reborn, and me, right along with him.

"You're very persuasive," I said, as she stroked me into A-Okay, ready to play.

Kia wiggled her eyebrows, and then bent to Hercules to give him a caressing tongue bath that made me see stars. By the time she'd licked him clean, my fatigue was forgotten, and my control with it.

I rolled her over, and slid my fingers home. Six orgasms are bound to leave a mark, and Kia squirmed at the tenderness she felt, but grabbed my hand when I tried to pull away.

"Don't you dare stop now. You're just getting started."

Kia was the right stuff. I hadn't had this much fun in . . . in ever, and as I looked down into her triumphant eyes and happy-you're-back-in-the-game grin, contentment blazed in my chest. I was no longer falling. I was there, and whatever Kia wanted, she was going to get.

I edged my way to my back and pulled Kia on top of me. Slowly, deliberately, I slid her down the hard, determined length of my shaft, and smiled when she purred at the pleasure. We fit together perfectly, and the power of our stroke was intoxicating. We did good things to each other. And we'd keep doing them.

"Remember, Kia," I said. "When I don't let you stop, it's because this is what you wanted."

"Promises, promises," she moaned, and I placed my hands on either side of her hips, holding on tight. She was more tired than she had let on, so I helped her stroke against me. Up and down, back to front, over and over. Until she was gasping, panting, and fighting for more.

Kia dug her nails into my chest, tipped her head back and went for gold. Rubbing, grinding, coaxing her sensitized flesh, and we didn't stop, even when she went incandescent and screamed my name. Not until every last wave had melted away, but even then, we kept on. Kissing, caressing, being as one.

I ran my fingers through her hair, her crystal beads long gone, and ravaged her mouth. Kia tasted like home and chocolate, and I burned with wanting more. Holding her tightly against me, I rolled us over onto her back, and never missing a beat, I drove into her, deeply, with a satisfaction I'd never known. She met me thrust for thrust. Again and again. Heat flushed my skin. My every nerve ending charged, vibrating intensely. I was about to supernova, and I felt Kia tense once more.

I smiled.

Our perfect storm was primed for maximal havoc, and Kia, goddess and vixen that she was, focused and intent, looked deeply into my eyes, grabbed hold of my heart, winked, and then shifted her tormenting little tush, raising her hips and angling them into . . . just . . . the right . . . spot.

"Oh my God."

Fierce and furious, blinding brilliance raged on a shudder. Sound ripped through my chest. And time ceased to exist.

Somewhere in the distance I heard a giggle. A happy, melodious, satisfied, Kia giggle.

Vixen, angel, princess, goddess, *indeed.* And all mine.

Kia

Hell and Holding, Part II

Jake was down for the count. He wasn't snoring so much as breathing deeply. His eyelids wiggled with REM sleep, and there was no way I was going to wake him, but I needed to get home. The sun was coming up, which in June time, meant it had to be around five-thirty. Chloe was coming home today, and I didn't want to miss her. I knew she was going to make a run for it, just as soon as the doctor gave her the okay, and my place would be first on her list.

I inched my way out of bed, and successfully escaped without disturbing Jake. He didn't even twitch, even when his ancient wood floors creaked as I tiptoed to my dress. I took one last look—he was an amazing, gorgeous, beautiful man, capable of doing the irresistible. And he was magnificent. And tasty. And we did it. And it was fantastic!

I breathed in the scent of him—it was everywhere—and closed my eyes. *Mmm, mmm, mmm.* Chloe had been right. He was a cupcake. And I wanted to keep him.

Wasn't sure how that was going to work, especially now that I was apparently without a job, but first things first.

I floated across the floor and quietly pulled his door closed, then made my way down the stairs and into the living room. I was still naked, carrying my dress across my arm, and I walked over to Bullet, who was giving me his suspicious eye.

"Hiya Bullet," I whispered, giving him scritches under his chin and behind his ears. "Please don't bark. I don't want to wake up Jake. He's had a long night, okay?"

Bullet swacked his tail around, and he silently worked his adorable snout, but he didn't bark.

"Thanks, Bullet. I'm just going to call a cab, so don't feel like you have to get up for me."

He gave me some more tail swack and a happy pant, so I gave him a few more scritches, and then, doing my best to avoid noisy floorboards, padded my way into the kitchen.

I didn't know where Jake lived, but I was hoping to find something with his address on it, like mail.

Last night we had explored his countertop and sink, but I'd missed everything else. It was dim in the kitchen, but I didn't want to turn on a light. Somehow turning on a light seemed like it would be sounding an alarm, so I walked around looking at the walls in the dark, searching for his phone. It was hanging on the wall near the mudroom entrance, and I got lucky. He'd laid his keys and yesterday's mail on the counter, presumably when he came in from walking Bullet. I dialed information and got the number for Checkered Cab, gave them Jake's address, and put on my dress while I waited.

It took about ten minutes, and I knelt down to give Bullet one last quick scritch.

"See you later, Bullet."

Silent bark and tail wag.

Bullet was a very cool dog.

I grabbed my shoes, locked the door, and bolted for the curb, so the driver wouldn't honk. Climbing in, I yawned, "Sorry. Please take me to Babbling Brook apartments on Plymouth."

I pulled my door closed, and the driver took off. Exhaustion I didn't have time for was settling in and making my eyes heavy. The hum of the tires on the road didn't help, and by the time we arrived, I'd managed a short catnap.

The driver cleared his throat quietly. "Ma'am, we're here."

I yawned again, and said, "I need you to keep the meter running. I'll be right back, I just have to get some cash."

I wrenched my door open, skittered out and up the stairs. I'd left my clutch and Jake's camera in my office, so I needed a key, and thankfully Chloe had convinced me to keep one hidden in my building's laundry room. It was Saturday morning, and no one else was up and moving yet, so I didn't bother with being overly stealthy. I just walked in and grabbed it.

I made my way into my apartment and pawed through my purse. I found a twenty and ran it back downstairs.

The cabbie said, "Thanks," and motored away.

I yawned again, this time louder. I was going to have to get a move on, or I was going to pass out before I did everything I needed to do.

I raced back up stairs, blew into the shower, threw on some tan khaki shorts and a celadon capped-sleeved tee, crammed a waffle in my face, and hot-footed it in Molly over to the Acer. The sun was up, and the museum would be opening for business in a couple of hours. I wanted to get there, grab my clutch and Jake's camera, and get out before anyone was the wiser. I wasn't prepared for any discussions about Phillip's behavior last night, and to be honest, I really was too tired to even think about it right now.

Yawning the whole way, I hustled up Plymouth, and shot up the drive to my usual spot. Andrew, our weekend security guy, had his car parked toward the back of lot, but no one else appeared to be here. That was good news.

I hopped out and beeped my Mini locked, and jetted up the sidewalk to the main entrance. Last night the museum had been open to all, and I hadn't needed my security pass or keys. Now, I had both. I followed after-hour's security protocol and dashed up to my office. I didn't see Andrew, but that didn't mean he didn't see me.

Scooting over to my desk, I keyed open my security drawer and retrieved the clutch and camera, and took a cursory look around to see if there was anything else I absolutely needed in the event I wasn't coming back.

Nope. Nothing I couldn't reproduce or recoup.

Of course, I was suppressing my devastation and still feeling crushed about my job, so I didn't allow myself to look around while I was passing through. I locked up and power walked back out to my car.

Now all I had to do was wait for Chloe to come home, then I could tell her all about Jake, the one thing still going right for me. She would never ask for details, but she would have fun harassing me with a number of *I-told-you-so's!* I was so happy about how well things were going with Jake that I was looking forward to taking the ribbing.

I hustled home again, and with hardly any cars on the road, made it in four minutes flat. My eyes felt like lead weights, and I'd practically sprained a cheek from all my yawning. I figured Chloe could be here any minute now, or it could take all day. Either way, I might as well try to get some sleep. Chloe would know where to find me.

I set everything down on my table, and dragged myself to bed. I was lights out long before my head hit my pillow.

Bang, bang, bang!

I pried my eyes open, overcoming the impossible task, and tried to figure out what was making all the noise. Grogginess fogged my brain, and I felt like I was being wrenched from a drug-induced sleep. My body was lethargic dead weight, and I laid there trying to get my bearings.

Wow, Jake really packed a punch. I was going to have to get a lot more sleep before we tried that again. I smiled at the thought.

Ding dong.

Chloe!

I hauled myself out of bed and crammed my feet into my spa slippers. I was the walking dead, but seeing Chloe would fix that!

"Coming," I hollered out and hurriedly flip-flacked my way to the door.

I didn't bother to throw on a robe, or check my hair, or brush my teeth. It was just Chloe after all, but as soon as I opened the door, I wished I had.

"Jake?" I said, surprised and confused. He looked as tired as I felt, but he was dressed in a black suit—strange for a Saturday morning—and he wasn't alone.

"Jake?" I asked again, but he didn't answer. He just stood there looking conflicted. He was mad-as-hell, but seemed uncertain.

There were three other men with him, all in black suits, and I got a chill down my spine. Something was wrong.

Oh God, not Chloe?

"Nothing's happened to Chloe has it?"

"Ms. Everet?" said the thirty-ish something, blonde, cold-emanating man in black standing to Jake's immediate left. He was tall, lean, and looked like he regularly ate sour fruit. He was a surly sort of man.

"Yes."

I looked back-and-forth between Jake and this imposing man, but still Jake said nothing.

"I'm Special Agent in Charge, Chris Jeffries with the FBI," he said, flashing his badge. "May we come in?"

This scene didn't compute, and I couldn't seem to grasp what was happening.

"I'm sorry. What?"

The four men didn't wait for my permission. With Agent Jeffries making way, the rest followed, and I stumbled some, trying to move backwards without getting trampled on.

"Can you account for your whereabouts between the hours of four and eight this morning?"

I looked at Jake, and his expression was blank, or rather bland. Like he was waiting for my answer, too.

"What's this about?" I asked, fully awake now, and although still quite confused, I knew I was somehow in trouble.

Agent Jeffries seemed poised for the kill—for what I didn't know—but he was impatient, and he stepped closer, going for increased intimidation and said, "Can you answer the question?"

Jake wasn't helping, and I didn't know why he was here with the FBI.

"Jake? Are we in trouble for something?"

He finally spoke, and there was a chilly tone of detachment in his voice that left me rubbing my arms for warmth. "Kia, you need to answer the question."

I recoiled in confusion, and flashed Jake a *what-the-hell* look. "I was with you until about five-forty-five, then I taxied home—"

"What company?" Jeffries asked, taking out a notepad.

"Checkered Cab."

"Then what?" he said.

"I came home, showered, and drove to the Acer Foundation Museum of Art History."

I saw Jake's face fall, then harden, but what for? None of this was making sense.

"Why are you asking me all these questions?"

Agent Jeffries ignored my question, but seemed grotesquely pleased with either my response or himself.

"What did you do next?"

I had no idea what was going on, but I was done.

"Are you charging me with a crime, here, or are you just out for some Saturday morning male bonding?"

"Are you going to answer the question?"

"No. We're done here. Please leave."

Agent Jeffries motioned his men with his finger and said, "Leave no stone unturned." Then he laughed at his own inside joke.

"You can't do that," I protested, and he handed me a search warrant. "Says right here that I can."

It was all legalese, but it mentioned the locket. And that got my attention. *It was missing.*

"You think I took Tsarina Alexandra's Garnet Love Locket?"

Special Agent in Charge, Chris Jeffries assumed the most contemptuous look I'd ever had the displeasure of seeing, and he narrowed his eyes at me. "I don't *think* anything. I know you took it, and we'll find it."

"I didn't take anything!"

This was ridiculous, and I was getting mad.

I turned to Jake and said, "Tell him. Tell him I didn't take it!"

Jake had a tortured look on his face, and before he could respond, Special Agent in Charge Jeffries dealt me the final incapacitating blow. Between Chloe's heart attack, Phillip, everything hinky with the locket, and now losing my job, I was so not prepared for the words that came out of his mouth next.

"Arrest her Jake."

"*What?*"

"I think you've already met, but let me properly introduce you. Ms. Everet, this is Special Agent Jake Davidson. He's here to arrest you."

Jake had the decency to flinch, but it didn't stop him from turning me around, and placing cuffs around my wrists.

"Jake?" No way was this happening!

"Kia Everet, you have the right to remain silent. Anything you say can and will be used against you in a court of law. You have the right to speak to an attorney. If you cannot afford an attorney, one will be appointed to you. Do you understand these rights as they have been read to you?"

I felt my legs give, and I heard a loud whooshing noise. The last thing I saw was my living room carpet and a hand.

Jake

This Can't Be Happening

I caught Kia on her way down. She surprised me, and I almost missed. I was mad, off my game from being rudely awakened by an overly cheerful Chris, and disconcerted by the morning's events thus far, but I didn't want her getting her clock cleaned from fainting just because Chris was a callous bastard enjoying the moment a bit too much.

I angled us onto her sofa, and gently tapped her face, bringing her back to reality. Not that her reality was something she probably wanted to see again.

Chris zeroed in as she blinked her eyes open, and said, "Good. Fainting isn't going to make this any less real for you Ms. Everet. You can save us all some time, and just tell us where the locket is, so we don't have to rip apart your apartment looking for it."

"I told you. I don't have it."

"Then who does, and where is it?"

"I couldn't tell you."

"Can't or won't?"

Kia shook her head, and her expression screamed her frustration.

She genuinely looked like she didn't have a clue what we were talking about, but that didn't mean she didn't. I needed to talk to her, alone. And Chris was making that impossible.

"I take it by your silence, that you meant *won't*," Chris said, high-handedly. "Fine." He shifted his attention to me, and said. "Jake, take her downtown, and get her booked. We'll finish up here, and I'll see you back at the office."

For a morning that had started out with Kia in my bed and in my arms, this day was really turning into shit.

I looked Kia square in the eyes, still trying to read her, but couldn't tell. My heart was telling me no, but my brain niggled with,

Then why in the hell did she sneak out in the middle of the night—no warning, no note, no nothing?

But there was pain and anger in her eyes, and I was pretty damn sure I was the cause.

Chris, making his fucking point, making me arrest her. What an ass.

I'm sure he felt like he was doing me a favor by making me face my demons once again, just like with Vicki. But I still wasn't certain Kia was a demon I needed to face. And I didn't want to call a spade a spade until I had better evidence than we did. If he found that damned locket in her apartment, my heart would split in two. It was bad enough I'd had to be here, getting outted from my cover this way, but to make me cuff her. If she was innocent, how was I ever coming back from that?

Chris had followed his guys into her bedroom, and Kia flinched at the sound of her drawers being searched. If she was innocent, and Chris was being overly zealous in his efforts, then this was a terrible invasion of her privacy. I couldn't stop it from happening, anymore than I could be certain of her guilt or innocence, but the murderous look in her eye told me being here was making it worse.

Kia was dressed for the beach, except for her slippers. She was going to freeze in the holding cell and interrogation room. "Kia, you need shoes and socks, and a sweater."

"Don't even pretend that you care."

I refused to add to her discomfort, just because she was angry at me. "Chris," I called out. "Find Ms. Everet some socks and tennis shoes. And a sweater. And toss them out here."

I heard Chris groan in irritation, but after some creative use of expletives and some slamming of drawers, he leaned out of Kia's bedroom and threw her stuff at me. "You've gone soft," he reprimanded. "Get your head out of your ass. She's guilty, using you, so you should stop giving a damn."

I bent to put socks on Kia's feet, paused, and said, "I know your mad, but don't self-defeat. Do not try to kick me or anything else stupid."

She rolled her eyes at me, something that used to be cute, but in this moment, wasn't cute at all.

"I'm serious, Kia."

"Just do it, then, and shut up. *Please.*" Sarcasm from Kia was not a pretty thing. But what did I expect? A medal?

I leaned down and slipped the socks over her feet, and followed with her shoes.

"I'll give you your sweater when we get there."

She stood up, not happy with me, and said, "Are we leaving yet?"

I sighed. This day so sucked.

I helped Kia balance down the stairs, and then put my hand up to tuck her head as she slid into the backseat of our waiting Agency cruiser.

I closed her door, and walked around to the driver side, angling into the seat, and pulled my door shut. I glanced in the rearview to find Kia's stony face staring back at me.

We were both hurting, angry, and confused. Some of our reasons were the same, some were different. Either way, neither of us wanted to be here. Not like this.

"Your friend's a real sweetheart," Kia said, not being friendly at all.

"He's my boss," I said by way of explanation.

"Well at least that's something," she said, taking comfort in my presumed negative circumstance.

This wasn't productive. I turned the engine over, and pulled out. We had a forty-five minute drive to Detroit. Plenty of time to talk.

"Why did you leave this morning?" I said, turning onto Plymouth, heading for US 23.

"Well, quite obviously to go steal myself a locket!"

"Kia," I warned. "Sarcasm is not going to help you."

"What?" she scoffed. "And you will?"

"I will if you're innocent."

"That you don't know the answer to that question, means you are useless to me."

Ouch. Direct hit to the heart.

She must have seen me wince, because she said, "The only thing you can do for me now is to keep Chloe from going to my apartment and seeing your friends tossing my place."

"I can't do that."

"Jake. She just had a heart attack. She's still in recovery!"

"What do expect me to do?"

"Try being human! Call my dad. Call Zoe. Call them all. Just don't let Chloe find her way to my place without me being there!"

"I could lose my job."

"Don't worry. Phillip's got your back."

I shook my head, and held her glare in the rearview. I could totally see how from her position I was an ass, but I really did care. In fact, I loved her, even if she was guilty.

Damn.

I yanked my phone out of my breast pocket, glanced at the readout, and selected Mr. Everet's cell, and thought to myself, *What are you doing Jake? This is so not a good idea.* I had the annoying audacity to answer myself with a mental slap to the back of my head and a, *You're the idiot who slept with a suspect!*

I punched the call button, checked the rearview—Kia wasn't giving an inch, and waited for her dad to answer. *What in the hell was I suppose to say?*

"Hello? Mr. Everet?"

"Yes. Who's this?"

"Jake Davidson, sir."

He sounded confused by my call, but replied politely enough. "What can I do for you Jake?"

I hesitated. I really didn't know what to say. I'd just arrested his daughter, so nothing that came out of my mouth was going to go over well.

"Well, sir. Kia's not home right now, and she wanted me to call you to intercept Chloe. Keep her from going to Kia's apartment today."

"What's this about, Jake?" He sounded suspect, and rightly so. "I can't see why Kia is having you call me."

I looked at Kia in the mirror again, and she stared back, expectant and ungiving.

Sigh.

This was just another crappy part of today, but I didn't want Chloe freaking and potentially ending up back in the hospital, or worse.

"Kia has been arrested and is being taken to Detroit."

There was a pause at the other end; I'm sure as Mr. Everet ran through his list of questions, trying to figure out what to ask first. Like, *Arrested? Detroit? What for?* But instead he came back with a very unexpected, "Are you the arresting officer?"

"Agent, and yes."

"To where shall I direct her lawyer?"

I relayed the information, and he disconnected.

I snapped my phone shut, and focused on the road. That might just be the last thing I do as an FBI Agent. Chris was not going to be pleased. He was going to be furious. My guess was that Kia's lawyer—most likely high-priced and top of the line—would be waiting for us when we got there. Kia's dad was very powerful, and even though he was corporate, I'm sure he knew all the right people.

Kia was probably going to be downtown only long enough to make bail. And I was running out of time to talk to her. I wanted to believe her—I really, really did—but she was going to have to help me get there. And her mood right now was monumentally less than cooperative. She'd disappeared without explanation, and all of sudden the locket's gone missing, after she's essentially been fired. As coincidences go, that was an awfully huge leap of faith to take.

Let's not even talk about the crushing pressure and pain that was clawing at my heart. Mixed in with my anger—I didn't like the idea of getting played again—I felt loss and fear and guilt. Kia had worked her way into me, and our survival was resting heavily on this moment never happening. But now I have to explain. You know how when you know you've irreversibly screwed up and you get that plummeting vacuum in the pit of your gut and your mouth goes sour? Well one look into Kia's face told me I was there, and to be honest, it was killing me. I didn't realize until Chris had me cuff her, just how hard I'd fallen for her, and now my brain was scrambling through an obstacle course of no turning back, trying to make time and cross the finish line.

And that's just my side of the story.

I sucked in a heavy sigh and merged onto I-94.

Kia was quiet and I glanced back at her. I just wanted her to tell me the truth, and I would believe her, somehow. And then somehow I would make everything better, whatever it took.

Where to start? *Well, Jake, that's easy. Just take a leap of faith.* Like that was just a piece of cake.

"Sooo," I stalled, and then went with the obvious. "Your dad's getting you a lawyer," I said forcing encouragement.

"Why am I not surprised you had my dad's number in your contacts?"

Kia was still working her cutting charm, and it made me want to pull over and shake her. Shake her to make her stop; hug her to make her listen; love her to get her back in my life, *happy*, not in this place, where my chest was ripping wide.

"Kia, just stop. Please."

"Stop what? Pretending to be someone I'm not? *Like guilty*?"

"I know I've hurt you, but you have to admit, it doesn't look good."

"That's your plan? You've hurt me, but you think I deserve it?"

"That's not what I meant."

"Then what did you mean, Jake? Did you mean to tell me that sleeping with me was just part of your job? Gain my trust or some bullshit like that?"

Tears weren't really my thing, but my eyes were stinging, and my head shook in this repetitive pattern of no, but she kept throwing punches.

"Now it all makes sense," she said, coldly. "Why you were so perfect to me. You were playing me the whole time. Really, you were just keeping me in your line of sight, waiting for me to slip up."

"It's not like that."

"The hell it wasn't. All that chocolate. Being exactly what I needed. Wanted. I'm sick at thinking how easily you hit your mark. Using me, baiting me for your job. You must think I'm—"

Kia blinked angrily at a tear she couldn't wipe away, and the hole in my chest got bigger.

"I don't know why I would care what you think about me. It's not like I know you. Not the real you. Just the lying, betraying, conniving you. You obviously don't respect me at all."

"That's not true," I bit back. "I do respect you. And not all of it was a lie."

"No, not all of it. Just the important part. And don't you dare try to tell me you care. You're a liar and a deceiver. And that's all I know about you."

This wasn't working, and my frustration was making me angry. I didn't mean to, but it came out anyway.

"Well, what about you?" I said with sarcasm sliding in just a bit too easily.

Kia tried rubbing her wet cheek against her shoulder. It didn't help much, and that just seem to irritate her even more.

"What about me?" she asked with smacking incredulous indignation.

This was a tough side of Kia to take, but I didn't back down. I needed the truth, and if getting her spitting mad was going to do the trick, then I was going to have to run with it.

"Kia," I said just has harshly. "The evidence we have against you is highly compelling. The FBI just doesn't send in an agent to go undercover on a whim."

"Well, Jake. I don't know what kind of evidence the FBI thinks it has against me, but since I didn't do this—and let me make myself clear—I. Did. Not. Steal. The locket. Or anything else for that matter. I love my job. I wouldn't do anything so stupid. And if you knew the real me, you'd know I wasn't a thief."

"I want to believe you. I really do."

"Well, it's pretty easy, Jake. You stripped me naked. Filled my heart. Fit into my life. Made me laugh. Had your way with me. *And now*, you don't think you can believe me? *Really?* What else would it take? You want me to slice my wrist for you or something?"

"God, Kia. You're such a ballbuster."

"I didn't ask for your opinion. Feel free to go to hell."

She said it with ice in her veins, but I glanced back and just caught the downward shift of her eye, and the vulnerability waiting there.

We were practically choking on pain, and it didn't feel like we were coming back from this, but I held on to that vulnerability, and hoped for the best.

"You can trust me, Kia. I want to help you."

Her eyes snapped up, and not in a nice way. The fight was back.

"I'm supposed to trust you, when you don't trust me," she scoffed and shook her head. "What I want to know, is who do I speak to about your misconduct with a suspect? You were out of line and unprofessional, and I have to believe that whatever happens to me, the FBI frowns on its Agents sleeping with suspects."

There was that. And just one more reason I wasn't likely to have a job tomorrow. But despite the solid wall she was building between us, I didn't want to lose her, so I stuck with hope.

"Kia, what can I do to prove to you that what happened between us is real and not because of my job?"

I'd like to think I saw a glimmer of hope shine through, but it was hard to tell behind all that venom.

"You can believe me and get out there and be the all-powerful FBI guy that you think you are and find the real person responsible for your missing locket. Because, quite frankly, I'm not your gal!"

Kia

Check, Please!

No job. No potential boyfriend. Charged with four counts of Grand Larceny. Each count worth up to ten years in a federal clink, and a fine, yet to be determined. I was ready for a do-over. This week was just getting worse and worse.

And just when I was thinking things were looking up.

I was sitting in a locked interview room, nothing like the drama shows, and everything like soul-exposing austerity. The walls were white and glaring from the skin-peeling fluorescents overhead. The steel table emanated cold, and the pleather cushioned metal chair I was sitting in begged the question of why they had bothered to pad it, uncomfortable being the nicest thing I could say about it. But I guess the intimidation scene was the whole point of an interrogation room.

Jake had booked me, and the whole process had been a smooth, well-oiled, anxiety-producing, sterile, alienating detachment machine. Fingerprints, mug shot, paperwork, abandonment, left for dead. I wasn't guilty, but Jake was right about something—if the FBI had enough to charge me for the theft of not one, but four missing lockets, then they had something. And it was damning enough for Jake to do his job without compunction.

I'd be lying if I said I wasn't scared. The system was a tricky and unreliable place to be. I knew my dad would get me the best lawyer in the state, so my chances were good, but still.

But worse than the fear I felt, was the unrepentant devastation shattering my will, rending my soul, and breaking my heart.

I clutched at my sweater, seeking comfort, and begged my tears not to come, but they were stubborn, and I was lost.

It was unbelievable to me that I could fall so hard, so fast, and not even know it. Jake was fun, and it seemed like it was going well, but I thought we were budding, not bursting. And when he pulled my hands behind my back and put those cuffs around my wrists, loss of the most unimaginable kind came flooding in, drowning me in what would never be, and I just hadn't been ready for that. I loved someone, or rather, the thought of someone who didn't love me back.

He didn't care. He wasn't falling. It was his job. Everything was a lie.

I bit into my lip, and pleaded for it to stop. Nuclear tear bombs slid down my face and kamikaze dropped into my lap. I couldn't take it. It just hurt so bad. Emptiness and heartache hacked at my control, and my shuddering was escalating toward all out sobs. I fell for the perfect guy, and I wanted him back. I *really* wanted him back.

How pathetic.

My whole body grieved. Complete total meltdown was imminent, and it was happening in an FBI interrogation chamber. How fitting for the purgatory taking over my life.

I was an avalanche of despair, and as the first wave of total agony hit, ripping a barely contained whimper from me, the door to my insult cell opened, and Jake entered with a tall, crisply-suited, salt and pepper man who could only be my lawyer.

I could have swiped at my tears, but I decided Jake should see first-hand the destruction he'd dealt. He was culpable, and he should know it.

"Kia, I'm Clayton Thayer. Your father has retained my services for you. If you agree to this, we can leave now."

Mr. Thayer pulled a handkerchief from his inside jacket pocket and handed it to me. I stood, definitely ready to leave, and he directed me toward the door. Jake followed our departing steps, staying to our rear, but didn't say a word.

My shoulders trembled, but I was a bit calmer, now. It didn't make sense to me, but I felt a little stronger with Clayton, a man I didn't know, standing next to me.

We entered the intake room, and I heard commotion to my left and looked to find Chloe and my dad at the elevator. Two FBI people were detaining them at the doors, and I heard my dad say, "It's alright mother, Clayton will have her out in just a minute. We can wait here in the elevator."

"I don't want to wait!" Chloe demanded.

My heart flip-flopped in relief, and my dam broke. I raced for Chloe, and she barged past the two men, meeting me, scooping me into a huge bear hug. I fell into her waiting arms, and sobbed. It was one of my more decorum-depleted moments in life, but I just didn't care.

"There, there," she soothed. "It's gonna be okay."

Chloe stroked my hair and rubbed my back, and I held on tight. I saw my dad walk over to Clayton, lean in, and have a quiet exchange. Mr. Thayer nodded, and so did my dad.

Chloe lifted her head, gave me a loving squeeze, and whispered, "I'll be right back."

She walked over to Jake who had pulled up the rear of our entourage and looked him in the eye.

If I had to place it, I'd say sadness. Sadness is what I saw in Jake's eyes. Well, at least he really cared about Chloe. Hard not to.

"I'm disappointed in you, Jake," she said, and he nodded. "I know, and I'm truly sorry."

"I'm not the one you have to apologize to."

Jake flashed his glance to me, and I stood my ground. I was a blubbery mess, but I managed an ungiving stare, which he met with determination, but no words. It was like we were breathing the same air, but in a different space.

He looked back to Chloe and said, "I'll fix this."

"I'd like to see you try," she said and shook her head. "And to think I had such high hopes for you."

I saw it, but I didn't believe it. The barest hint of agony darkened his face, and he looked back to me.

Chloe turned away from Jake and came back to take my arm in hers. "Let's go home, honey."

My dad drove us to Chloe's house and suggested I stay the night with her. My mom and Zoe would come by with dinner, and he was going to go talk law with Clayton. He instructed me to stay away from my apartment until Clayton's team could assess the damage and actions taken by the FBI search team. I agreed.

My grief was taking a backseat to an encroaching numbness and surreal disbelief. It didn't seem like any of this could be happening. Maybe if I went to sleep, I'd wake up and find this was all just a bad dream, and everything was really okay. Maybe, but not likely.

Jake

Time Out

I was getting ready to break my cardinal rule of never drinking hard alone, but if I could drink this day into non-existence, I'd be very grateful.

Bullet sat at my feet, giving me his *you-okay?* look, and I shook my head, "No. Not so much." Bullet raised his brows, and being the best dog in the world, scootched up against my foot, dropped his head, and quietly reached out his paw—completely *I'm-here-for-you-buddy.*

"Thanks Bullet," I said leaning down to give him a much appreciated ear rub.

Leaning back, I settled into the buttery soft cushions of my couch, attempting calm, but failing—staring at my recently acquired bottle of Balvenie Signature 12 Year Old Scotch. Its golden-honey rich hues calling out to me with promises I knew it couldn't keep. *Thanks dad, for proving problem-solving miracles don't jump out of alcohol bottles.*

I should be more grateful, but the problem was— Well . . . there were really so many to choose from. But front and center, it was that I couldn't get Kia's tear streaked face to stop popping up every time I closed my eyes, and every time it happened I flinched at the memory.

Today had turned into a full-body twitch. And I thought I might be able to sleep better if I took the edge off with a bottle of Scotch.

The sum total of today's events, right after I'd fallen asleep with Kia in my arms, had amounted to disaster, disappointment, and pain. Every which way I turned, I fumbled, letting myself and everyone else around me down, and worse, hurting some of them. My personal and professional failures were at an all time high, and I needed a moment to get balls-to-the-wall blitzed, hammered, shitfaced, stoned-drunk. Then I could wake up to a new day and try again.

But so far my solutions weren't making the situation any better.

Just like I expected, when Chris got back and found Kia released on bail, he was stunned and pissed as hell.

I was still shocked by how quickly Kia's lawyer had been able to see a judge and arrange bail, and on a Saturday no less.

So in his infinite understanding of the situation at hand, Chris had rewarded my stupidity with an unpaid suspension. Now I was badgeless and no gun.

I was certain that was going to impede my ability to track down Kia's mystery thief. If there really was one. Without access to the Acer, I wouldn't be able to establish any new leads. So then I went and did the second most stupid thing—or third, or fourth . . . really who's counting anymore—I did all day. I called Dr. Phillip Mann and asked him if his job offer was still open.

Yeah, that's right. I took Kia's job.

If you're thinking, *Hoooly Shit*, then I'm right there with you.

I heavy sighed, but it didn't make me feel any better, so I cracked open my Balvenie and poured a four finger shot to take the edge off. No use bothering to enjoy it. That was something you earned. This was a purely medicinal approach to dealing with my awe-inspiring lapse in judgment. I downed it all on one burning drag, and poured myself another.

I didn't know how I was going to explain to Kia that in order for me to help her keep her job, I needed to take it first.

I was thinking that was going to go over like a steak dinner in a room full of vegans.

There was no guarantee that she would talk to me, much less hear me out, and even less, be willing to help me keep my cover and take the demotion. Even if I was to help her clear her name. Of course, this is all assuming she isn't sending me on a wild goose chase, and that it's even possible to clear her name. But hey, remember, this is me having faith. And a drink.

If I'd gotten anything out of today—seeing Kia crash and burn in agony—it was that I was back to believing her. She sucked as a suspect. None of this made sense, and people who stole shit didn't rank a breaking heart over impending jail time.

It was me who had crushed her today. Not the threat of prison. Not at being caught. But at me not being who she thought, and *that* knocking the floor out from underneath of her.

Federal prison was no joke, and with the amount of time Kia was looking at, if she was guilty, she was the type to show her fear. If convicted on all counts to be served concurrent, Kia could be looking at upwards of 40 years and a zillion dollar fine. She wasn't trying to figure out how to hide from this. She was watching the pieces crumble and fall, and wondering how she was going pick them all up again. And that was my fault.

I belted back my second drink and capped the bottle. Enough of that. Another walk for Bullet, and then sleep. I'd told Chloe I was going to fix this, and for Kia, and her, I meant it.

Going on a hunch, I pulled up in front of Chloe's. No way did Kia go home alone last night, so I was betting dollars to donuts she was holed up here.

I don't know what qualifies as a suitable offering of apology to the woman whose life you've unintentionally turned upside down, but I was thinking my head on a stick and not the chocolate in my bag was the better choice. But for obvious reasons, I went with the chocolate. Besides, I might be able to get her to give in to her sweet tooth, even if not me.

I rang the doorbell, and Chloe answered.

"You don't look so good, Jake," she said by way of good morning.

I took in my wrinkled jeans and white T, ran my fingers through my hair that felt like it was standing on end, and shrugged.

"Is Kia here?"

"That's not a good idea, Jake."

"Probably not, but we need to talk."

Chloe shook her head at me, reluctant to invite me in. "That was yesterday. Today, she needs a break."

"Chloe, I know I've screwed up, but I want to help Kia, and I can't do that out here."

"She doesn't want to see you."

"Understood, but I'm willing to take that chance. Are you?"

"Jake, you're the arresting officer. How is your being here, not a conflict of interests?"

"I've been suspended, Chloe," I said, and her expression turned thoughtful. "Please let me in."

"Sorry, Jake. I'm going to have to ask Kia first."

I sighed, but said, "I'll wait here all day if I have to."

Chloe nodded and closed the door.

I stood there waiting, minutes ticking by. After fifteen, I took a seat in my Jeep and waited. I was serious. I wasn't going anywhere until Kia and I had the chance to talk.

The June morning sun was warm, but a chill lingered in the air. Big creature-shaped clouds morphed and crept along the bright blue sky, giving me something to occupy my time, because Kia wasn't taking me up on my offer. My morning coffee had found its way through me and was showing signs of impatience, but I wasn't leaving and giving Kia the chance to sneak away. I considered knocking on Chloe's door again, but figured hospitality wasn't high on either her or Kia's list today.

King Triton turned into a dragon. A school of fish shifted into a giant bear. Ho hum. Beat a drum.

Oh come on Kia! At least come out here and sizzle me with your fiery wit.

She must have heard, because she appeared in Chloe's doorway, casual indifference marking her stride, and it was the last thing I would have expected. She was rallying her war defenses with polish and disinterest. It had been over two hours since I arrived, and Kia had taken the opportunity to get pretty. Feathery-light white babydoll sundress, barely there sandals, shimmering bouncy curls, and rosy cheeks. It was her battle cry, and what I heard was, *See what you can't have?*

Kia walked over to my Jeep, practiced disinterest plastered on her face, and leaned in to ask, "What do you want, Jake?"

"I want to talk."

"We talked yesterday. Seemed productive. I thought we were done."

I contemplated getting out and coming around to face her, but didn't want to unsettle the balance she was fighting for.

"I believe you." I had a *teeny* bit of doubt, but that was cynic in me, so I threw heap-loads of conviction into my voice, and went with hope.

"Yesterday was the day for that. Today, you're somebody my lawyer tells me I shouldn't speak to without him present."

"Kia," I said, really pushing the boundaries of info sharing. "Chris, my boss, has been driving this case from the very beginning. I always had my doubts, but he's got his sights set on his future. I think he jumped the gun. I believe you and want to help."

"Why?"

I didn't know what to say to that. I didn't think she wanted to hear the truth, because she didn't believe the truth, and I didn't want to turn this conversation south. So I gave her something she could accept, and I'd have to work on the rest later.

"I don't send innocent people to federal prison, Kia. I've had consistent doubt about your guilt, and I think Chris overshot. But someone is stealing lockets, and doing a damn good job making it look like it's you. So before this gets anymore out of control, I want to find out who it is, and right the wrong that's been done to you."

I thought I handled it well, but Kia's eyes hardened, and the line of her lip went flat.

Uh-oh.

Jerk, slapped me from the other side of my Jeep, and I steeled myself, waiting for her digging reply. And it came.

"You will never be able to right the wrongs you've done to me."

"Agreed."

She was right there. Nothing I could say or do would ever undo that damage.

"But will you let me help you?"

Kia

Do I Have To?

Note to self. New side of Jake—calm, play-free, exploitive FBI guy wants to make good, clear his conscience, and finally do his job for real, and all on my time. *Great. Just great.* Like 'em, lust 'em, dupe 'em Jake rides to my rescue.

This should be fun.

Or not.

The thing is. Clayton, my top-of-the-line lawyer, is prepared to kick ass, but he warned me that the circumstantial evidence against me was *very* damning. And that even though he felt he had a decent chance of winning my case—decent, not absolute . . . courts of law and all that jazz—he's concerned about the negative impact—or more to the point, the trust issues future employers might have with me if irrefutable evidence of my innocence doesn't present itself. Meaning that my grad school plus two jobs gone really terminal were going to be the very likely end to my art history, curating, and museum career.

And that was really depressing.

I wasn't sure what universe impaling transgression I'd committed to warrant such a violent karmic retaliation, but to show me love in my work—the most awesome job, minus Phillip—and bring me the "perfect" guy, and then pull a *just kidding* . . . seriously, who in the hell's parade did I rain on?

I didn't want Jake's help—wasn't sure I could handle having Mr. Beautiful in the vicinity—but I apparently needed it.

And here he was offering.

Well, isn't that just dandy?

Jake was just sitting there, waiting, not pushing, but looking a little tense, and I got the distinct impression, he had more bad news for me.

Oh, for the love of Christ.

"Do you smell chocolate?"

The corner of Jake's mouth tipped into an almost smile. *We* weren't back, but this was a game he knew well. He was still working his *play it safe*, far from his comfort zone, but he sure had my ticket, and he reached into a large, brown-paper gift bag and pulled out the most gigantic box of chocolates I'd ever seen.

"It's the five pound starter kit, and it comes with a chocolates-of-the-month club. I got yours for life, figuring it was the least I could do."

Chocolate Charmer.

Luscious cocoa fumes saturated my senses, and I had to fight the mini-euphoric high trying to ruin my perfectly obstinate attitude. I hated that my mouth watered and that my nose was doing chocolate-endorphin inspired somersaults. Traitors! The both of them. I refused to like Jake. Absolutely refused to! No matter how many cards he played. For me, he was so yesterday. And he had to stay that way!

"So I'm guessing you have a plan."

"I do, but you're not going to like it."

"Gee, that sounds so promising. Can't wait to hear it."

From the scrunchy *just great* expression on his face, I could tell he was loving my new frosty drollness. Bitter sarcasm at it's best, but he'd earned it. *So get used to it buddy.*

Jake sighed, but went with determination and said, "Okay then. Would it be okay if I used the facilities first?"

I shrugged, blasé, and said, "You'll have to ask Chloe. And I don't think she likes you anymore."

Chloe had had more heart than me. Now Jake and I were walking Chloe's sub, two feet apart, uncomfortable as hell. My apartment was off limits. So was his place—*absolutely off limits.* So that left the great outdoors. He'd suggested we continue our discussion in private, not wanting to risk upsetting Chloe with her heart. And all I could think was, *This conversation's going to suck.*

"Okay, so let's hear it. This great plan of yours."

Jake glanced over—hesitated—dragged in a requisite preparatory breath—resigned himself to the impending carnage—and dropped his bomb.

"Did Chloe mention to you that I have been suspended from the FBI?"

"Only suspended? Well, that's too bad. I'd hoped for worse."

I saw him smash his lips together. He was obviously having a difficult time keeping his cool.

Good.

"Well, the problem with that is," he said fighting frustration. "If I'm suspended, I no longer have access to the Acer, and thus," he stressed emphatically, "no further access to the real thief."

I hadn't thought of that, and I didn't like where this was going.

"So I called Phillip and took him up on his job offer."

"You did *what*?"

I was floored. And red was my new favorite color.

No amount of chocolate was going to make up for this!

"There's no other way, Kia. I messed up Chris's chance to interrogate you, and this is his payback."

"Well, can't you go over his head?"

"Over his head is pissed at me, too. They want you bad."

My head was swimming, and my legs were wobbly. "I need to sit down," I said glaring at him. "You did this on purpose!" I raged, waving my hand around at our good-for-nothing surroundings.

Jake looked around, and did well not to contradict me. "There's no where to sit," he said, holding out his hand, in a useless gesture to me. Of course I ignored it.

I walked a few steps further to an old maple in the easement and leaned up against it, breathing, angry, and duly shocked. Could this not get any worse?

"Besides," Jake said, sounding convinced he was doing the right thing. "Without me, the Acer isn't taking you back anyway. The Board believes it's you, too."

"*What*—because the all-mighty powers that be incorrectly fingered me?"

"No Kia, because all four lockets that have gone missing have come from collections you coordinated and brought to the Acer. All four lockets came up missing when you were key-carded in and working alone. Because, they don't have any reason to believe it's anybody else."

I looked to the sky. This just couldn't be happening.

Jake added, all matter of fact, "Their reputation is on the line. The Board has kept the thefts quiet, but they called in the FBI."

"Why not just fire me? It's not like Phillip doesn't think I'm incompetent enough as it is."

"One. Only the Board knows. Phillip isn't in the loop. And two. They didn't have enough evidence for just cause, and with your dad being who he is and all—" Jake left it hanging as self-explanatory.

I shook my head, ready to pop a gasket. "This sucks, Jake. I haven't done a damn thing wrong, and my whole life is turned upside down."

"So let's fix this."

"Like it's my responsibility?" I nearly spat.

"No. But it is your life, and if you want it back, buck up."

My jaw dropped, but he didn't stop.

"You know Kia, I don't have to help you. You might want to think about that while you keep clawing at me."

I was really starting to feel sick now.

"No. You don't."

"I'm trying to fix this."

"Well, it wouldn't need fixing if you'd done your job right in the first place."

"That's complicated."

"Oh, cry me a river. Your boss is a jerk. Get in line. You had choices. You made them, and in the process you—you—you *know* what you did!"

Jake stood still. Staring at me. Sad. Heart rupturing in his eyes. *Like I could believe that.* Barely breathing. He blinked, and took a microscopic step toward me.

I backed away. "Oh no you don't. You can help me. But you don't get me. Is that understood?"

I waited.

He just breathed.

"You can clear your conscience and do the right thing, but don't think for a second that I buy your whole *I really do care* act. Try selling it to someone you didn't sleep with on a lie!"

Jake took two steps back and nodded.

And I felt disappointed that he didn't try harder.

Oh, shut up. I was such an idiot.

I needed to wrap this up. He was getting to me, and I couldn't take it.

"Okay," I said. "So—you're my new boss? They think I'm a criminal, but they're going to let you keep me?"

"I've cleared it with the Board. You have a few hopeful supporters, and I convinced them they didn't want to ruin your career without being one-hundred percent certain it was you. A number of them think it's folly. But you're being permitted to return to work under my supervision, minus key-card, keys, and anything that would allow you unsupervised access to artifacts."

"Well, isn't that lovely?" I shook my head, wanting to cry. "I stand corrected. I guess I owe you a thanks for rooting for me."

"You don't owe me anything."

Jake

That Went Well–Note the Sarcasm

I walked Kia back to Chloe's in silence. It was a lot for her to digest—and considering—I was grateful my head was still attached.

We followed Chloe's sidewalk to her front door, and Kia reached out to open it.

"Kia?"

She dropped a heavy sigh, not looking at me, and said, "What?"

"This is only going to work if you don't blow my cover. Only the Board knows. Not even Karen. I'm taking your job, so being mad at me works."

Kia rolled her eyes at me, and I smiled on the inside. Her sense of humor was just trapped under the heavy weight of disillusionment and distrust. She'd bounce back.

"There's likely to be a lot of commotion on Monday. Your main showpiece is M.I.A., and that's going to be big news. The Acer isn't closing the show, but they've taken tremendous rebuke from Moscow. Moscow wants the locket back, and somebody's head."

"What do you want me to do?"

"What you do best. Curate and sell your show. Talk about your arrest, but keep it low key. If people know you are suspected, then maybe the person working hard to make this look like you, will feel cocky enough to slip up. I want someone thinking they're getting away with it."

"Do you really think that'll work?"

"Maybe. But I'll throw out a wider net, check backgrounds, financials, see if anyone turns up suspicious. We had so much on you, we didn't focus on anyone else."

Processing, processing. Kia's picture wasn't a pretty one, and she was working her grip.

"Okay," she said, and pushed the door open.

"One more thing, Kia."

"Just one more?" she said heavily.

"Expect the unexpected from me, and go with it. I know you're angry with me, and justly so, but this is your life, not mine. Be open to following my lead, even if it doesn't make sense. Even if you don't like it. I'm going to be testing the waters, trying to flush this person out. I'm not sure how much help I'm going to get from Chris, if any, so I need you to have my back."

Kia looked even less happy. I'm sure as she was feeling a complete total loss of control. And it made me feel even worse.

Someone was raking her over the coals, and I'd been a part of that. All I could do now is find the opportunistic Ivan the Terrible, and make him or her pay.

"Can I go now?"

"Yes."

Kia walked through the door without giving me another look, and I called out before I could think better of it. "Kia, for what it's worth, I'm sorry. Really, truly, very, soul-rending sorry."

She paused long enough to listen, but that was the only acknowledgement I got. The door closed, *not harshly*, in my face, and I stood there, shaken, trying, determined, and scared.

What if I couldn't win her back?

I hopped in my Jeep and headed for the highway. There was lots to do between now and tomorrow morning, and first up, a call to Chris. *Yeah, not my favorite either.*

I punched 1 on my speed dial and waited for Chris to pick-up.

"I'm not talking to you," he said, all attitude and no hello.

"Oh, grow up, Chris. I know you're all about your career, but seriously. What happened to doing the job and getting the bad guy?"

"We got her, and she's not a him."

"If we have her, then why were you so hell-bent on questioning her without a lawyer present? And like in your wildest dreams that was ever going to happen. Even though it happened faster than you thought, you knew you didn't stand a chance. She would have shut you down faster than hitting *off* on your computer."

"Still, you showed our hand and have weakened our case. You overstepped your authority."

"Maybe. But if we had anything better than circumstantial it wouldn't matter."

"Why are you calling me? It's my day off, and you're irritating me."

"Then maybe you should grab yourself a drink or two, because I'm betting it's about to get worse."

"Now what?" he demanded.

"Well, since you've so kindly suspended me, I've found another way to work this case."

"Oh no you don't!"

"Already doing it. And you can help me or not. Maybe it'll be Kia; maybe it'll be somebody else. But it will be the person who is really stealing the lockets, and we'll have proof."

"We've made a case. You're supposed to leave it to a court of law to decide."

"When we have proof. I will."

"How do you plan on working it?"

"I've been given a position at the Acer."

"You're going to dismantle our case."

"No. I'm going to make it. And not just because you said so."

"Do you want me to bring you up on charges of insubordination?"

"I guess you'll do what you have to do. But rest assured, so will I."

"You're just being love-dumb."

"No, I'm not. If anything, you're just being shortsighted and career happy."

"Fine. But you're still suspended. If the Acer wants to foot the bill, so be it. If she's guilty, your FBI career is over."

"Understood. But I need something from you, and you're going to give it to me, or we're going to find ourselves in a pissing match in front of the review board."

"And what's that?" Chris asked, peeved, and not really containing it.

"I want deep background on all Acer employees including financials, and I want it today."

Chris bellowed his favorite expletives in a verbal tantrum and then yelled at me. "It's my day off!"

"If only I weren't suspended."

Chris grunted into the phone, and instead of giving in, he said, "Fine, I'll call Check-In and Mandy. You'll have an escort, and Mandy will get you your files."

"Thank you."

"Jake?"

"Yeah?"

"Don't fucking call me again until you have someone hogtied to a big sign that says, 'Here I am. I did it. And here's the evidence to prove it!'"

No problem.

Chris disconnected, and I was on my way into the office.

Kia

Another Day, Another Dollar

Chloe breakfast, new work clothes from a feel-better shopping spree with Chloe, and a dozen of the chocolates Jake had brought me, and I was standing at the front door of the Acer, waiting to be let in. Demoralized. Embarrassed. And suffering a total blow to my psyche.

I was hoping to catch Karen, but of course got Phillip instead.

How perfect.

Phillip came sauntering up, happy as a clam at high tide, oozing glee, making me want to vomit. "Good morning, Ms. Everet. I imagine that you've found your key no longer works."

Vomit.

No, I hadn't; since it had been taken away. But for the full intent and purposes of following Jake's instructions, I just let Phillip see it his way. Only curators, department heads, and security had passes. Now, I was only a lowly assistant. No keys.

I just smiled, and he continued, pompous and tripping on his own ego. "I'm sure you understand. I had to put the museum ahead of my own personal interest, and Mr. Davidson is perfectly suited for the position; whereas—" Phillip paused, as though searching for the right words. "You seem to have been having a very difficult time staying afloat."

Phillip patted my shoulder, condescension at its best, and said like the gelatinous slime mold that he was, "Maybe spending some time working as Jake's assistant will help you to improve your skills, and maybe someday, if you pay enough attention and are able to learn, you might be able to rise to curator again. It's probably going to take a very long time. So it might be best to start with a more reasonable goal. Senior assistant perhaps."

In my mind, my hands and fists pulled a Mohammed Ali, and Phillip went down like a sack of potatoes. And much to my great pleasure, no one came to revive him.

In reality, Jake walked up and intervened. Oh, Good. Here we go with the *My Savior* routine. Just another notch in Phillip's mental belt, proving how incompetent I am.

But then Jake didn't say a word to me. He didn't even acknowledge my presence. He just key-carded us all in, and said, "Good morning, Phillip. I trust you had a pleasant weekend."

"Jake!" he said, slapping him on the back. "So glad you came to your senses."

Jake smiled an oily smile. "You're offer was too good to refuse."

I started walking to the reception desk, but Phillip halted me. "Ms. Everet. Your new I.D. badge and employment paperwork are upstairs in the admin offices. You and Jake can follow me, and I'll get you both set-up."

Grrrr. Grumble. Mother-freaking, arghhhh!

I turned to him and smiled, obsequious and miffed. "Thank you, Dr. Mann." It was all I could manage without ripping his bloated, arrogant head off.

I looked to Jake, but he was already past me, taking the stairs two at a time, a vision of fitting right in.

Heavy sigh.

I was thinking it was going to be a very long day.

New photo, new "Assistant" badge, paperwork complete, and I was feeling low. Jake, in his black, silk suit and oceanic, eye-matching blue tie, was dazzling, impressive, still gorgeous, larger-than-life and blowing me off. He was acting like I didn't exist, and even though I was still mad as hell at him, mostly I was hurt. I liked, really liked him, even more—I just couldn't bring myself to admit it, especially now, because I'm stuck with *What do I really know about him?*

What I really know about him is that he melts my insides, brings me chocolate, is witty, charming, has the cutest dog, is an Olympic straight 10 in bed, and up until Saturday afternoon, he made me happy.

Now, I'd drawn a line, and he was following it. *Now.* Now when he should be fighting like crazy to tell me how wrong he was, fighting like crazy to explain, fighting like crazy to make it better. But in truth, I wasn't sure there was a better, could be a better, so I don't know. Maybe blowing me off was the smart thing to do. Cut and run before it really got ugly.

I was low and down at what was and what wasn't. If only he weren't such a cupcake—

"Ms. Everet. I'll need to see you in my office." Jake looked over at me, assessing and detached.

Whose office? My office!

Scratch that, he was a cold, mud pie in my face!

I gave him my best *you've got to be kidding* look, and he didn't budge, flinch an inch, nothing, just straight up *cool as a cucumber* expectation of obedience.

I rolled my eyes, hunched my shoulders, and thought, *Kill me now. Death had to be better than this.*

Jake took no notice of my protest. He just turned on his heel, and purposefully strode off. I trudged behind, feeling petulant. If there was a stone to kick, I would have, and hoped it hit Jake square in the back of his head.

We were on the third floor, leaving H.R., and I caught Karen's quizzical *what-the-hell* stare as she gaped at our bizarre procession. I rolled my eyes, shrugged, and mouthed, "I'll be back." She nodded, and I plodded on.

I moseyed down the stairs, mentally dragged across the show floor, catching the darkened, empty display case where the Tsarina's locket should be, fought the sick feeling that skittered up my throat, and found Jake comfortable in my chair, sitting at my desk. Waiting.

Oh joy. More fun.

"Kia, if you would please take a seat," Jake said, indicating the same chair he sat in all last week, as my assistant.

Heavy sigh.

I traipsed over, and hunkered down.

Jake's expression softened and he said, "Will you please follow-up with Karen Daniels in Curriculum," he sure was being awfully formal, "about your No-Locket contingency plan?"

Jake picked up a pencil and pulled a sheet of paper toward him and wrote while he gave me my instructions.

"Until the locket is hopefully returned to the museum, we should think about the flow of the presentation."

I nodded, and he slid his paper over to me and tapped his forefinger for me to read it.

What happened to angry? You're acting like Chloe died.

"My back-up file is in my—your—bottom, right desk drawer," I said and wrote back.

This is harder than I thought. Why are we writing?

Jake reached down into my drawer and pulled out the file. He slid it across the table and said, "Here. Please keep me apprised of your progress." And wrote,

I'm sorry. Hang-in-there. Just in case someone is watching or listening.

I suppressed the urge to shudder at the thought, mostly ignored Jake's potentially genuine compassion, and said, "I can meet with Karen now. I'll let you know."

He took the paper back, folded it up and put it into his breast pocket.

"Thank you Ms. Everet. I'll see about getting you a desk set up in the lab," he said pointing at my lab, and I shook my head. "If it would be alright, I'd like to see if Karen has some space upstairs."

Jake hesitated, apparently caught off guard by the request, and said, "We'll have to talk about that later."

"Okay. You're the boss." And I telegraphed, *How's that for angry?*

He took on his flat-lipped look, and it was my turn to turn on my heel and flounce out.

Karen was sitting at her work table when I walked in, doodling, passing time, and maternally concerned.

"Kia!" she said, hopping up from her chair and coming over to me, like I might be frail. "What is going on? I came in and found the locket is missing, and Phillip tells me he's hired Jake to be your supervisor. What's that about?"

I walked us back to her work table and said, "You're gonna want to sit down for this. Trust me."

"That doesn't sound good," Karen said, dropping into her chair, and I followed.

"It's not."

I cleared my throat, not sure if I was ready to relive this all over again, and Karen said, "Okay, you're really starting to freak me out."

"Uhhh, okay, soooo—you remember the gala Friday night?"

She gave me her *Duh* look, and I said, "Right. Well, the night was going fabulously, amazing in fact, and I was on top of the world, or so I thought." I paused to remember the time. "I think it was about nine, and I was taking a break from all of the hullaballooing and schmoozing, and went to find Jake. He was up by my office sipping club soda, and Phillip came over. From his tone, I was shocked thinking he was about to congratulate me on a job well done."

"Aaand?" Karen prompted.

"He offered my job to Jake instead, giving him all the credit for the show."

"He didn't!"

"He did," I said nodding my head.

"What an asshole."

"It gets worse."

"Yeah, I can see that. Jake has your job! And I thought he was a nice guy. What the hell was he thinking?"

I couldn't bring myself to tell her about Jake and me. I just wasn't prepared to deal with the humiliation, so I skipped to Saturday afternoon.

"But, so, then, you don't know about the locket?"

"No! It was here when I left on Friday night, and gone when I came into work this morning. No one is saying a thing."

"Well, so then on Saturday, I was taking a nap and waiting for Chloe to come home from the hospital. The doorbell rang, and I jumped up to get it, and when I opened the door, the FBI was standing there."

"What?" Karen's face said it all, and I had lived it.

"Yeah. Apparently, the locket has been stolen, along with a few others, all from collections I have curated, so I'm their primary suspect, and they arrested me, and searched my apartment, and are in the process of trying to ruin my life."

"Get out! This is so not true; it can't be."

"Ooooh, it is. And I now have the mental scars to prove it!"

"Kia, this is ridiculous! You're the most honest person I know. You wouldn't even steal a paperclip from here."

"Tell that to the FBI."

Karen shook her head. "I can't believe this," she said and put a supportive hand on my arm. "Are you okay? What are you going to do?"

"I'm not okay, but I wish I were. My dad got me the best defense lawyer in Michigan, and he's going to do his best to work his magic, but it appears the FBI has one doozy of a circumstantial case against me, and he's not sure if he can pull it off."

"Holy shit, Kia."

"I know. I'm looking at forty years." The tears started to bubble again, and Karen handed me a Kleenex.

"You tell your lawyer about me. I'm an Acer. This is our museum, and I know you didn't do this. I'll be a character witness for you!"

Now my tears really started, and Karen gave me a supportive hug. "Don't you worry. We'll get this all worked out."

"But I thought you already knew, because the Board are the one's who contacted the FBI, and they think I'm guilty, too."

Karen's mom and grandmother sat on the Board, and I was surprised they hadn't told her.

"There's been a mistake," Karen said with a will of stone. "This is so wrong, Kia."

I sat back and blew my nose. "And to top it all off, Mr. Wonderful is my boss. But apparently this is the Board's attempt to avoid a civil suit. They wanted to just fire me, but since there isn't concrete proof that I did this, they are keeping me on, as long as I am not in a position of having any unsupervised access to artifacts. Phillip offering Jake my job, just worked out for everyone involved."

Karen was still in denial. "No, Kia. I'm going to talk to my family. No way is this okay."

I loved that she was on my side, but I was thinking that if she was out of the loop, it's because they knew we were friends, and didn't want to put Karen in a funky position.

But it still felt good having her so indignant on my behalf.

"So what's Jake saying about all this?" Karen asked. "I thought you two had something going there."

We did, but then he lied. I guess that's what FBI guys do.

"He's telling me to do my job, *assisting him.*"

Karen's face darkened. "This is just idiotic."

"What's idiotic?" Jake asked coming up from behind and scaring the bejeezus out of us. "I thought Kia pretty much had a plan B worked out already."

Karen shot up and shot in between Jake and me, and I thought, *Everybody keeps trying to protect me. That's just silly. I can take care of myself.*

"I can't believe I gave you my vote," Karen said coldly.

"I didn't realize I was in the running for something," Jake countered, smooth as silk.

"You're a despicable man, Jake." Karen was biting for blood.

I wiped my nose, making sure I didn't look like a sniveling Benedict Arnold, and swiveled around to find them in a stand-off. Jake glanced at me, *Really?* And I shrugged. He was on his own. He told me angry worked, so he was getting some.

"I'm sure you think I'm scum—"

"No," Karen slighted, "scum is too good for you."

"Maybe so," Jake said, brushing off Karen's verbal slap and moving on. "But I need to know whether you two have a plan I can present to Dr. Mann for his approval."

"Since when does Kia need a middle man to do her dirty work?" Karen was hopping mad, and Jake's little announcement wasn't sitting well with either one of us. We hated Phillip and didn't go to him for approval. He just tried to interfere frequently, which I dealt with and Karen ignored.

If this was going to be Jake's approach to supervision, he wasn't going to have anyone left on his side except Phillip. And Phillip wasn't good company to keep.

Nonetheless, this had to stop.

I stepped into the space separating them and gently pushed Karen back. She looked at me, and I small-smiled her. "It's okay," I said, and she said, "No. It's not Kia. You don't have to take this."

She was right about that.

I took my place in her face-off with Jake and went for my most dismissive tone.

"Shhhhh," I said drawing my hand down the length of his body without touching him. "Just be beautiful. Don't say anything. You'll ruin it."

Jake's eyes bugged out of his head, and I smiled fake pleasant at him and said, "When Karen and I finish working out the kinks, I'll update you. Just like you asked. You don't need to worry one pretty little hair on your head."

I must've hit a nerve—*finally*—because his eyes darkened to unfriendly, and he leaned in *real* close to me. So close that I could smell his mesmerizing scent, and almost forget I was mad at him—almost.

"Don't forget what we talked about," he said, shredding the intoxicating impact he was having on me.

He stepped back, gave me a look that could freeze liquid steel, and marched off, and Karen chimed in merrily. "Gosh, he sure is touchy; isn't he?"

And I thought, *Jake, this isn't working. You better find your guy fast.*

Two hours later, Karen and I were done, and she said, "I'll submit these new narrative boards to Theo, and he should be able to get something here by this afternoon."

I rolled my eyes and scoffed, "What? You're not going to wait for Phillip's approval?"

"Kia, I do declare. You are getting yourself an attitude problem."

I smiled all innocent like, and she said, "I approve."

"You getting lunch?" I asked, and she said, "Working through. Classical needs help incorporating some new pieces into their regular display. How 'bout you?"

"Chloe packed me something. I'll probably eat while setting up my new desk."

"Har har," she said, shaking her head. "Don't play too nice."

"Not likely."

I found Jake pouring over something at *his* desk, and when I sauntered in, he didn't bother looking up.

I grabbed my lunch-tote, *for one*, and sidled off to find someplace to eat. Maybe the reflection path, as it seemed fitting. Apparently I needed to do some serious self-reflecting, and that was as good a place as any.

"Have dinner with me."

Jake's chest warming, soul resonating voice called out to my back, inviting-not commanding, friendly-not hostile, sincere, and without presumption.

My eyes sank shut, and I thought, *Why, Jake? Why?*

Jake

Not Giving Up

Kia stood stock still, half in the doorway, half out, and I wasn't sure if she was seething at the thought or worse, suffering. I hadn't meant to catch her so last second there, but after her kicking me in the teeth, it'd taken some working up of the ol' nerve.

I needed to bring her up to speed—reviewing those files had been illuminating—and I know how selfish this sounds, but I wanted to be near her, even if it meant taking her ill-tempered attitude. We could get through this. We just had to.

She still hadn't turned around, so I explained, "There are some *things* I need to go over with you, and I don't think we should do it here."

I saw her take a deep breath, and I added quickly, "Take out, my place, you can meet me there. I'll give you a map."

Kia kept her back to me, and I watched her shoulders fall—*suffering—damn*—and she said, "I'm not comfortable with your place."

"I know. But Bullet will protect you, and besides everything is there. No hanky panky." I almost added, *I promise*, but I stopped. I didn't think it would go over well, since she thinks I'm a self-serving liar. So I let it ride.

"Have you decided on my desk?"

"I think you should set it up in the lab—"

Kia's body tensed, coiled, prepared to pounce, and I hastened to clarify. "However, given how much work you and Karen will be doing together, I'll understand if you spend the bulk of your time working in the C.O.D."

She took another deep breath.

"What time do you want me there?" she asked.

She'd kept her back to me the entire time, and it was a crappy thing being on this side of Kia. She was such a fun, happy person.

Seeing her like this came with its own can of whoop-ass. And it made my stomach grind glass.

"Do you need to work late?" I was attempting accommodating, but she whipped around, miffy ire gone gusto, and asked, "I don't know, do I?"

Not good.

Breathe Jake, breathe. This isn't getting fixed overnight.

I lowered my voice to completely non-combative and said, "No, Kia. I just didn't want to infringe on any more of your time than necessary."

She looked for a cutting retort, but apparently couldn't find one, and went with, "How's six."

"Six is fine."

Kia's stone cold glare softened to tolerant gaze, and I wondered, "What?"

She shook her head, and her mouth opened, but then no words. She shook her head again, patted her lunch as explanation, and left me.

I firmly came to the decision that I did not like watching Kia walk away from me. It smacked, and I did not like the sinking, cold feeling that spread through me and choked my air.

No. I did not like it all.

I checked my wall clock. Six-twelve. "She's not coming, Bullet."

He wagged his tail, *Of course she is.*

I'd gone all out where take-out was concerned, dropping a cool hundred and bringing home beef tenderloin from my favorite restaurant, The Common Grill, in Chelsea. They had the best beef tenderloin and white cheddar mashers around, and the shoe string onion rings were hand-dipped delicacies. Throw in the merlot, and Warm Chocolate Fallen Cake with caramel sauce, toffee-pecans, and vanilla ice cream, and it was perfection in a meal, and it was my hopeful hook for getting on more stable footing with Kia.

But first, she had to show up.

It took another seven minutes, and felt like a small lifetime, but the doorbell rang, and Bullet flew over into the foyer, barking his fool head off. I pretty much felt the same way.

I took a deep breath, hoped for the best, and pulled the door wide.

Despite the staid look she gave me, in the June sun she simply gleamed, radiant and beautiful. She'd let her hair down, and it spilled across her back, a few strands dancing with the breeze, and her eyes were sparkling again, *sun magic.* Kia had changed from her earlier strict, black pant suit and top knot hair, to a softer, more Kia-like sundress, the same lulling green as her eyes. She was a sight, but her face read, *Unavailable.*

"I came all this way. You gonna invite me in or just stand there staring?"

Bark!

Kia smiled at Bullet and stooped down to give him some friendly ear scrubbas. Bullet dropped to the floor and rolled to his back, *lucky dog,* obviously in heaven, and I thought, *I want some of that.*

Temporarily sated, Bullet flopped back over and raced inside. His way of saying, *Come in, come in!*

I stepped aside, and said, pointing at Bullet, "What he said."

Kia's smile sagged, but she came in, and I thought, *Well, it's a start.*

"I have dinner in the oven, warming. Did you want food first, or dessert?"

She was pulling off somber and uncommitted better than a disillusioned free agent, and I was back to wanting to shake her.

"It's an easy choice. Steak or cake first?"

"Steak."

I led her into my dining room. I had the table all set. And I offered her a seat.

"You look great," I said, and she said, "Yeah, I got that."

This falling flat thing was hard.

"Let me just grab dinner. Wine's on the table, would you mind to pour?"

Maybe a few glasses would take the edge off. Her. And me.

"So what did you need to talk to me about, Jake?"

I came back into the dining room, pot-holder and plates in each hand, and set hers down first. "Please be careful. These are hot."

I set mine down, and took my seat. My table sat eight, not that I'd ever had eight people over for dinner. Not even two. But I was hopeful, so I'd gone big. But for tonight, I sat our seats right next to each other. I was prepared to defend with, "Didn't want to have to yell across the room," but, it's just because I wanted to be by her.

I waited until Kia picked up her fork and took her first bite. I was thinking she might offer an, *Mmmm, this is good Jake*, to give me encouragement or at least an opening, but she didn't, so I just went with it.

"First, I'd like to start with an apology."

Kia looked up from her plate, tentative, but kept eating, small, non-interfering bites, just in case she needed to rip my head off, or so I assumed.

Okay.

"I'm sorry. I'm sorry I hurt you. And I'm sorry I had to arrest you. But I'm not sorry for how I feel about you."

She swallowed and reached for her wine. Cool and steady.

"It's true, I had the upper-hand. But meeting you, and my reaction to you is real, and if it took this case for me to get to know you, then I'm only sorry if we can't get past the unpleasant parts. Because everything else, I've loved and wouldn't give back."

Kia downed her glass of wine and poured another.

Okay, maybe not so cool and steady.

"My name is Jake Matthew Davidson. I have a Bachelor's in both accounting and art history. I have my CPA, and am a forensic accountant and special agent with the FBI."

Kia listened, but didn't interrupt. She just continued taking her tiny bites.

Her look was bland, but her eyes were heavily focused on me. I took that to be my encouragement, but I downed my glass of wine and poured another just for good measure.

"My mother, Jane, and my father, Thomas, are both passed-on. She of cancer; he of alcoholism. I have two brothers, Ethan and Connor. Ethan is a math professor out East, and Connor is a Navy Seal. We're not close, and I haven't seen either of them in about five years, since our mother's funeral."

My plate was untouched, but Kia was managing slowly. I'm sure this isn't what she expected, but it was necessary to help clean the slate.

"I'm single, never married. Thirty-two. I've had a few relationships along the way, but nothing stuck. If you want the itemized chick list, I'll write it all down for you. I own this house. I have about forty thousand saved up, and maintain a diversified portfolio for retirement. Bullet is my dog, and everything else you've seen about me is true. I did investigate you. I did withhold my undercover status from you, and I did sleep with you. But not for my job, but because—"

Kia had stopped eating, and she'd laid her fork down onto the table. I watched her wipe her hands on her napkin, and I wasn't sure what any of it meant. Was she about to bolt? Throw her glass of wine at me? What?

"Because, you took me by surprise, because you've got *Wham*, and because I've fallen for you. It wasn't supposed to happen, and I fought it like crazy. But being near—being near you—is the closest thing to home I've known in a really long time, and I wanted it. I want you."

Her eyes had turned glassy, but her face was still bland and holding.

"But what if I'm guilty?"

"You're not."

"How can you know that now, and two days ago—"

"Two days ago, I was doing my job, because I was doing as expected. When we started this investigation, you looked good for the thefts. But as I got to know you, it just didn't add up. You didn't fit the profile. I raised concern, but it was dismissed, because I liked you. Then the locket went missing the morning after Phillip offered me your job. It still didn't seem right, but the coincidence was a killer. It didn't look good, and even though it was all still circumstantial, Chris demanded we move. He planned to interview you, thinking he could intimidate you into confessing. It was a bad plan. But he's so hell-bent on a promotion, and this case is his chance. So it was a whirlwind of go-get-her, and I did, and you got burned."

"I can't do this," Kia said, springing up from her chair, and I leapt to follow.

"Please Kia, just let me finish."

She shook her head, wary, but from the torment on her face, she was fighting hope. The same hope I was counting on.

"Kia," I said, reaching out to her, but she threw up her hand in a recoil that would make a Smith and Wesson Magnum jealous.

I held my hands up in surrender and took a firm step back.

"Kia. I'm just trying to level the playing field. I had a file on you. It was an unfair advantage, and I know this isn't the same, but no matter which way this goes, you deserve to know the bits and pieces of me."

Unwanted tears rolled down her porcelain cheeks, and she doggedly whisked them away.

"I'm not trying to hurt you." I skimmed into the bathroom for Kleenex, and keeping my distance, passed them to her.

"Please just come back to dinner. I'll stop talking, and you can finish your meal. Then we'll see what you want to do."

Kia wiped at her eyes and nose, blinking back the flow, *deciding*, one eye on the door, one eye on me.

Bullet hadn't made a sound, but he'd hopped up on the couch, front paws on the top, concerned and curious.

Kia held up her hand in a silent *please just stop*, and I nodded, *okay*.

Hesitantly she started for the table, and I turned to Bullet and said, "It's okay, Bullet. Get down from the couch."

Bark!

Bullet jumped down, did his walk-in-circles routine, and snuggled up into his blanket, happy again, thinking his people were on the mend.

I could only hope.

We took our seats, and in silence, quiet but not strained, we finished our meal.

Kia waited until I had finished my plate, having gotten a head start, and then said, "Thank you, Jake. Dinner was delicious."

Still hovering at subdued.

"You're welcome. I'm glad you liked it. Can I interest you in some dessert? You can have your own plate and everything."

That got a hint of a smile, and I said, "Is that a yes?"

"Sure. Dessert would be nice."

I gathered up our dishes. "Be right back."

"I'm just going to use your bathroom."

"Okay," I said and went to get our cake.

I heard my front door open and close and my heart sank. I dropped everything into the sink and ran outside. Kia was getting into her car, and I sprinted the distance.

My chest was swelling, burning, and I felt like I was crashing. *No, no, no!*

I jumped in front of Kia's Mini, and said, "Please, Kia. Don't go."

"Jake," she said, tears welling up again. "I. Can't. Do. This."

She turned her engine over, and cold fear at losing her clawed up my spine, and propelled me forward. I surprised us both, grabbing for her door, and pulling her out of her seat and into me. "And I can't let you leave. Not like this."

I nestled Kia's head into my shoulder and hugged her tight, whispering, "Give me a chance. I can make this better."

I felt her shake her head, no, and I nodded. "Yes, I can. And the only upside to our pain right now, is that it proves we care."

"I don't care," she sniffled.

I smiled at that silliness. "Yes, you do, and so do I. And I don't want to lose you. I'll fight to the death if I have to."

Kia snorted into my sleeve. "Yeah, I'd like to see you do that."

Sassy, sassy.

I pulled back just far enough to look into her tear-soaked eyes, and said, "Kia Emily Everet, I am sorrier than life that I ever hurt you. Believe that. And know that I . . . I . . . I love you."

There. Said it. Then I dove for her mouth before she could deny that too, and kissed the silliness right out of her.

I reached my hands into her hair and pulled her face to mine, not wanting to ever let her go, and I fed her desperate kiss after desperate kiss, until she relaxed into me, and kissed me like she meant it.

When the racing in my heart switched from the cold-sweats to heated eagerness, I bent down into Kia's car, cut the engine, extracted her keys, and locked her door.

"Come with me," I said, holding her hand. "I'll show you how I can make this better."

Kia

The Unusual Suspects

Okay, Chloe. You said to be hopeful. Well, this is as leap-of-faithish as I get.

I'm scared, and the hurt is heart-consuming, but I'm finding myself wanting to believe—*just in case.*

As far as signs go, Jake was going all out, really working it, even when I kept shutting him down. Who does that? Who takes hit after hit after hit and keeps coming back for more?

"You know, you're glutton for punishment," I said, as he pulled me back inside his house, and he said, "Whatever it takes," then flashed me his perfect smile.

My brain had been frozen in time, trying to grasp at the ammunition Jake was throwing at me, and failing. And it wasn't until we were back inside his house that reality hit again, and I heard Bullet frantically barking and jumping all over, trying to land a perfect 10 for high-jumps.

Jake closed the door, locked it, gave me a stern, wry eye—totally, *I'm watching you*—and then bent to Bullet, and said, "Heya Bullet. I know. It's lots of excitement today." Bullet panted energetically, and wagged his tail, swacking it back and forth so hard I thought the momentum might flip him over. Jake stroked his ears, calming him, and looked back up to me, and said, "But I think we're good now."

Bark!

"Well, let's ask her," and they both shifted to look at me.

"Are we good now?" Jake asked, still soothing Bullet, moving him back over to his blanket.

"Better—but I'm not sure about good."

"Fair enough," Jake said, keeping his tone even. "See Bullet. All better."

Bullet gave me a questioning brow, and I mimicked him in response, smiling.

His look said, *Sass. I recognize that.*

I laughed. "You're funny, Bullet."

Bark!

Bullet settled back into his blanket, and Jake came over to me and took my hand.

I dug in my heels, not sure what Jake was thinking, and blurted, "I'm not ready."

"Ready for what?" he asked, giving me a knowing look, playing, but not pushing it. "Dessert?"

I closed my eyes and took a deep breath. *Playful Jake, the one you like. Eat some dessert, Kia. Relax.*

"Dessert?"

"Dessert," he said, all like, *Yeah, what'd you think?*

"Chocolate?"

"Like there's any other kind?"

"I can do dessert."

"Inside or out?" he asked, kidding, but I heard the note of uncertainty.

"Inside, but I'd like to wash my hands."

He gave me his *I wasn't born yesterday* look and said, "There's a fresh towel and soap in the kitchen."

"Ha. Ha."

"Come on you potential escapee. We'll get you cleaned up and saturated in chocolate. You'll be happy. Then I'll tell you all about what I've found out and see what you think."

We scrubbed up, and as promised, Jake brought out two plates of heavenly smelling chocolate cake.

"What's all this?" I asked, and Jake said, "One of my favorites. Lemme know what you think."

My plate had more, and I arched my brow inquisitively. Jake always fought for his fair share.

"Part of my penance," he explained.

I spooned off a chunk of cake, followed it with a dab of ice cream, and attempted to fill my spoon the rest of the way with the caramel sauce, and then shoveled it all into my mouth. Not lady-like, but devouring chocolate rarely is.

"*Mmmmmm.*" It was excellent cake. "I like this you making up to me stuff."

Jake chuckled and said, "Thought you might."

"What's on the pecans?"

"Toffee. They're delicious and crunchy."

I picked up a cluster and bit off a chunk. Buttery goodness to be sure. "Is this your chocolate guy, too?"

"Nope. The whole meal comes from my favorite restaurant around. If you're nice to me, maybe I'll take you there someday."

"I think you should tell me, so I can go there myself," I said spooning in another perfect bite.

"I don't think so. That would not be wise. Cutting out the middle-man like that."

"What about your penance?"

"Did you not see how much more dessert you got than me? That's penance!"

I laughed; he smiled, and we finished our dessert in peace.

This time, when we were done, Jake didn't seem to trust me enough to clear the dishes. He just moved them off to the side of the table, and pulled a pile of files off of his sidebar.

"Did you want to take the dishes into the kitchen?" I razzed.

He gave me squinty brow, and said, "Tried that once. I'm good, thanks."

"I'm not going anywhere, Jake," I said, trying for meeting him halfway.

"Glad to hear it, but we'll give it a little while longer. Let the feel of your seat make you comfortable, and all that."

Doofus.

"Okay then. So what do you have there?"

"Lots of interesting information turned up when I started peeking into the lives of the Acer folk. Thought you might like to know, and maybe you might be able to help."

"Like what?"

"Well, essentially, I've come up with three possible lines of inquiry to start with. I was hoping you could tell me what you think."

"Okay. Let's hear 'em."

"Do you know Anders Schmidt in the Modern and Contemporary department?"

I shrugged. "The Acer is small enough. I've met everyone, but Anders and I aren't friends. Nothing in common."

"Anything ever strike you as odd about him?"

"Not really. But I don't see him enough to notice."

"Well, he has curiously questionable finances. Some really bizarre deposits have been made into his account over the last couple of years, and I can't find any reason for them. They're sizable, to say the least, and worth following-up on."

"Do you think it's him?"

It was Jake's turn to shrug. "Hard to say. His file is pretty clean. Just the finances. He's smart and has overseas connections. So—leaving no stone unturned, I'll check it out."

"Okay. Who's next?"

"Benjamin Nice."

"Ben?"

"Yeah. Fun and affable Ben has a secret side something. Regular deposits, often times quite large, are finding their way into his account. He's fronting something lucrative. It could definitely be pinching artifacts. The Acer houses tens of thousands of pieces. Most of which are in storage. He has access to any and all of those pieces, and he knows the system."

"I can't believe Ben. He's too fun and friendly."

"Those are usually the ones. No one suspects a thing."

"Hmmm," I gave a small supportive whimper for Ben. "I hope it's not him."

"Yeah, me too. But better him than you."

I sighed. "True. And the third?"

I know you like Ben, so this possibility is going to be one you like even less. But it's a real eye catcher."

"Oh-kay." I said, not liking the sound of that, but not liking the sound of jail either.

"The Acer family."

"Karen? No way."

"Not necessarily. But more likely her mom or grandmother on the Board. The economic downturn has been causing problems for most, and generous pockets are becoming less generous. The Acer is experiencing cash flow problems. The Board is keeping a lid on it—most likely hoping things will turn around. But the four missing lockets are worth a lot of money, and are small enough to move easily. *And* all come heavily insured. We could be looking at insurance fraud."

"Wow. That's hard to get your head around. It just doesn't seem like something they would do. Not Karen for sure."

I bit my lip, pensive.

"What?" Jake asked.

"Well, I was surprised Karen didn't know about the locket. Or you getting my position; or my getting arrested; since, you had told me it was the Board who contacted you about the missing lockets. I just figured the whole family would know and think I'm a terrible person, but Karen was truly shocked. She said she was going to speak to her family and was willing to testify on my behalf."

Jake found that interesting and wrote a note in his Acer file.

"What's that mean?" I asked, and Jake said, "I don't know. But it's interesting."

"I thought maybe they just didn't tell Karen because she was my friend, and they didn't want to upset her."

"Could be," Jake shrugged. "Well, that's what I found out, aaaannnd why I was so rude to you at work. Sorry, I couldn't give you a heads-up, but we weren't communicating very well. I'm trying to distance myself from you in front of these people, thinking that will increase the right person's comfort with me. If I'm not for you, then I fit in with their game plan. Maybe I can get someone to overshoot in over-confidence. And I'm sorry I had to be mean. You don't deserve it, but I'm trying to clear your name."

"Oooooh," I said, teasing. "The ol' I'm doing this for your own good routine!"

Jake smiled apology and said, "Something like that. Sorry."

He closed up the files and pushed them off to the side. "Don't suppose I could interest you in a little bit of a walk?"

"Trying to keep me around for a while?"

Jake looked guilty as charged, but not sorry about it. I had to give it to him. He was really trying, and that's more than I can say for most. No other man had even so much as lifted a finger to order me flowers, much less get to know me and still like me. Mind you, Jake got a head start with a file, and he arrested me for something I didn't do. But, hey—nobody's perfect, right?

At the sound of the word *walk*, Bullet came bounding in—excitement galore, and I thought, *This must be part of their regular routine, and I'm being invited in.* Warm fuzzies crept in, bustling their way into the lingering recesses of doubt and worked at melting away the remaining chill.

Jake stood and held out his hand to me. "Bullet will not be happy if you don't come along."

Bark!

I took Jake's hand, and said, totally onto his tricksy ways, "Well, I wouldn't want to disappoint *Bullet*."

I bent down to give Bullet-the-Jumping-Bean-Beagle an enthusiastic scritch, and added, "Or his *Charming Conniver* of an owner."

"Charming Conniver?"

"Among many other things, yes."

"How about scuttling my way back into your good favor?" And it was all right there in his voice. Hope, fear, love, *question.* He really did care, and he knew he'd seriously dropped the ball.

"Well, you do keep feeding me chocolate, and I am rather fond of your kisses. Sooo." I wasn't going to let him off the hook that easily. "*Maybe.*"

He smiled, happy and relieved, and said, "I like the sound of that."

Jake pulled me in, going for a kiss, but I smiled back and dodged. "Walk first. Then, we'll see."

"Did you hear that Bullet? We're going for a walk."

Bullet did a few victory laps around the table and dashed for the mudroom door.

We walked, talked, held hands, smooched, and hit all of Bullet's favorite spots—every so often, Jake would drape his arm around me and scrunch me in a hug, being sure of me, knowing I was there, whispering sweet somethings into my ear. When the sun dipped low, we walked back, and Jake got me settled into Molly. He reached into his pocket and pulled out his card, on the back, he'd written his home and cell numbers. "I'm always accessible to you. Every day, every night. Starting tonight—call me as soon as you get tucked in." Jake leaned in, kissed me good and sound, smiled wickedly, and said, "And tell me what you're *not* wearing!"

I drove all the way home with a light-hearted pitter patter skipping around, bumping into all the right places, every bit of me beaming. Maybe this could work. Maybe.

Kia

Playing Hooky

I woke to the sounds of Chloe humming and tinkering about in my kitchen, the sunshine shining, and the smell of something yummy blueberry tickling my nose, and smiled, *She's back.*

It took less than a blink to throw on my slippers and skedaddle out to greet her.

"Hiya, Chloe," I said, zooming in for a big hug. "How are you feeling today, and what smells soooo good?"

Chloe gave me a big hug back. "I'm fine. I miss you, and it's blueberry muffins. My hospital dietician gave me a cookbook with low-fat, low-cholesterol, heart-healthy recipes, and so we're trying these."

"Well, they smell amazing!"

She nodded, *Yeah*, and said, "I was thinking. How about you take the day off? I've booked us massages, just in case. And I thought we could girl around."

Chloe had never asked me to take a day off before. "Are you sure you're alright?"

"I'm fine. It's just been a difficult week, and I thought we could use a treat."

I gave her squinty eye. "You wouldn't fib to your best friend now would you?" And she laughed, "Like I could ever get away with it!"

Still some more squinty eye. "Alright," I said. "I'll just call Jake, and let him know."

Chloe made a grimace face and asked, "How's that going?"

I shrugged, *enh*. "Not as bad as you'd think. But I don't know. I'll tell you all about it."

I picked up the phone, and Chloe opened my oven door, releasing breakfast heaven into my apartment. *Yum!*

Jake picked up on the first ring, sleepy still in his voice, and sexy.

"Did I wake you?" I asked.

"What's that smell? Is Chloe making you breakfast again?"

I chuckled. "Nope. Just cold cereal for me."

Chloe put a plate of fresh berry-melon medley with strawberries and a giant crumbly-crusted, piping hot blueberry muffin in front of me, and said, "Be careful. It's hot," and Jake said, "I knew it. I'll be right over!"

I smiled. "Nuh-unh-uh. Sorry, none for you. She only made enough for me."

"Cold, Kia. That's just cold. You know how I love a good Chloe meal."

"Speaking of Chloe—" I segued to, "Since you're my supervisor now, and all . . ."

"Ouch. *Really?* First thing in the morning?"

". . . I'd like to spend the day with Chloe. She has massages booked for us, and Karen has it under control. And you wouldn't know this—" I didn't say it meanly, "but I've never asked for a day off."

"Okay."

"Just like that?"

"I'm your new and improved boss. No walking on coals."

"Wow. Okay, thanks."

"Just one second there little missy . . . on one condition." Jake sounded like he was enjoying himself immensely.

What a doofus.

"What happened to my new and improved boss? No coals?"

"Here today, gone tomorrow."

"It's still today!"

"But could be gone tomorrow, if you don't meet my demands."

"Fine!" I said, playfully petulant, and he said, "That's more like it."

"So what do you want?" I laughed.

"You have to tell Chloe that I want some of whatever she's got in front of you right now."

"Does it have to be from my plate specifically, or just a sampling? Because I'm not good with sharing."

"And here I thought you wanted the day off," he said all *La-tee-da.*

"Fine. I'll have her scoop my plate into a bag, and make me something fresh."

Jake chuckled, "You sasser! So I'll call you later?"

"Okay."

"Have fun with Chloe."

"Have fun at the Acer."

"Ahhh. That would be your dry wit."

"Hee hee."

We hung up, and Chloe gave me her thoughtful look.

"So there's been a change in the weather?" she asked.

I smiled. "Maybe. Kind of. I think we're working on it."

"Well, that sounds hopeful, but what about your case?"

"Jake's on our team now."

"Really? Can you be sure?" Chloe said, kind of doubtful, and I nodded. "He seems truly genuine. If it's a set-up, then it's a good one, because I find myself believing. He wants to find who really did it, and clear my name."

"Well, then," Chloe said with a smile, and raised her orange juice to mine in a toast. "Here's to finding the real culprit, Jake, and—" She wiggled her eyebrows at me. "Your hopeful future."

Clink.

I smiled back, and took a big bite of my muffin. "Mmmmmmm. These are delicious."

"And nutritious," Chloe said. "Made with egg whites, apple sauce, and super-food blueberries. We can eat lots, and they're good for us."

"We should send your dietician a Thank You note."

"Mmm-hmm," Chloe said around a mouthful.

"So what's on our agenda for the day," I asked, and Chloe beamed. "Actually, I booked us a full day at the spa. If that sounds good to you. A day of total rejuvenation, head-to-toe."

Bliss!

"That sounds perfect and wonderful, Chloe!"

"Then chop, chop, kid. We've got a date at the spa."

Breakfast and a quick shower later, and Chloe and I were on our way to Serenity Spa.

"Thanks, Chloe. This is a really nice surprise. I've never had a full day at the spa."

"Me neither. But I figure a little pampering never hurt anybody. And besides, sounds like we have some stuff to talk about," she said, giving me her knowing eye look.

"I'm sure that would be *Jake* stuff," I chuckled, totally on to her.

Chloe nodded big time and said, "Can't wait."

We pulled in and parked in the shade provided by some very large oak and maples trees. Serenity Spa was truly serene looking. An old Victorian, white with sage green and mellow blue accents and a giant wrap around porch, nestled in and amongst leaf and pine trees, and sporting gorgeous rose and flower gardens, calming chimes and a trickling fountain welcomed us. And as first impressions go, I breathed a deep, refreshing sigh.

"Right there with you," Chloe said, and I said, "Let's go in!"

We walked up the wooden steps to the front door, and were pleasantly greeted by a lovely, relaxed, middle-aged woman, dressed all in white.

"Hello. Welcome to Serenity Spa. Chloe and Kia Everet?"

"Yes," Chloe said, and she said, "My name is Charity. I'll be your personal Serenity assistant for the day. If you need anything, just let me know."

Charity motioned for us to follow. "You'll be in our Tranquility for Two suite on the second floor. I have your baths already prepared, so if you'd like to begin."

Would we ever!

Ahhhhhhhh. Lavender mineral baths—overlooking the rose garden and copper, cherub fountain—hot stone massages, facials, baked Mahi Mahi and steamed vegetables with rose-infused water, manicures, pedicures, and fresh do's later, and you could have floated us home. Chloe and I were blissed out to the max, and I said, "Where's our chauffer when we need him?"

Chloe smiled and said, "What's next?"

"How about we go laze about in your backyard, and see where that gets us?"

"Sounds good," she said, and I said, "This sure beats any day at work." Chloe grinned. "How do you think Jake faired without you?"

I shrugged indifferent and chuckled. "He's getting your homemade blueberry muffins. He'll be fine!"

Jake

Jake-in' Things Up

A full day of nada. The Acer without Kia was not fun. I'd done everything Kia usually did, with the exception of avoiding Phillip. Him, I sought out. Keeping up appearances was important, but it bordered on self-sacrifice for finding a thief. It's just that Kia was more important than scratching an itch. And dear ol' Phil was proving to be an itch I wanted to pummel. Even when Kia wasn't there, Dr. Mann was a self-righteous pig and ass, constantly ready with a Kia-slam. He either really didn't like women, or he *really* didn't like Kia. Either way, he was not good for her, and I wished she'd work things out with the Board when this was all said and done, because she deserved better. A lot better.

As it was, I kept my cool and made the rounds.

I couldn't just walk up to folks and say, "*Hey, you steal a locket lately?*" So I'd chit-chatted them up, hoping something might spontaneously pop out. But no. Nothing conclusively damning, just more things to consider.

Anders Schmidt turned out to be a nicotine-saturated aloof elitist, and I could totally understand why Kia didn't hang with him. He was as warm and social as a dead fish, and about the only thing I could get out of him was that he was the artistic answer to all the world's problems, if only anyone would be smart enough to ask. His narcissistic streak ran deep and was reasonably consistent with what I would expect from a criminal.

Ben, on the other hand, was so cool and laid back. I genuinely liked him, which had my guard up. I wasn't kidding when I'd told Kia, it was usually his type.

The Board wasn't in-house today, but it wouldn't have mattered. They're the ones who contacted the FBI in the first place. Ballsy if I called it with the insurance fraud, and if I wanted to check that out, I'd have to be a helluva lot more subtle than taking my questions to them. Meeting directly with the insurance companies was the way to go there.

For now, I was following-up old school, tracking down fences. Seeing if anyone might be looking to hock a locket. If we hadn't been so intent on bringing Kia down, this would have been a fairly easy line of investigation to follow. I was flying solo, down three with one left to go, and losing hope, but my fingers were crossed.

Marcus was a first-rate shyster, and a smart one. He was one of my least favorite people to lean on in the play-land of criminals. He was always well protected by muscle that only came out under pressure, and if that wasn't enough, he had connections of the unfriendly kind. Being FBI didn't mean you didn't end up dead, so back-up was always nice, but Chris wasn't playing. Not yet. So here I was, no badge, no federally-issued gun—*well, I'm not stupid*—my personal Glock was keeping me company today, and on my way to see if Marcus would play nice.

I rolled into the parking lot of his legal pawn shop hoping for the best.

Some parts of Detroit were less safe than others, and Marcus' Buy & Sell was in one of the lesser safe parts. It was an industrial-grade, cinder-brick, stand-alone building painted all the colors of the rainbow, graffitied attractively, with heavily barred, bullet-proof windows and entrance door.

I cut the engine, checked my Glock, reached for my folder of photo arrays, and said, on a preparatory sigh, "Well, Chuck. I'll be back in a minute."

Or so let's hope so.

I walked in to an apparently empty shop, and refused to check my gun again. Instead, I called out, "Marcus? How's business?"

"Well, well, if it isn't Mr. FBI guy," Marcus said, coming out from behind his back wall, dapper in slick black and heavily banded gold. He was tall, black, all business, about my height, and a good fifty pounds of muscle heavier. "Where's your partner?" he asked taking a curious look around, trying for intimidation, and pretty much hitting his mark—just a little, but enough. "You wouldn't be trying anything—funny; now wouldya?"

Showing no fear. Confident, but not cocky in another man's house, I said, "Nope. Nothing funny. Not here for you today."

"Interesting, but not sure I can be of help."

I waved my folder, and said, "Just wondering if you could take a look at a few pictures?"

"Sure, I can look. Doesn't mean I'm gonna recognize nobody."

I pulled out my two page photo array of all the Acer employees, Kia included, and repeated the same routine I'd been pulling for the last three fences.

He took a look, but then said, "Nah, man. I don't know these white people."

But I caught a glimmer of recognition in his eye and felt hope. "You're sure? Because if you know something, I'd consider it a personal favor." I was playing with fire, but hope does that to you.

"What kind of personal favor?"

"Nothing death, otherwise, potentially negotiable. I'd have to know before I agree."

"How 'bout I got a cousin—" *Why is it always a cousin?* "And he needs some slack."

"What kind of slack?"

"The kind of slack that gets him community service and time served."

"What's the charge?"

"Dealin'."

"Dealing what?"

"Meth. X. The usual," Marcus shrugged, *It's nothing, man.* "But he's prepared to go legit under my excellent tutelage."

Unh-hunh. Translation—muscle—the mean kind . . . often, frequently, and resulting in more than a few bumps and bruises. Well, that's a fight for another day.

"I'll see what I can do. Take another look?"

"Lucky for you," he said. "I just happen to see a familiar face."

Yes!

"Who?"

Marcus pointed, and my chest did flip-flops. *Damn.*

"Don't suppose you have any upcoming business planned with this upstanding citizen?"

Please, oh please, don't let him have dumped it already.

"As a matter of fact—" Marcus paused, considering, sizing me up. He clicked his tongue off the back of his teeth, and rolled his head off to the side. "I tell you this, and I come out clean, right? You get your man, and we're good?"

"That's how confidential informant works," I said, and he said, "It's a one-time deal, and just because I don't like the dude. He's got an attitude problem."

Oh, that's funny. But I didn't laugh.

"I'm cool for that. So whatcha got?"

"What I got is a meeting with this here particular *business*-man tomorrow night, seven. He's got something for a pre-arranged buyer—and I'm not getting in that game. You want *him*, you talk to your guy. Deal?"

"Deal. I need to know the particulars, and you'll have to wear a wire."

"You're not going to forget my cousin?"

"Got it. See you tomorrow. Early."

I walked out of Marcus' Buy & Sell, totally suppressing my relief and my excitement. Just get in your Jeep, and clear the war-zone. I slid in, cranked my engine, and headed for the highway.

Kia was off the hook. The buy for the locket was going down tomorrow, and she wasn't the one selling it. *Excellent.*

I jetted onto the Jeffries Freeway and headed for Ann Arbor, punching my speed-dial for Chris.

He picked up and said, "You better have someone hogtied."

"Not yet, but how's tomorrow, with the locket?"

This got his attention.

"You found the locket?"

"I've got the fence and the seller. Buy's going down tomorrow at seven. You ready to play or what?"

"So it's not your girl, then?"

"No, it's not Kia."

"Fine," he said not happy. "Tell me about it."

"We're cutting the fence a deal, and he's willing to wear a wire."

"And this is happening tomorrow?"

"Yes," I said, and then proceeded to bring a kicking and screaming Chris up to speed. He didn't like being wrong, but the upside to that, the chip on his shoulder fueled his anger, and now he was extra willing to go the distance to get our man.

Kia was next up.

I checked my watch. It was just after eight, and I hadn't had any dinner, yet. I was betting on leftover breakfast, and gave her a quick call.

She picked up, and I said, "I'm starved. What's for breakfast?"

"Sorry. We're fresh out. We've got boiled nothing, but I hear it's good."

"Well, that's too bad. I was going to bring my good news by, but if you're all out, I'll stop somewhere on my way home. I'll tell you tomorrow."

I made like I was going to hang up, and smiled when I heard Kia say, "Hey, hey. Wait, wait. Hold on there just a second, mister. I'm just getting word from the kitchen. Turns out, we've got a bounty in there."

I chuckled, "How quickly our stories change."

"Is this good news something I'm going to like? We're talking primo Chloe fare here, I just want to make sure what you're selling is worth the really good stuff!"

"Honey, with the news I've got, I'll be set in Chloe-ville for life."

I heard Kia breathe out a sigh of relief, and her tone dropped to serious. "Really, Jake? Like the kind of good news that proves I'm not guilty."

"Yeah. That kind of good news."

Kia was taking a few deep breaths, processing the potential, and I said, "I'm about five minutes out. I'll tell what I can when I get there. But you better have dinner on the table!"

We disconnected, and I broke the sound barrier closing the distance between us. Kia would be in a huggy, grateful mood, and I wanted to be there getting my due, and my breakfast, and there was the whole *she's recovering from shock* moment. I definitely needed to be there for that!

I swung into her lot, parked, and raced for her door.

She opened it before I could ring the bell and said, "Really?"

I pulled her into a giant bear hug, and said, "Yes," walking her backwards into her apartment and closing the door. "But there's a lot I can't tell you."

She nodded into my shoulder, taking that a little better than I thought she would, and said, "Okay. Tell me what you can."

I sat us down on her sofa, and said, "I can't tell you who. I can't tell you where. I can't tell you when. But I can tell you, I need you acting normal at all times when at the Acer. Don't blow my cover. Still bite my head off. Still do your avoidance thing and hang with Karen. And if all goes well, we're going to have the perp and the locket."

"So you know it's not me?"

"That I already knew. Now, so does my boss."

"Does this mean the charges against me are getting dropped?"

"Almost. Not yet."

"What? Why not now?"

"Chris wants to wait until we have the thief in hand. And I agree." Kia started to protest, and I said holding up my hand, "I know. It sucks. But we need to keep the charges in place to avoid spooking our suspect. So you can't tell anybody about this. If you need to vent, talk about it, decompress, whatever, until this is all over, I'm your guy. Day or night. Okay?"

Kia nodded, and I said, "What I've got is very promising, but until we have an arrest and the locket in hand—"

"I get it."

"You sure?"

"Yeah. This is good news. I just have to wait for the all clear."

"Exactly. And I know that might be tough at times, so I'm your verbal punching bag for when it gets stressful."

"That's very brave of you."

"True, and it will require substantial endurance. Feeding me, might be a great first step!"

Kia smiled. "Thank you, Jake."

"Well, it's not over, yet."

"I know, but thank you."

"Not even, Chloe," I warned, and she nodded.

"I know that will be extra hard, but it's your freedom we're talking about here. I don't want our excitement accidentally screwing it all up."

"Got it, and it's cool."

Kia got up and walked into her kitchen. "Do you want your muffin warmed up, or just out of the fridge?"

"Warm," I said, totally *silly-question*. "How many do I get?"

"I have five left."

"Does my heroism get me three?"

"Only if you don't want melon, too!"

"Okay, then. Four! *And* Chloe's fruit salad."

"You want four muffins?" she asked, and I nodded. "I haven't eaten since lunch."

"Jake! You need something more than muffins!"

"True, but I'm not sure it's on the menu yet," I said giving her my hungry look.

Kia rolled her eyes at me, and I laughed.

"You want some soup to go with all that? I've got Chloe's homemade chicken noodle. I can zap it up for you in a jiffy."

I'd held back long enough. "Yes to the soup, the muffins, the fruit, *and you.*" I long-strided it over to her, and before I knew it, I was kissing Kia senseless. Warmth, relief, and desire all pooled in the pit of my stomach, and even though we were in Kia's apartment, I felt like I was home.

Jake

Shake Down, Take Down

We'd survived another day at the Acer. Kia had held up her end of the bargain magnificently. I'd asked her to re-review her and Karen's proposed display changes—the one's Karen had already sent over to her digital wizard—*and* the corrections *I felt* were important—something like Phillip would have done, and Kia obliged me with scathing, low, dismissive cracks, calling into question my education, experience, and intellect, all topped off with her squinty eye roll and her flouncing off irritably to go find Karen. I'd asserted my superiority over her, reminding her I was her supervisor, eliciting from her a barely restrained sneer. And our *getting-along-so-well* status made the Acer grapevine. It hadn't been too long after that and Dr. Mann had strolled by with his *Attaboys*. Meanwhile, everyone else in the Acer had started skirting me and my comings and goings, just like Phillip. All in all, a job well done.

By two, I'd gotten a text from Chris stating that he and the tech team were getting set up, and they'd be in position when I arrived. I made busy, every once in a while poking my head out and stirring up trouble, and I stayed late a few extra minutes, just in case anyone was watching. Kia knew I'd be going home to walk Bullet before coming over for dinner with her and Chloe, but in truth, I wasn't going to make it to dinner. I had some fish to fry, but I had faith Kia would figure it out and lay low.

And now here I was. Bullet walked, Kia and Chloe unwittingly on hold, sitting with Chris in the tech van, getting briefed on the take down.

Chris was pointing to a schematic of the surrounding streets and the inside layout of Marcus' Buy & Sell.

"We've got eyes and ears set and live. We'll wait until we see the locket, and our Marcus cue is, 'That's a really nice piece.' When we get the go, we'll go in from here, here, and here."

I nodded. "Did Marcus give you any trouble with his paperwork or wire?"

"No. But he wasn't pleased that I reduced his firepower to zero. I left his guys in place for show, but we took their ammo until this is over."

"Smart," I said, and Chris said, "Yeah. I'd hate for you to get shot, now that you got your girl."

I wish I could say his tone was friendly or supportive, but still no. *Totally a wiseass.*

"It's so nice that you care," I said sarcasm heavy, and Chris threw me his disgusted get-real look and said, "I'm still recommending disciplinary action be taken against you."

I telepathed him, *Whatever*, and looked to the store-front counter monitor in high hopes of seeing the star of our day. I could argue with Chris, but I'd save it for the review board, *if* ever it came to that. Right now, all I cared about was the person getting ready to walk into Marcus' Buy & Sell, and clearing Kia's name.

It was six fifty-two, as recorded by our cam equipment, and I watched triumphantly as our mystery guest arrived, pulling the door wide, not a care in the world, ready to do business and walked in, doing just as I had done, calling out for Marcus—who never just hung around in the front.

"Marcus?"

We watched as Marcus materialized from the back room, just as usual, slick as oil on water, and said, "Hey," by way of an upward nod. "You go it?"

Kia's *Frame-Master J* didn't even bother to look around. No qualms. No nervous anticipation, just business as usual. He pulled a cloth sack out of his pants pocket, and laid the locket out on the counter, bright as day for everyone in the world to see.

I so couldn't wait to get my hands on him.

Marcus said, nodding, "Cool man, that's a really nice piece—"

Chris signaled the go, and we descended upon Marcus' Buy & Sell like the Roman army. Calculated, strategic offensive, surrounding the building, preventing escape, and capturing our prize without even flinching.

It was perfect.

And as Chris called out, "FBI, get your hands in the air," I sauntered forward, satisfaction ringing true, and said, "Hi, Phillip. Guess you weren't expecting a party."

Turns out, Phillip's a little thick.

"Jake? What are you doing here?"

"I think the better question is, what are *you* doing here?"

Ahh, there you go.

Dr. Mann's eyes darted as reality sank in.

"Hey, hey. It's not what you think," he tried evasively.

"Oh, really? Then what is it?"

Then the Phillip I'd gotten to know and loathe came slithering back. "What? All this for a skirt? What's one stupid locket?"

One, my ass.

While Chris and his team stood guns ready and taking down Marcus and team, *for show*, I frisked our friendly Dr. Mann, cuffed him and read him his rights. Then I leaned in real close, and said, "She's too good for you, and you know it!"

Phillip jeered something low—I couldn't hear it, so I jacked up his cuffs a little, and said, "What was that?"

"Nothing," he fumed.

"That's what I thought."

Two hours later, we had the locket in safe keeping and Phillip in-processed and lawyered up. We'd waited for his counsel to arrive, and Phillip wanted to deal.

This was Chris's moment in the spotlight, so he took over questioning, but I sat second chair.

"I didn't steal the locket. It was the Everet woman, but she needed help moving it."

"As much as I would like to believe you," Chris said, "and I *really* would like to. I don't. You're going to have to do better than that."

"It was all her idea."

"Whose idea?" Chris asked.

"Kia Everet's."

Even now, the slimy bastard was going at Kia. I wasn't having it. Any of it.

"Dr. Mann," I said. "Perhaps you don't realize the gravity of your situation. This is only going to get easier for you if you start telling the truth."

Phillip looked from me to Chris and back again. Shifty, considering, and his lawyer leaned in, whispering in his ear.

Phillip tried shaking him off, and I said, "You want to try again?"

His look turned sulky and angry, but he said, "What are you offering?"

"You're currently facing four counts of felony larceny—" Chris said before Phillip cut him off.

"Four!" Phillip tried for shocked indignation, but we'd seen it too many times before, and Chris continued, unmoved. "That's up to forty years in a federal pen, and a sizable fine. Sure to put you back a few houses."

"You can't prove four," Phillip blustered.

"Maybe, but we can prove one, and that's going to lead the jury nicely to the other three," Chris said, disimpassioned. "Ask your lawyer. I'm sure he can explain."

Phillip's lawyer did his lean-in-whisper thing again, and Phillip looked over, unhappy.

"I see you're beginning to grasp your situation, Dr. Mann. What we want from you is the name of your buyer. We want the other three lockets back as well. And nothing less is going to help your case."

Phillip was a weasel. A glowering, sycophantic, womanizing weasel. And he just sat there like an idiot, apparently thinking he could wait out my egotistical, career hungry boss. The cocky battle of chicken between two reasonably equal self-serving jerks.

This should be fun.

"Let me help you decide," Chris said, opening the file folder in front of him. "This here is a duplicate copy of Ms. Everet's personal security swipe card," he said, laying out an evidence bag. "And here is a duplicate copy of her door key." Another evidence bag. "These are electronic clip cables for looping video feed." Another bag. "All of which was found in your home, and all with your fingerprints. Finally helping to make all the pieces in our puzzle fit."

Phillip shifted his position in his seat, but still held firm, and Chris smiled his gotcha smile.

"And my personal favorite," he said, going in for the kill, and enjoying it, "Video feed from Marcus' Buy & Sell with a perfect view of you," Chris stressed emphasis in his next words gaily, "*each* of the *four* times you have come to him with *each* of the four lockets. So, in my book, pretty much signed, sealed, and delivered after all. You sure you don't have a name for me?"

Finally Phillip paled and caved. Game up. No turning back, only time for damage control.

"Ian MacAllistor. He's British, and each locket was a specific request from him."

"What's he want with the lockets?"

Now that Phillip had spilled, he was gushing like a geyser. He waxed eloquent for over an hour, telling us how MacAllistor contacted him, set up the buys, the works. Kia just got caught in the fringe. And her thesis work and interests fell spot-on into MacAllistor's lap. All of which was way too convenient for Phillip, especially given she took the job he had put in place for a junior level lackey of his choosing. Her dad had pulled strings he shouldn't have, and Phillip was just repaying the favor.

It's one of those things you just never got used to. You come to expect it. But still, people's personal disregard for others still came as a shock to me, every time. Chris had once said that it was this romantic optimism that made me good at my job—that I held out hope—and even when smacked with reality, still hoped. Chris admitted he lost that long ago. But so here I was listening to Phillip and feeling sick. All for a buck. He hadn't cared one way or the other what happened to Kia, and worse, he'd done everything he could to put it all on her. He'd almost succeeded. We'd almost bought it.

Hell.

Who am I kidding?

We did buy it, and Kia—wonderful, amazing, *Wham*-filled Kia almost, *almost*, got lost in a system apathetic to her pleas.

If I hadn't cared—

Phillip wound down his story, and Chris got down to the business of wheeling and dealing.

I had to get to Kia, tell her the good news, and—and anything else she wanted.

I turned to Chris and said, "You got this?"

He looked over, happier than a lone vulture with fresh road kill, and waved me off, my presence now redundant and unnecessary, except for doing paperwork. So this was the time to bolt. Before I got stuck with the bureaucratic red tape of sticking it to Dr. Phillip Mann. I'd already pulled the long shift. So let Chris earn his promotion. I was going home.

Kia

Waiting . . .

Chloe and I had settled into her living room, passing time staring at the boob tube. I don't think either one of us could tell you a thing we'd seen in the past few hours. We were distracted waiting for Jake to call. When he hadn't shown for dinner, I suspected something might be up. It was almost eleven, and still no word.

Chloe and I were exhausted, running on fumes, but eager to know Jake was okay. Hoping to hear I was off the hook.

The phone rang, and a second later there was a knock at the door. Chloe went for the phone. I went for the door.

Chloe picked up and said, "Jake!" at the same time I opened the door and said, "Jake!"

He stood there smiling, and Chloe hung up.

"I tried Kia's place first," he said, "but of course, you're both here." He grinned wide and sucked me into a huzza-huzza-three-cheers hug. "I have good news!"

I laughed at the excitement and heard Chloe clap in delight. "Tell us, Jake. What is it?" she said.

Jake gave me a happy spin, a giant kiss, and put me down next to Chloe, and said, "We got him. And the locket!"

"I'm off the hook?"

"You're off the hook!"

Jubilation!!!

I did a little victory dance, and Chloe and I were a cacophony of gleeful squeals.

Chloe took a seat on her couch, put a hand to her heart, catching her breath, and Jake and I asked in unison, "Are you alright?"

Chloe nodded, "Just need to sit down and take it all in." She looked at Jake, sincere and tender gratitude sparkling, and said, "Thank you, Jake. Thank you so much. Thank you for taking care of Kia!"

Jake leaned down and gave her a gentle hug and whispered something in her ear that I couldn't quite catch, but it made Chloe beam and pat him on the shoulder. "Kia's right," she said, "You are a chocolate charmer."

He grinned. "And proud of it."

I gave them both my suspicious eye, but they went all innocent on me. I chuckled, "You, two. Connivers, the both of you."

Jake's look was all like, *What?* And Chloe was right there with him.

"Sooo," I said, "Jake, we saved your dinner. Just in case."

His relief was practically comical.

"I take it you haven't eaten since lunch again."

"Not unless you count drive-thru Mickey D's."

Chloe tsked, tsked. "That will never do. Let's go into the dining room. Kia, will you—"

"Got it," I said, and we all made our way to the table.

"Don't suppose there's any chocolate to go with that dinner?" Jake asked, and I said, "Don't suppose," on a grin. "Only if you tell us everything. Well, everything that you can."

I was still waiting to hear who did it and was itching with anticipation. Now that I was off the hook, it felt like gossip, the sick-fascination kind, where you don't want to look, but you can't seem to help yourself.

Besides, since it felt personal, I wanted to know, *who?*

I brought Jake's dinner to the table and said, "This here is Chloe's ridiculously delicious chicken-vegetables and rice. You're gonna love it."

"My mouth is watering already," he said taking the fork I handed him.

We all got situated, and Jake took one look at his plate, and then wolfed down his dinner. No time to talk. Hunger had apparently taken over.

I gave him a sympathetic chuckle and asked, "Would you like some more?"

Jake wiped his hands and mouth on his napkin, and shook his head, no. "But that hit the spot. Thanks."

"How about dessert?" I said, clearing his dishes, and Jake said, "Now you're talking!"

"We cheated," Chloe said. "I'm still having to take it easy, so we bakery bought today. Hope you like cream cheese cake with chocolate sauce."

"Nothing wrong with that," Jake said, completely affable, eyes goggling at the portion I brought him.

"I think you're hungrier than you're letting on, so this should do the trick."

"And then some," he said, but that didn't stop him from diving in. "Mmmm. Not bad at all. Good save, Chloe!"

"Glad you like it, but if you don't start talking, I'm going to take that plate away from you!"

"Banish the thought," he said, and swallowed. "Okay, so here's the low down. Apparently there's some guy in England who's bent for trinkets, lockets especially, that originate in the Royal family, most specifically from Queen Victoria. These lockets were either gifts directly from her, or from her fairly immediate family members."

Jake looked pointedly at me, and said, "Which is why Kia turned out to be such an attractive addition to the Acer. You were better at pulling in collections that suited his purpose than Phillip."

"Phillip?"

"Yes. Dear ol' Dr. Mann. He was just getting into the business of making money on the side at the Acer's expense, when you arrived. He'd posted your position in hopes of getting a dupe in place. But then your dad stepped in, and voilà, you became Phillip's scapegoat. You were set up before you even took your first steps into the Acer. Phillip duplicated all your security keys and passes, and once he noticed that you liked to work late, he knew it would be easy pickings."

"Phillip?" I was stunned, but somehow not surprised. "So is that why he treats me so badly?"

"I'm sure it didn't help."

Then it dawned. *Phillip.* "And he's under arrest?"

"Yup. In custody as we speak, and not going anywhere anytime soon."

"So I'm thinking this means he's not going to be my boss anymore?" I said, a note of cheerful slipping out, and Jake grinned, "Probably not. And me either. Other than wrapping up with the Board, I'm going back to my regular day job."

"So I'm currently without a boss?" That sounded soooo good.

Jake nodded, and Chloe said, "No more terrible Phillip, Kia! That's excellent news."

"And what about the locket?"

"Well, the Tsarina's locket is currently evidence. I'm sure the Acer isn't going to like that, and neither is Moscow. But I'm not sure if Chris will be able to do anything about it. That's up to the prosecutor and other powers that be."

Jake scraped his fork against his dish, unwilling to leave any trace of chocolate behind, and licked at the tines. "As for the other lockets. My guess is Chris, along with the two governments, and the responsible insurance companies are going to be blasting their way through to Mr. British, sooner than he can say, '*Blimey*.'"

Jake finished his dessert. "That was great! Thank you."

"Do you think you'll have to go to England, Jake," Chloe asked, and he shrugged, "It's possible. Chris isn't thrilled with me, but I also made his career, so it depends on his mood. All he has to do is the clean-up. But he's so damn lazy and incompetent in the field. He might "request" I go."

Jake looked at me, smiled, all happiness and heat, and my pulse ratcheted up a notch.

Chloe chuckled, obviously onto the both of us. "Well, this is good news indeed, and we'll have to celebrate. But not tonight."

She muffled a yawn, real or convenient, I'm not sure. Hard to tell with Chloe. My bet was that she was back in the Jake game, giving him a big hint.

I would have put up a fight, buuut—it's Jake. And I was thinking . . . maybe. He *was* a cupcake. Maybe he'd be mine.

Jake looked from me to Chloe and back, sizing up the moment, nodding, and said, all contemplative squint, "I think I like where you're going with this."

Delectable Doofus.

He slid his chair back and said, "Kia and I can wash up my dishes real quick, if you want to get ready for bed. We can lock up on our way out."

I hugged Chloe goodnight, and Jake came around to do the same. Chloe whispered in his ear again, with Jake nodding, and I said, all melodious taunt, "I can hear you," even though I couldn't, and she said, "I hope so," with her playful eye wiggle.

That Chloe!

She yawned again, hand-covered, this one real for sure, and her tired lines billboarded her fatigue.

"I'll see you in the morning," I said with another hug, and Chloe nodded. "Now, shoo. Off to bed with you, and we'll be out of here in a jiffy."

Chloe padded off, and Jake grabbed my hand, pulling me tight to him, whispering enticingly in my ear, sending warm somethings hurtling through me, "Come home with me, Kia. Stay the night."

Jake

Stay, Don't Go

"Mmm," Kia hummed. "But I have to go to work in the morning."

"I'll make sure you get to work," I said dropping a tongue teasing kiss onto her shoulder.

God how I loved her sundresses.

"Tempting, truly tempting."

Was that a bit of a purr?

I moved my kisses up the delicate curve of her neck to settle on her lips and threaded one hand into her hair, massaging her head, letting the other trickle down the long length of her back and cup her perfectly rounded cheek.

"You know you want to," I said, biting back at her kisses, and she threw a little more tongue into the mix to prove my point.

I played my fingertips along her skin, and found my way back to the sensitive hollow of her throat. She tilted her head, smiling so very sultry-like, and offered me better access.

Oh-ho-ho. Kia was Hot, Hot, Hot!

She liked this spot. And so did I.

"I'll take that as a yes," I said, yanking her into the kitchen, and we made fast work of the dishes.

Chloe, my co-conspirator in all things Kia, had made like a thief in the night, and thoroughly disappeared.

I hurried Kia toward the front door, and she called out, "Love you, Chloe. Sweet dreams."

Chloe called back, a lilting smile in her voice, "Love you, too, honey. Good night."

Kia closed and locked Chloe's door with her key, and I piled her into my Jeep.

"Want to grab an overnight bag, first?"

She bit her lip, calling my neglectful mouth back to hers, and nodded. How could I resist? I kissed her again, and my body went into a full solar flare.

"Okay, but you have to hurry. And I'm going to keep feeding you kisses, so you don't lose momentum or get side-tracked."

She nibbled a little more, and then went for full-on devour.

How I got us to her place, I don't know, but I followed her up the stairs, and when she opened her door, I walked her through, engaged the lock, and swooped her up, my lips never leaving hers.

This time, I knew the drill. Bedroom, through the doorway, off to the back left, bed. Tumble.

No laughs, no giggles, just straight up heat.

Kia tore at my clothes, and I fisted the cottony fabric of her dress in the small of her back into my hand and clutched her to me, full possession, and fed her kiss, after fiery kiss.

We rolled, and she landed on top. Without pause, all the buttons on my shirt flew. She ripped it wide and hot-palmed my chest.

Ache and impatient need drove us.

I pushed her hands toward my belt, and raked her dress up her thighs.

And there they were. Another pair of her barely there panties.

"Put 'em on my tab," I said, and flicked my wrist.

Kia got her hands under the elastic waist of my boxer briefs, and doing a careful shimmy, pushed my pants down my legs. With a little flip-kick of my shoes, the rest followed.

Kia was back to her biting kisses, and I slid a tentative finger inside her, testing the waters, finding them ready and waiting, but waiting no more.

Gripping her hips, I lifted her up and slid her slickly home.

A few more licks of her tongue and a lip craving kiss later, Kia rose up, anchoring her hands on my chest, with my hands still at her hips, and together we slid. We ground. We found our rhythm and pushed harder. Driven by the intense pleasure. It was all glide, grind, glide, grind, glide, grind. And as we kept increasing the pace, I felt Kia tense. She was getting close, and I wanted to go with her.

I grasped her bottom, tilted my hips up, *just right*, and increased her thrusts.

"Mmmm," I said, and she said, "More Jake. More."

No problem.

Grind, glide, stroke.

"Yes, Jake," she breathed.

Grind, glide, stroke.

"More Jake," she panted.

And I pushed us harder. Kia was almost there.

I squeezed my hands tighter, grinding her deeper, and that's all it took. Kia locked into a tight coil of exquisite body spasm, cresting her Mount Everest, and groaned my name. I pressed my head back, and pushed at Kia's hips. She was almost rigid in her rapture, but I kept us moving—tightly and restrained. My blood pounded, my body pulsed, and then, concentrated release. Surging wave after surging wave. Pulling a throaty groan from deep in my chest.

Kia collapsed onto me, and I wrapped my arms around her, placing a kiss into her hair.

We were a heap of sweaty, heavy breathing, limp limbs, and it was right where I wanted to be.

"I thought I was just going to pack a bag," Kia grinned, panting, and I said, deflecting guilt, "*You* bit me."

I felt her silent laugh against my chest, and I smiled.

"So you gonna pack that bag or what?"

More silent laughter.

"Just let me get Bullet settled in for the night, and I'll be up," I said as we pulled into my garage. "I haven't had a chance to give him a walk yet, so we'll make a quick run around the block."

Kia yawned and nodded, and I said, "Make yourself at home; get ready for bed—whatever you want. Just don't fall asleep. We're not done yet!"

Kia smiled. "And we're not likely to be any time soon."

I sure liked the sound of that!

We piled out of my Jeep, and I reached into the backseat for Kia's bag and favorite pillow, which she had encased in soft, snowman-print flannel. *How cute.*

"So why flannel? It's almost summer," I asked, handing her things to her, to open my door. Bullet was already doing his excited greeting thing, and Kia said, "It's comfy and helps me sleep. Is he always this excited to see you?"

I chuckled, "Aren't you?"

"Not really," she said, giving it back, all airy and aloof, and I said, grinning, "Sure you are."

Kia yawned again, smiled, and cut, "Hey. Whatever gets you through the day."

I held onto the door, keeping Bullet at bay on the other side, and pulled Kia in for an ice-melting kiss, and she leaned in, taking the bait, kissing me back like she wanted more.

I broke our lip-lock and she said, "Heyyy!" and I said, "That's what I thought."

"You suckered me." She yawned again, bigger this time.

"Literally," I nodded. "And I'm warning you. Do. Not. Fall. Asleep."

"I won't."

I didn't believe her. Her eyes were already hanging at half-mast.

Bullet was going into a frenzy inside the house, so I said, "Brace yourself. He's going to be happy to see you, too."

I opened the door, and Bullet went ballistic. Jump. Jump. Jump. Run into the house. Run back. And a happy resounding, *Bark!*

"Heya, Bullet. Look who I brought home!"

Bark!

Kia bent down, keeping her bag and pillow up and away, and petted Bullet with some behind-the-ear scrubbas. "Hi Bullet. Have you had a good day?"

Bark!

"Well, I'm glad to hear it. And it's about to get better. Jake says he's gonna take you for a walk!"

Bark!

And Bullet went nuts. Of course. Kia'd said the magic word.

Kia laughed, and I reached for Bullet's lead and a scoop bag, and said, "We'll be back. See you in a few."

Kia nodded, and I added, "I'm gonna lock this door again."

"Okay." Kia bent and gave Bullet another scrubba and said, "You two have fun."

Bark!

Kia headed in, and Bullet and I headed out. Bullet had been cooped up for the better part of the day with only quick trips out, and this wasn't going to be stupendous, but it was special circumstances. He was a guy. He'd get it.

"Okay, Bullet. We've got a lady staying over. Let's do double time."

Bullet wagged his tail, grinned, and took off for his oak. When he was done there, he took me for a light jog up and around the long block in my neighborhood. Every once in a while, stopping for some business, but then getting back at it. When we got back to the house, he looked like he still had some excess energy, so I stopped us in the yard, dropped down, removed his lead, and said, "Have at it."

Bullet rolled his eyes at me, like, *Really, this is it?* But then took off, tearing circles around my postage stamp of a front yard. After about a hundred laps, he came trotting back over to me, tongue lolling, tail wagging, appeased.

"Good?" I asked, and he panted his happiness. I tossed his scoop bag in the trash, and we went back inside. I got everything closed and locked up; Bullet fed and watered for the night; and headed upstairs to find Kia.

When I got there, I found her all snuggled up, blanket up to her chin, comfy, head on her flannel pillow, on my side, sleeping, and I thought, *You little sneaker.*

I light-footed it into my bathroom and found her toothbrush in a cup on my counter and an overnight goo bag at the sink. Organized Kia in my space. The now familiar homey warmth I felt with Kia settled deep in my chest, and I smiled.

In under five, I'd motored through my nighttime routine. And wiping my face with my hand towel, I took a good look at the man in the mirror. Same mug, different guy. I'd gone from finding purpose on the job, to finding contentment in life. And she was taking up space in my bed. We'd made it to second base in the grand ol' ballgame of love—falling together, falling apart, both under contrived circumstances—the big question was—*Could we make it to home base in regular season?* I'd be going back to work, doing my FBI thing, and she'd stay at the Acer, normal everyday domestic life, without all of the drama and trauma.

Kia in my home, in my bed, in my life. I'd had her here before, but woke to an empty bed and an empty house, and a broken life. And that had sucked. This time, I'd made sure she had her things about her, proactively lessening her potential need to run, and as far as I knew there was no more *ugly* hidden and waiting. I hung my towel up, and shrugged. The only way to find out was to get in there and give it a try.

So here's hoping.

Kia

Curtain Call

Jake's place. It was another sunny day, and bright beams framed the heavy drapes hanging in the window above, blocking out most of the sun. Not that it did much good. Jake's skylight wasn't covered, and it was like a day at the beach already in his room. I could see clear blue skies and the occasional wispy cloud floated by.

If we were going to make this a habit—and it would be nice if we did—I was going to need a sleep mask. I shuffled down under the covers, trying for darkness, and Jake said, halting my descent, "Good morning."

He rolled up next to me and scrunched close. "How'd you sleep?"

He was of course cover model gorgeous, even first thing in the morning. Not a hair out of place, and his oceanic blues were bright and cheerful. I eyed him suspiciously.

"Do you wake up this beautiful every morning?"

"Ah," he said, bright-eyed and bushy-tailed. "Chloe withdrawals. I should have suspected as much. I can get some breakfast on, if that will help."

I reached up and pushed my hair back, smoothing it away from my face, hoping I didn't look like a crazy woman.

Jake smiled, *Cute*, and kissed me, reminding me where we left off last night. "Mmmm, this is better than breakfast," I said, and he said, "I won't tell Chloe you said that!"

He was lying on his side, propped up on his elbow, looking down at me, and I got the solar eclipse effect of his head. I blinked at the brightness, and asked "How do you sleep with all this light pouring in?"

Jake leaned in, kissed me again, and reached over and pushed a remote, and the skylight went black. "I thought the sunshine would be a nicer way to wake up than my nasty, ol' machine-gun beeper of an alarm clock."

"Ohh, that *is* nice. Does it have a dim?"

Jake pushed the remote again, and soft light glowed from the skylight.

"That's pretty cool."

"Yeah. I had it installed when I moved in. I like to watch the stars at night, when I'm falling asleep."

"That's kind of romantic. How come that wasn't part of my deal?"

Jake grinned and bent to kiss me again. "Because you fell asleep silly."

"Well, I'm not asleep *now*."

Good thing Jake was FBI. It made him good with hints and clues. And he was reading mine *just right.*

He made quick work of my boxers and tee, and I toe-scrunched off my socks. I felt around and made contact with—nothing. Well, at least not his clothes. He was already in the buff, so I wrapped my hand around him and said, all playful like, "What's this?"

He was hard as a rock!

And he said, playful back, "Here, let me show you."

One thing I can say for Jake—he looked good, tasted good, sounded good, and felt, ohmigod, *So* good.

For only visiting twice before, he'd learned his way around quick, and before I could say *Chocolate*, I was ringing incandescent and biting my pleasure into his well muscled shoulder, begging for more.

As my rock-n-roll waves faded to ripples, and I felt myself floating back to earth, Jake nibble-kissed me the way he always did, infusing me with more and more enticing heat and want, and said, "Come with me."

I chuckled, following him into the bathroom, and said, "I thought I just did."

"Har, har. There's more where that came from, now into the shower with you, or we'll be late."

"Late?"

"For work. You remember. That place you go. Practically day-in, day-out."

"Ohhh, work. Right. Well aren't you still my boss? Can't you just give me the day off and then call in sick?"

"Very tempting, but not today."

Jake turned the water on and pulled the shower lever up. He reached into the closet for a couple of towels and washcloths, and then checked the water temp.

"Perfect. Now hop in," he said and followed right behind me.

The water was warm, and I ducked my head under the flowing rain shower and let it pour down over me. I closed my eyes and stepped backward, letting the water wash my hair down my back.

"Oh crap," I said, my eyes flashing open. "I forgot my shampoo and conditioner."

Jake was standing there, staring at me again. Curious, intent, watching the water sluice. I smiled. I liked how he looked at me. It made me feel pretty. Sexy.

I bit my lip, and let him look.

"That's a nice birthmark you've got there." His voice had turned thick, and the sound sent a heated flutter to my stomach.

I looked down at my pelvic bone and the nickel-sized brown oval resting there. It was my own sneaky, natural tattoo.

"Chloe told my dad when I was born, that God had marked me good. That he was gonna be keeping a close eye on me."

I smiled at Jake and the memory, and he said, "I like it."

Jake reached out to touch it with his thumb. "It's like a little on-off button. What happens when I push here?" he said pressing his thumb into me gently, and then using it as a pivot point, he rotated his hand, so that he could slide his fingers inside me. One, then two.

I bit my lip again. "*Mmmm.*"

"You like that?" he asked, and I nodded. "Because I like how you respond."

Jake stepped in closer to me, and leaned me back against the wall.

"We might be late after all," he said dropping a wash cloth on the tub floor and kneeling down in front of me, never taking his fingers away.

I bit my lip again, and watched as the water coursed through his thick, almost black hair, and down his long, beautiful back. He glanced up, right before going in, and said, "I love everything about you, and right now, you look good enough to eat."

His mouth made contact, and his fingers did their magic, and my brain went blank. I reached out, grabbing for anything, needing balance, and found the wall and his shoulder. With one hand plastered against the cool tile, and the other gripping his muscles tight, I held on for dear life, vaguely wondering if he might drown—

this had never worked for me before, but who knew. Maybe this time. But whatever. It felt sooooooo good.

All on their own, my legs locked, keeping me upright, while delicious tingling waves raced through me and stole my breath.

Oooooh my!

Jake was patient, persistent, and taking his time, paying careful attention to every sensitized inch of me. And right when I thought we might have to call in the rescue crew, he did something new. I don't know what, but it hit ground zero, and my head practically popped off. I dug my nails into Jake's poor, tortured flesh, and pounded at the ceramic. My voice had gone hoarse, and I cried out at the intensity. My body swelled and I rode the tide until my legs started to give.

"Beautiful, just beautiful," Jake said, and stood, keeping me afloat, and hoisting me up. "Wrap you legs around my waist."

I did, and he said, "Yeah, just like that. Not too tight."

No problem. I didn't have legs anymore, I had rubber bands.

Jake looked into my eyes, *ravenous*, happy, and smiled his sexy, sly smile, then stepped into me, and plunged deep.

Ho-lee cow.

It was all I could do to hold on. Every stroke was heaven and perfection, but my body had gone spaghetti. Jake was dealing out the really good stuff, and I could feel the nuclear bomb building inside me.

"Jake," I warned.

"Right there with you, babe," he groaned.

Another deep plunge. Then another.

He'd pushed himself to the limit, and I went mushroom clouds. Jake ground out my name, and fought his body's rigid reaction. I reached out to pound on the wall again, the force and impact of my orgasm seeking more than one way out, and ended up bringing Jake's shower curtain down.

When the shockwaves subsided, Jake carefully lowered me to my feet, and examined the aftermath.

"Maybe sleepovers on school nights aren't such a good idea."

We burst out laughing.

"I'd say I'm sorry, but you started it!"

Jake flipped off the water, grabbed our towels and handed me my overnight bag. "We'll have to finish this up down the hall."

Well, that sounded promising, I thought, glowing, ready for more.

Jake

Wrapping Up

Kia was upstairs finishing up. All that hair took time. And I was in the kitchen scrounging together some quick breakfast for us. No way was I going to live up to Chloe's culinary magnificence, but I could pull off edible.

I had fresh, crisp apples, some eggs, and bread.

"No O.J.," I said to Bullet, and he blinked, unaware of the magnitude of this faux pas.

I grimaced. *Oops.*

Well, maybe being all blissed out, she wouldn't notice.

Unh-hunh. Sure.

I dropped the bread into the toaster, and scrambled us up some eggs.

I'd already taken Bullet out, and he'd powered through his Halo crunchies, happy and content once more.

My phone rang, and I picked-up.

"Why's your cell going to voice mail?"

Chris. Joy of joys.

"Good morning to you, too."

"I've been trying to reach you all morning."

"It's not even eight yet," I said, all get-a-grip.

"I'm on my way London. After I wrapped with Dr. Mann last night, I called Scotland Yard, and this morning I got a call that they have MacAllistor in custody."

"Wow, that was fast."

"Seems they didn't like the idea of someone nicking jewels connected with the Royal family. I'm on my way to see about recovering the other lockets."

"So your career's on the up and up after all."

He was as smug as the day is long.

"Looks that way, and if you want to keep yours, I suggest you head on over to the Acer with your update, and then mosey on down to the courthouse. Dr. Mann is being arraigned today. We've got A.D.A. Fleischman, and she's going for remand."

"Think she's going to get it?" Remand seemed like a long shot.

"No, but we'll see. I want you to call me as soon as it's done and let me know."

Kia drifted into the kitchen, breathtaking in another feather-light babydoll sundress—this one printed with tiny peach and pink, five-petal fun flowers. Very sunny and happy. She was an uplift after listening to Chris drone on at the other end.

"Anything else?" I asked, and he said, "I want constant updates."

"Will do."

"And you can tell the Acer that as soon as the locket is processed as evidence, we'll be getting it back to them. Day or two at most."

"Okay. Safe flight. Call you later."

"Can the sarcasm," he said and clicked off to my get-real eye roll.

"Your boss?" Kia asked, and I nodded. "He's on his way to that career I was telling you about."

"Good for him," she said, and looked at my breakfast in the works.

"O.J.?"

I pinched my lips and shook my head, and she said, "So much for the perfect date."

I lickity split us to the Acer, and informed Kia, "We have a meeting with the Board this morning at ten."

"We?"

"We. I need to bring them up to date, and I want you to be present when I inform them that all charges against you have been dropped. And that you were never complicit to any part of the thefts."

"I wonder if I'll get my job back."

"Can't see why you wouldn't. It's not like Phillip wasn't off his rocker."

"And I'm good at my job, too."

I smiled and gave her a little chuck across the chin, "Yeah, that, too."

We rocketed into the parking lot, and I said, checking my watch, "After that, I have to go to Detroit—Phillip's being arraigned today—and then I'll be back to pick you up. Want to have dinner with me?"

We got out of my Jeep, and Kia smiled *you're-so-in-big-trouble.* "What?" she teased. "No lunch? Chloe will not be pleased."

"Yeah, about lunches—" I gave her my *sorry about that* look. "I have to hand the reins back to Chloe, unless you want me to pack you PB and J every day."

I beeped Chuck locked, and we high-tailed it inside.

"PB and J?" Kia scoffed.

"Yeah, I know. Doesn't compare with Chloe cuisine."

She sighed dramatically. "I guess all good things must come to an end."

"Hey," I said, not wanting to be included in that generality. "Not *all* good things come to an end."

Kia's smile was mischievous on the surface, but her hope was peeking through, and it made my heart do a little jig.

Yay!

"Well, that went really well," Kia said, and I said, "Of course it did."

Kia was doing *her* security thing and opening the door to *her* office.

"It was extra nice of them to offer me a seat on the selection committee for the new director." She grinned, *incoming wit*, and I braced myself. "Here's hoping the third time is a charm."

"I thought *I* was your third time."

"Oh, right," she chuckled. "Hmm." Like she was tsk, tsking me contemplatively. "Yeah. Wrong kind of charm. Maybe you should work on that!"

"I'm totally offended," I said, and she laughed, "No, you're not. You didn't want to be my boss either."

"No. I did not." I sidled up close to her, and dropped my voice to bedroom and said, "Where you're concerned, I'm all about equal partnership."

"Equal?" Her tone was *as if?* And then she added, "So you're going to give up your chocolate source."

I winced apology. "Yeah. No can do. Confidential Informant and all that."

"Gross!" Karen smiled, strolling in. "Get a room."

Last I checked, Karen thought I was scum, so her jovial hello meant word was traveling fast.

"Sooo, bottom feeder. Turns out you're FBI come to save the day," she said.

"Turns out," I said dryly.

Karen apologized, friendly-like. "Don't mind the blonde. She was just protecting her friend. And thanks. My mom says you're getting the locket back."

She looked at Kia and beamed. "Beyond the obvious, you must be so excited. Your show's a hit, temporarily delayed, but no more Phillip! I know that makes me happy."

Kia nodded triumphant, and said. "And I met your grandmother. She's nice, but a bit fierce."

"That's the Acer in her," Karen agreed. "She gets it from her mom. We're four generations of kick-ass women, not about to compromise, and always looking to conquer."

Karen punched me playfully in the arm. "That's why I had to step in," she said. "Just in case you were aspiring to being a chip off the ol' Phillip block. Couldn't stand for that. He was already one obnoxious asshole too many around here."

Hear, hear to that.

I leaned into Kia and gave her a quick kiss. "Looks like you're back in good hands."

Karen and I exchanged quiet smiles, buddies again, and Kia nodded.

"I've gotta go," I said.

"Okay."

"But I'll see you for dinner. Call me and let me know when you want me to pick you up."

I kissed her again, quick, but for good measure, and headed for the door.

"Have fun catching bad guys," Kia called. "And I'm just saying, but seems like you've gotten a little remiss with your friendship dues."

I paused and turned. "Any special requests?" She was such a sasser!

Kia shrugged *you're the chocolate charmer.* "You know what I like."

I grinned.

Yes, I do.

And from there, regular season commenced. Dr. Mann wasn't remanded, but he couldn't afford his bail, so it was pretty much the same thing. Chris returned from England, three missing lockets in hand, and MacAllistor was being dealt with by Scotland Yard. Phillip had a deal on the table. He was getting off easy with seven to ten years and a hundred-fifty thousand dollar fine. But the icing on the cake for Kia was that his credentials were toast, and he'd never work in the museum world again.

Chris had gone off the deep end of power control freak, and sent me up to the review board. I couldn't believe he did it, but he just kept riding his high horse. I got a slap on the wrist, and Kia got a chance to stick it to me. She passed, and I'm still in the field where I want to be, on hold for a new partner. Chris went up the ladder, and with any luck he'd tip over.

Chloe continued being spectacular, and on the sly, I'd started looking for a house closer to her. She was teaching Kia and me both how to cook her recipes, and everyday was a new day of amazing food bliss.

I'd survived the Fourth of July party at Kia's parents' house, and her dad's interrogation. He wasn't so bad, once he'd explained his *Sugarplum's* needs, and threatened my life and career, should I fail to meet those needs. Fun guy really. But I got it. He cared. And so did I, so it was a no brainer. Kia's mom managed aloof better than any wafer thin runway model, but she'd taken me aside and given me career tips, proving who really wore the pants in James Everet's rising political career. Zoe had turned out funny like Kia, but quieter, always thinking, and a bit of a cynic. I knew we were cool when she'd told me her parents were a real piece of work, but that Kia was worth the price.

I thought so, too.

It had been a little funky getting back to work and not going to the Acer, sparring with Kia everyday. She'd been the most fun I'd ever had on the job, but the thrill of the hunt was still there, and it felt good righting the wrongs of the bad guys. I was just as bad as Kia about working late, but she'd found a way to discourage my regular tardiness.

"Have you seen my panties. I can't seem to find them anywhere."

I'd reach into my jacket pocket, my fingers making contact with gossamer silk, and groan, and she'd say, "Oh, there they are. When are you coming home? I might catch cold."

Wham, and more Wham!

My dainty destruction tab was off the charts, and Kia always made me pay. Not that I minded. No, not at all, but one of these days, Kia was going to run out of panties.

Days at work, evenings shared with Chloe, walks with Bullet, and steamy, fun-filled nights with Kia. Brownies, cakes, cookies, ice cream, éclairs, chocolate chip pancakes, cheesecake, mousse, in the bed, in the shower, on the couch, up against the wall, bent over the counter, biting, nibbling, teasing, laughing, playing, loving, and living in fun.

But I still hadn't given up my chocolate guy. Until now.

Kia

A Night to Remember

"But you can't be late! You're my date! *Check your pocket!*"

Jake chuckled—he knew my tricks—but he said all too seriously, "I'm sorry, Kia. I *will* be there, but I can't leave here until I get this guy processed. Once he's in the tank, I'm on my way."

"Your new partner can't do it?"

"My collar, my credit, my work. Have Chloe bring you, and I'll be out of here as fast as I can."

"But my new dress," I protested.

"Is beautiful, and I can't wait to see you in it!"

"You're in big trouble."

"Have been since the day I met you!"

"You're lucky I love you."

"Yes, I am!"

"Hurry, Jake. I don't want you to miss it."

"I will."

I snapped my cell phone shut, tipped my head back, and blew out a grumbly breath of acceptance. Chloe and Bethany rolled their eyes, girls sticking together.

"Not tonight," Chloe lamented with a supportive pout.

"I know. But he finally caught the guy he's been chasing all month. He should get to be the one to rub it in."

"True," Chloe said. "But Bethany, I think you should give Kia your Super Sexy Special."

Bethany laughed. "Definitely. But with Kia in that dress, you're gonna have to mop this poor schmuck up off the floor."

"Perfect," I said, and Bethany said, "Close your eyes, and don't open them until I say so."

Twenty minutes later, Bethany magic, my dress, and four inch, spikey sandal heels, and Jake was in big, big trouble.

My eyes were dark, alluring, and smokin' sexy. My hair hung long with big, loose, flowing curls that were just messy enough to beg for Jake's touch. My lips were pinkish-natural, plump and oh, so bitable. It was Bethany's Triple S, and she'd set the volume to max. Jake wouldn't be able to resist. And my dress wasn't helping either.

It was a floor length, white chiffon gown with another thigh-high split. Seeing as how Jake seemed to like those a lot. And I'd added drop diamond earrings to accent the crystal encrusted round-strap neckline and waist.

"Turn around," Chloe said. "I want to see the back."

I laughed and rotated. "There isn't one."

"I've come to the conclusion that you look radiant in chiffon," Chloe smiled, pleasantly satisfied.

"I could say the same about you," I said, giving her my hot-mama look, and she grinned.

Bethany'd done Chloe's hair and make-up, too, and she looked sassy with a whole lot of spunk. She was wearing a creamy blush chiffon, three piece pant set, and it fit her perfectly.

"You'd better be careful. Some of those benefactors are grabby grabsters. You get your butt pinched, and I don't want hear about it!"

Chloe chuckled. "If anybody's getting their butt pinched, it's you, not me!"

Bethany stepped back from us, taking in the whole picture. "Aren't you two the pair? Not bad, if I don't say so myself."

Hugs, big tips, and promises to send Bethany Jake's E.R. bill, and we were on our way to the Acer.

It was the final night of the Tsarists' Treasures exhibit, and the Acer's were throwing a closing party celebrating its success and the return of the locket. And my whole family was coming.

On Monday, Chloe and I were flying with Karen and her mom, Eloise, to Moscow to promote goodwill and personally return the locket on behalf of the Acer. Since Phillip had disclosed how he'd stolen the lockets in full detail, as part of his deal, the Board had brought in a new security specialist, and the problems had been addressed. Karen and Eloise were going to instill surety of future confidence, and I was going to give my heartfelt thanks. Chloe was with me and thought Moscow would be interesting to visit.

Chloe, my partner in crime!

"Are you excited about tonight?" she asked.

"Yeah," I nodded. "No Phillip!"

"That *is* an improvement," Chloe agreed.

"And mom and dad are coming for the first time."

"Well, it's not everyday your kid gets arrested on suspicion of theft working at a museum."

"True."

"And they love you, and this visit is long overdue."

"True again."

"But mostly, I'm sure it's just their curiosity what all of the hullaballoo was about."

I laughed. "Most likely true!"

Chloe reached over and squeezed my hand. "Are you happy, Kia?"

I squinty-eyed her, suspicious, "You're not gonna have another heart attack are you?"

She laughed, "Heavens, no. I hope not. I just want to know if you're happy."

"Yeah," I said and smiled. "I'm happy."

"And Jake. It's going well with him?"

"I think so. I haven't seen him much in the last couple of days. He's been staking out his most recent prey. And I miss him."

"But it's good?"

I bit my lip, nodded, and then rolled my eyes at her. "But I'm not giving you any details."

Chloe chuckled, and our driver pulled to a halt. Chloe had gone all out and gotten us a limo.

"Ladies, we're here. I'll be right around to help you with the door."

The driver came around—a complete gentleman—and extended his hand to Chloe first, and when she was standing steady, did the same for me.

We thanked him, and I led Chloe inside.

As always, most of the festivities were held on the first floor, but my exhibit was upstairs. A number of our regular benefactors were already mingling about, and it took a little finagling and fancy footwork to get over to the coat check. By the time we got there, and I'd checked our bags, Chloe leaned into me and whispered. "My word."

"What?" I asked, a picture of innocence, already knowing, because I was all too used to Mr. Gunderson's overly grabby hands.

"That man clapped my bottom!"

I winked and said, "I warned ya."

"Where's Jake when we need him?"

"Exactly!"

I taught Chloe my shimmy-hip-twist trick, and together we were able to deflect most of the additional grabby hands. Throw in a few polite regrets, and we worked our way to the second floor in under ten.

"Not bad, Chloe. Maybe you should volunteer. You're a donor magnet."

"I'm not the magnet," she said quite confidently. "Jake better hurry, or he might lose his chance."

"Sugarplum!"

I looked up—careful to sidestep Mr. Zucker, or as I knew him, Mr. Touchy-Feely, who didn't seem to have as much courage without Phillip doling out unwarranted permissions—and found my mom and dad standing by the locket.

"Hi dad. Hi mom," I said with big hugs. "Where's Zoe?"

"Sugarplum, you look beautiful," my dad said, and my mom nodded, and then pointed toward the back.

"She didn't bring a date, but there's apparently a number of interested gentlemen trying to get her attention," my mom said.

"Oh no," I chuckled. "Any of them her age?"

"I don't think so."

Chloe said, "I'll go save her; you stay here."

"Good plan," I said, and Chloe took off for poor Zoe.

"Where's Jake?" my mom asked, and my dad zeroed in with hawk-like vision.

"He's not here yet. He closed a case today, so he's going to be a little late."

My dad didn't look appeased, always watching out for me, so I said, "I'm sure he'll be here soon." I shot my dad some warning daggers. "And this time, no cornering him with one of your courtroom kill speeches."

My dad shrugged, like it was no big deal, and said, "It's nothing. He likes it. We talk shop."

"Unh-hunh. Like I was born yesterday. This is your daughter you're talking to."

"So this is it?" my dad asked, wisely changing the subject, taking in the locket.

"Yep."

"Well, it is a very attractive piece, but we're glad it's back where it belongs."

"Me, too."

"Your father and I have already meandered through the show," my mom said. "Kia, you did a wonderful job. It's all so fascinating, and Alexandra was quite influential in her marriage."

My mom!

"It's true, but I was suckered in by the romance. I found their relationship interesting and inspiring."

"But it ended in tragedy," my mom said, wrinkling her nose.

"But it's a love story, and that's Kia through and through."

We all turned to find Jake standing there, smiling, a sucker for me. And I don't know about them, but my heart stuttered. He was in his tux again, and he'd picked up a tiny bit of a tan, making his eyes cool blue pools I wanted to jump into. He was a gorgeous day at the beach. The room faded into the background and the voices became distant.

I bit my lip, and he grinned. "I told you I'd make it," he said kissing me.

"So Jake—" my dad said, and I blinked back to reality. "Don't you dare!" I warned.

Jake laughed, and shook my dad's hand. "Hello, Mr. Everet. More Q and A?" Then he gave my mom a delicate hug and a quick peck on the cheek. "Mrs. Everet. You're looking lovely this evening."

"Jake," she said, almost monotone. "How nice to see you."

My mother. I'm telling you. A piece of work that woman!

Jake leaned in and whispered in my ear, "I think I'm starting to rub off on her."

I laughed, "Not likely."

"Jake! You made it!" Chloe came bounding back with a grateful Zoe in tow, and Zoe said, "Remind me to avoid fundraisers from now on. This place is a zoo!"

"Don't worry, Zoe," Chloe said. "I'll teach you Kia's patented shimmy-hip-twist, and you'll be mowing these guys down in no time."

"Well, the gang's all here," Jake said, pleased, confident, and strangely a little deer-in-the-headlights. He edged closer to me, and my brain fizzled. He was doing his smell good thing again, and I tried to shake it off, certain something hinky was up.

God, he wasn't going to break up with me right here in front of my family, was he?

"Don't tell me you don't like the dress," I said. "It's got the slit and everything."

"I love the dress—we'll talk about that later—and I love you."

He unbuttoned his jacket pocket, reaching for something, and my nose dove for happy.

"Do you smell chocolate?" I asked, and he laughed and gently tweaked my nose.

"Those highly attuned senses," he said. "Always giving me away."

He pulled a card from his pocket and gave me a sly grin. "I have something for you."

My family had gone silent, apparently onto something my chocolate bombed brain wasn't detecting.

Jake handed me the card, and I read it out loud, "Charlie's Choc-O-lats."

I looked up, merriment and smiles. "This is serious, Jake. Are you sure you want to do this. It's your only real leverage, and you're just going to give it up, because you're a little late? That's crazy talk."

My brain was trying to reach me . . . *Earth to Kia!* But my happy fog was dense.

Jake pulled something else out of his pocket, and knelt down on one knee. I heard Chloe giggle and clap excitement, my mother gasp, and my father murmur approval. As usual, Zoe was observant and quiet. I just stood there, stunned.

"Kia Emily Everet, you are the *Wham!* in my life, the home and shelter I seek, the fun and desire I crave. I love you, like you, respect you, and want you. Will you marry me?"

I smiled, rolled my eyes, and shook my head, pulling Jake up, and then kissed him. "*Yes! Absolutely yes!* There better be some chocolate in that box."

He grinned and pulled the top off. It was a chocolate locket, just like the Love Locket, and he said, "Open it."

"Don't I get to eat it?"

Jake laughed, "Yes, but open it first."

I opened it, and on the inside was a gigantic, hand-eclipsing, beautiful princess-cut diamond engagement ring, and Jake said, "A princess and her love story."

Ahhh, a true chocolate charmer and my very own cupcake.

Jake smiled, his heart in his eyes, and slid the ring on my finger, kissing me, to the delight of my whole family, and whispering against my lips, "You licked me, now you have to keep me!"

About the Author

Mary Kate Kopec lives in Dexter, Michigan with her husband, Paul, and their Bear-ific, Bear-tastic, Bear-abulous cat, Bear–who thinks he's human, and they don't have the heart to tell him that he's not. Mary Kate has earned Master's degrees in Human Genetics and Educational Studies. She has spent lots of time teaching in the community college classroom and advising university students on how to make good choices–all the while keeping them laughing and entertained with her stories and antics. She is an advocate for community, family, and friends. You can visit her at www.MaryKateKopec.com.